In this character-driven crime thriller, police corruption, a paranoid militia and a decades-old cold case haunt the woods of southern Vermont.

Five years into her retirement, former U.S. Border Patrol agent Jill Benoit finds her quiet rural life intruded upon in the most annoying way: an early morning phone call from a private investigator demanding to meet with her. Jill feels all the more irritated by a mysterious package, a panicked neighbor and the discovery of poached deer carcasses concealing explosives. Soon a 25-year-old bank robbery and murder case is reopened. along with Jill's memories and old wounds from her early days at the Washington State border. Is there a cross-country connection? And why are dead bodies and messy break-ins following P.I. Bill Robinson as he travels into the Vermont backwoods? Questions build up with much cogitating, but the story takes its time unfolding, as if, like Jill, it needs to first regain a law officer's mindset-not to mention a whole lot of coffee and pastries. Fortunately, despite the lack of narrative urgency, what readers get is a heady peek into the world of law enforcement from a woman's point of view: the lack of respect from superiors and peers, the extra smarts necessary to offset the physicality of male officers, the double standards. The novel also offers insight into how law agencies compete instead of cooperate and into the poignant pain of survivor's guilt The untangling of threads connected to the reopened case will be a pleasure for readers who love puzzling out a crime, and the novel depicts its characters and all their tetchiness and foibles with a pragmatic sensibility that reveals their psyches in real time. By the conclusion, with its welcome if too brief action, the reader's relationship with the protagonist has developed deeply enough to make the epilogue notably affecting. It also offers teasing potential for a Jill Benoit series.

Your novel does fit those categories, but I believe it transcends the genre - or I should probably say it belongs in with the best of them. After all, Edgar Allan Poe is credited with writing the first detective mystery, and your story is as intriguing as some of the outstanding ones by Agatha Christie.

You have written a real page turner. I found myself wanting to get back to the book to see the mystery unravel, as it does with just the right amount of suspense and most satisfactorily - at the very end! But like all good novels, you have created memorable characters whose idiosyncrasies make them intensely human and likeable. Jill Beloit is a remarkably independent woman whose back story is revealed skillfully with only tangential reference to a daughter and a divorce, but whose integrity, courage and even wisdom is clearly evident in the choices she makes and the life she has managed to create for herself. She's found fulfillment on all levels, including an amazing love relationship that combines fidelity and freedom.

The setting also comes alive in your description of the natural beauty of southern Vermont. Of course, I recognized all the locations you named in the Bennington area, and kept exclaiming to my husband about each one as I came across it. Equally effective as part of the setting is the insider's look from a woman's perspective that you provide into the workings of several overlapping law enforcement agencies, fascinating details about the rules and the commitment of the officers involved - as well as the inevitable exception.

I could go on and on, but perhaps I should adapt my comments to a review on your Amazon website. I looked it up and was most impressed. If you think it's a good idea, I can submit one. Let me know.

Little Spiders Big Web

S. J. Gero

ARPress

Copyright © 2019 by S. J. Gero.

All rights reserved. No part of this publication may be reproduced, distributed, or transmitted in any form or by any means, including photocopying, recording, or other electronic or mechanical methods, without the prior written permission of the publisher, except in the case of brief quotations embodied in critical reviews and certain other noncommercial uses permitted by copyright law. For permission requests, write to the publisher, addressed "Attention: Permissions Coordinator," at the address below.

ARPress
45 Dan Road Suite 36
Canton MA 02021

Hotline: 1(800) 220-7660
Fax: 1(855) 752-6001

Ordering Information:
Quantity sales. Special discounts are available on quantity purchases by corporations, associations, and others. For details, contact the publisher at the address above.

Printed in the United States of America.

ISBN-13:   Paperback   979-8-89389-869-9
           eBook   979-8-89389-870-5

Library of Congress Control Number: 2024923854

CONTENTS

SPECIAL ACKNOWLEDGEMENT

Since the original publication of Little Spiders Big Web, by dear friend Margaret "Peg" Murphy passed away. After a hard battle with breast cancer, we called it a day on thirty-eight years of friendship.

Peg was a unique person with a heart of gold and an intellect that never stopped seeing possibilities. Together we made a team that made single parenthood manageable, built homes, fought inequality in economics and the workplace, and fostered an environment of adventure for our friends and families.

This book would have never been written without her and she lived through many of the experiences in it. I owe her a great debt and profound thank for many years of care, love, and friendship. I miss her and hope wherever she may be that she enjoys this reprint. And no, Peg, I haven't written a sequel yet!

Your BFF Always,

Sue

ACKNOWLEDGEMENTS

At the top of my list, I thank Jennifer M Wolfe for her editing skills and taking time above and beyond to guide me through the rewrites. Her insights, knowledge, and patience with a first time writer like me were crucial to the completion of this book. Without her, this would never have gone to publication. Thank you, Jen, you are the best.

I also want to thank Patricia McHugh for having read the first drafts and suggesting I might have some talent! Your kind words of encouragement and knowing your talented background as a writer and editor also inspired me to continue on a course that was pretty scary to me.

It would be sinful for me to ignore the support, patience and help of friends and family who have put up with my silence and ranting over the past few years. To Peg, Wanda, Chris, Susanne, Julia, Jill and Tim, I am in your debt.

DEDICATION

For Bert and Lucille who always believed.

CHAPTER

1

It wasn't supposed to be quite so cold this morning, at least that's what that they said last night just before predicting another dusting of snow after midnight. Dusting, my ass. I was getting tired of plowing and shoveling "dust" out of the mile long, private driveway and paths to the house and barns. Not that the weatherman or anyone else cared.

That didn't stop the little white stuff from drifting down silently and relentlessly overnight to cover, ever so slightly, the surrounding countryside with its not-so-soothing blanket of cotton-looking fluff. There it laid waiting for those inevitable black rubber monsters with teeth of steel to come rolling through, causing clouds of white powder to fly off to each side of the vehicle while leaving underneath a hardened track of packed snow. The first run always looked like a violation, an environmental rape of a perfect snow carpet. The second set of tracks looked like someone coloring outside the lines. After that, who cared? The road crew would obliterate all traces of trespass with the mighty blade of justice, and the slate would be ready for the next snow crime scene.

The coffeepot had to be washed out again before a fresh pot could be made. It was a bad habit I really should break although I couldn't think of a good reason why. Brinker's car went down the driveway in front of the house as the coffee started to drip into the pot that brought my attention to the clock on the stove. Why on earth was Brinker leaving so early? Even lawyers didn't have to appear in court until 8:00 am. So why leave at 5:30 am? Plus he didn't usually take the car. He was more the SUV type, but hey, what did I know? *There you go with the cop stuff again. Mind your own business, and you'll be happier with much less to remember. Not that you remember much these days anyhow.*

With coffee in hand it was time to tickle the satellite and see what disasters the administration had gotten us into overnight. Seemed our capacity to meddle into everyone else's business was endless and lead to countless conflicts of wills as well. No surprises there. Let's see, we shot a couple of people here and there, and arrested two suspected of terrorism (against who or what I'm not sure). We're still rattling sabers at Iraq, the anti-war folks are ticked off at the 'Hawks', the pro-war folks are ticked off at the 'Doves', this person was suing that one for that, the rich were richer the poor poorer, and the beat goes on. Man, is this world screwed up.

The phone doesn't normally sound like an alarm bell in an empty room, but at 6:15 am in the backwoods of Vermont anything above the bark of a dog wakes you up a bit. I was tempted to ignore it, but it was disturbing my quality time.

"Hello?"

"Agent Benoit?"

"Retired."

"Is this retired Agent Jill Benoit of the US Border Patrol?"

"At six in the morning I'm retired from everything including nosey questions from unidentified people on telephones. Who are you and what is it that you want?"

"I'm sorry, Agent Benoit, my name is Bill Robinson. I'm a Private Investigator working on a case that you may have some information about. The reason I'm calling at this hour is because I have to be in California for an 11:00 am meeting and my flight leaves shortly.

I wanted to catch you before leaving to make arrangements for a meeting on my return. What would be a good time for you?"

"Whoa there, first of all, you're talking to someone who's just barely had a cup of coffee. This is not good. Two, I never agreed to meet with you. Three, I have no idea what case you are talking about. Four, even if I know, I may not be able to divulge information on that particular case. It would depend on the case. Why don't you start by telling me what case you're investigating, and I'll tell you if I can help. Then we can discuss if there will be any meetings, and at what kind of reasonable hours they will happen."

"Agent Benoit this is extremely serious, I assure you. We must meet, and soon. Several lives may depend on it. Please."

Now, this wasn't the sort of breakfast conversation I was used to. Yes, I had spent the better part of my life doing what I thought was a great job – serving with the US Border Patrol. After 25 years of service, I had heard my share of weird and scary conversations. There were plenty of interrogations that gave goose bumps reason to head for cover. There were stalkers who liked the uniform and thought public service meant something totally different for them. Every police officer I knew got death threats, and I was no exception. Most of those came over the phone or in unpleasant conversations of sorts in dark cars at different border crossings.

In all those years I was hard put to recall a case where my life or the life of another was in any danger as a direct result of information. Robinson wasn't setting off any bells either. His voice was polite, strong, and persuasive, but not in a car salesman way. Perhaps he had some law enforcement background before turning PI. Regardless of his credentials it was still 6:20 am and I needed to get a grip and get off the phone before this jerk got me involved in something that was none of my business. So said THE little voice, and of course, I always listened to THE little voice.

"Mr. Robinson, I'm inclined to think you are being a little dramatic. This is a bit much for me at this hour of the morning and I'm not interested in playing the game right now, but thank you for calling. Perhaps some other officer can help you."

"Agent Benoit, why in hell would I waste our time making up such an absurd story?" His voice was clearly showing great irritation. "I assure you the difference between a retired Border Patrol Officer and a Private Investigator will be negligible when they start sorting out body parts. I am desperately trying to solve this case. I need your help and that is as honest a statement as I can make from one retired officer to another."

He sounded sincere and a touch panicked. There was no mistaking the note of desperation lying under the surface of his plea for assistance. *Why do these guys always find me? Better yet, why do they find me before my second cup of coffee?*

"Look, Mr. Robinson, give me a call when you return from California and I'll find a way to meet up with you. Can you at least tell me something to point me in the right direction like a name or date? How about an incident or case file number?"

"No. It's too risky over the phone." Now his voice was almost shaky, as if someone caught him in the closet talking to his girlfriend. I could hear the flight numbers being called over the loudspeakers so it was obvious he was in a public phone bank. Maybe someone had come to the phone next to his or he thought someone was watching him.

"Fine, well you have a nice trip and call me when you get back. Meanwhile try to get your blood pressure down. You'll feel better." But he didn't hear my last well wishes as the dial tone attested to. As I hung up the receiver, I couldn't help wondering why he couldn't give the name of the case over the phone. He was obviously calling from the airport so a tap was out of the question. Did he think I was tapped? Was he using a cell phone? Being watched? Maybe he was being watched by a lip reader. I have no idea how he would know if a lip reader were watching him!

I need more coffee and less TV. As the second cup of Ethiopian bean aroma began to drift upward towards my befuddled brain, it became obvious this was going to be a bad day regardless of the weather. Routine may be boring and humdrum, but it gives one a sense of prediction and comfort and, yes, safety. You wake up, have your coffee, feed the horses, do the chores, check the mail, go fishing or read or travel to a friend's house for the rest of the day, come home, feed the horses, eat dinner, watch a little mindless TV, and go to bed. What's wrong with that? Life didn't have to be constantly exciting and upside down all the time. It wasn't necessary to have your sleep disturbed at all hours of the day and night so you could take an unpleasant ride in a car to speak with unpleasant people about unpleasant things.

It was amazing how fast everything was coming back. How long has it been? At least five years have passed since I've turned in my resignation.

Now there was the feeling of urgency and anxiety that was creeping all over me. I could feel the nerve endings in my legs and arms activate and fire as if they were getting ready to do a workout or test run just to be sure they could still function. Lord knows, the rest of me wasn't ready for active duty. Well, not much of it. My stomach was tensing and starting that pre- heartburn acidic belching only good strong coffee and shot nerves can bring on. The headache wasn't in full bloom yet but it was early. Let's see, about another 20 minutes or so and it should be a real crusher. The kind that starts at the back of the neck crawls up inside your skull then shoots straight across your brain to your eyes and explodes out your temples. Love those guys. They're so painful you don't dare shoot yourself in the head because you're afraid it will hurt too much.

That wasn't all that bothered me as I put on my winter outdoor gear and pulled wool-lined boots on. I opened the door and stepped out into the gray cold making sure the house door closed behind me. Fundy went charging out to the road as usual, sniffing out whatever scent he could, hoping against hope that something fast and mobile would provide him with a little entertainment before breakfast. As the gods would have it, none appeared and he was forced to stick with me and trotted down to the barn wagging his yellow lab tail in total acceptance of life's disappointments. What a dog. The horses weren't particularly interested in Fundy either unless he intended to feed them. Fundy, of course, not only did *not* intend to feed them, but endeavored to eat their feed if he could. It could all get very complicated and loud and confusing so I usually tied Fundy to the barn door. After feeding him several treats, I went about the business of cleaning stalls, feeding grain, tossing hay, and checking the water supply.

All the while I was working, my mind kept going over the phone call. Who could I possibly know that would pose a threat not only to me but also to a PI that I never even heard of? This had better not be one of those pranks that Tom Martins over in New York dreamed up. He had a reputation for pulling some real beauties on retired troopers. I'm not a trooper and he doesn't know me that well anyhow. Still, maybe I'll call Marion over in Salem to see what she knows.

As I walked back to the house I saw two squirrels racing across the driveway making one last desperate leap for the pine tree on my left. Not one inch behind was Fundy stretched out in greyhound form giving chase with great ease and grace. God, what a beautiful dog. He was so long and strong and beautiful, like a mountain cat. His stride at full bore had to be five feet. His head was massive but soft and classic in its features. There wasn't a print or picture of a Labrador retriever in any magazine or catalog that could match this guy. His coat was so light in color it was almost white in some places. His eyes were the color of a pair of tiger-eye earrings I once had. I think my daughter has them now. They were striking in their depth and richness and reminded me of a Sugar Daddy when it was snapped clean in two. His nose was brown too, which surprised me at first. I had never seen a dog with a brown nose. Sheltered life, I guess. When he stood at attention it was easy to see where the 80 pounds were distributed on his rather large frame.

As I opened the door to enter the house, I called Fundy to stop chasing the squirrels and come in for breakfast. Anticipating the routine, he was there before I could adjust my position and bolted inside leaving one cat clawing frantically at the wood stack for safety and me somewhat arched backward between door and doorframe. Crap! I'm going to have to train that dog someday.

He ate his breakfast in seconds and curled up next to the wood stove for his morning nap. I finished my cereal, took a shower, had a quick chat with Marion Innes, the dispatcher over in Salem, New York, and started to clean out some old boxes stored in the attic. If it was going to be a bad day, I might as well be doing what annoys me the most, reliving the past.

While cleaning the dishes from breakfast, a group of three deer wandered through the pines across the ravine towards the only other house on this side of the Hollow. The Brinkers had moved into that house six or seven years ago when I had been stationed in Richford on Vermont's northern border with Canada before my retirement. We had met casually once or twice while riding or walking by the yard, and they seemed okay. At least they didn't imitate the previous renters who frequently invited their dead beat friends to crash for a month, drank themselves blind, had gigantic bonfire/keg parties, and got themselves arrested and evicted for non-payment of rent. I wonder if it was that "anonymous tip" that brought the State Police out to bag those idiots before the forest burned down.

Once I moved back on a full-time basis, I had made it a point to get better acquainted with the Brinkers, just to be neighborly. In retrospect, that turned out to be more than either of us had wanted. Joseph Brinker was a defense attorney practicing criminal law, and came from a place out west that he declined to specify. Gretchen, his wife of unknown years (she was his second wife), came from a small town in the Midwest, didn't work at anything on a paid basis and, surprise surprise, there were no specifics on where she came from either. She seemed very reclusive and almost afraid to share any details of their lives although friendly enough to offer coffee and sit for an hour's chat. I had conducted enough interrogations and sat in on sufficient domestic cases to sense that maybe something nasty was lying below the surface of Mr. and Mrs. Joseph Brinkers' background. So far it was none of my business and there was nothing to spur on any active inquiry or action, but it certainly made me uncomfortable. The obvious omission of seemingly innocent information to someone who didn't matter, like a neighbor, was enough to punch my alarm button.

Then there were the children, Joseph Jr., the 15 year old 'Stepford' son, and Tracey, the 19 year old daughter attending Southern Vermont College. Joe Junior was tall for his age although teenage boys didn't really have a regulation height once hormones kicked in. Still, judging by mom and pop's physique, he was going to be well above their genetic contribution. His muscular development looked to be enhanced by something other than good home cooking and store bought vitamins. It would not be much of a stretch to see him in heavy competitions requiring strength as in wrestling, or team sports like football. But Gretchen said he was not at all interested in school sports or any other activities with kids his own age. He much preferred to be with his dad at the local private shooting club and went on trips organized by a private club he belonged to that was geared to outdoor sports all year long involving the whole family. They traveled all over the state and country with other families camping, fishing, and hunting, sightseeing and generally enjoying each other's company. Often they would exchange houses, and sometimes kids, for the summer or extended vacations to experience different areas and lifestyles. They were a very patriotic and health-oriented organization, but loosely structured and private. Membership was by invitation only and had to be approved, although she didn't know by whom. It all sounded very hinky to me.

Tracey appeared to be a little more "normal," in that the few times I had spoken with her she had actually smiled and engaged in meaningful conversation in return. Her brother had just glared and grunted. Tracey's goal in life was to get an Associate Degree in Business and transfer to any college she could get into that would take her out of this section of the country. Emphasis was on "any". It was obvious that she liked her family, but was not enthralled with her family life or their geographic location. As she put it, "Life in the Hollow is like an out-of-body experience. You can see yourself living, but you know you're just about to die. It can go either way." Not a flattering commentary on life in rural Vermont, but an accurate one coming from a young woman who had spent her teens in school or at home 24/7/365 for the past six years without a date or social life to speak of. Mom didn't approve of the local selection of friends, and neither invited nor accepted invitations for her children to attend functions outside of the home. It must have been hell for Tracey, although Joe Jr. didn't seem upset at all. For some reason, that didn't surprise me.

For the second time that morning the phone rang with an alarming sound that made me jump and almost drop the mug I was rinsing. The mug went in the strainer and, grabbing the towel from the handle on the stove, I stomped to the phone muttering to myself, "Gee, we must have won the lottery again. Damn I've got to tell those people to stop calling me. I've got too much money already."

"Hello."

I made a mental note for myself to start turning off the ringer on the phone and leave the answering machine on. This much phone activity at this hour was definitely going to cause the aging process to speed up and ruin my retirement. My grandchildren would be denied a warm and cuddly *Memere*.

"Hi Jill, this is Gretchen next door. Did I wake you?"

The voice was soft and quiet, almost distracted as if she were thinking of something else and not particularly interested in making the call. This did nothing to curry favor with her now totally irritated neighbor.

"I've been up with the horses, but that doesn't mean I'm awake. What can I do for you?" I tried to keep my voice non-committal and civil, but feared I was failing miserably.

"You have such beautiful horses. I just love that pinto you have, what's its name, Nevada? Just gorgeous. Reminds me of a horse I saw on this ranch we were on once down south. He used to run in this huge pasture with his mane and tail flying in the wind and looked like it could fly away into the sky. The other day I......"

"Gretchen," I had to raise my voice a couple of decibels to be heard over the ongoing narrative that wasn't going to end soon, "is there another reason for your call other than Nevada?"

"Oh, I'm so sorry Jill. I do tend to wander off the point sometimes, especially when I get upset."

"Why are you upset, and what can I do about it?"

This wasn't going to be good, two unsolicited crappy phone calls on the same day before 8:00 am. Nope, not good at all.

"Well, Joe Sr. left this morning to go on some sort of trip and took my car instead of his SUV. That means I have to drive his SUV to take Junior to school and run errands. But, on the news I saw where they are blowing up dealerships and bombing those HumVs, and SUVs are just as bad, and I'm afraid to drive the SUV into Bennington. Some woman in Arlington was shot at yesterday by the road to Kelley Stand and she had an SUV. What should I do? Can you help? Joe won't be back until late tonight. I just don't know what......"

I had to cut her off before my fuse reached the detonator and my mouth exploded with all those expletives deleted one shouldn't say to a neighbor. "Gretchen, you've got to get a hold of yourself." Good grief the woman was annoying.

Okay, breathe deep, count to ten, and calmly continue. "First of all, this SUV thing you are talking about is not what you think it is. Some idiots out on the coast, of which California seems to have a whole bunch of, have decided to protest America's gross consumption of crude oil by blowing up dealerships selling Hummers."

This was going to take forever. *Breathe, count to ten* ... "HumVs are the square looking Jeep type thing that's supposed to go anywhere and drinks gasoline by the foot instead of the mile. They are ugly, expensive to buy and expensive to keep on the road. If you ask me, they should shoot the guy that decided to sell them on the commercial market, but hey, I'm only one person."

I was making progress, she didn't chime in. "The lady that was shot at in Arlington was driving a van, not a Hummer. She was not shot at on purpose. Another idiot up on Kelley Stand Road was sighting in a rifle next to the brook, of all places, and hit the boulders with a high velocity bullet. It ricocheted off the boulder and went whizzing across the road she was driving on striking her van on the corner of the windshield fracturing the glass. Scared the crap out of her and she hit a small tree, but no one was hurt. The shooter was cited and has been scheduled to appear in court. Nice to see the East and West coast share the idiot population.

"As for people shooting at you, think about it, Gretchen. There are probably more SUVs per capita in Vermont than most other states except maybe Alaska. Shooting at them or their drivers would be like shooting one of our own. Would we really do that? How would we get around in the wintertime, dog sled? I don't think so."

The pause on the other end of the line was so long I thought I may have gone a bit too far. Well tough, it was barely 7:15 and I had already been disturbed twice by people who didn't seem able to live their lives without someone else to prop them up. Worse than that, they expected that someone to be me. Well too damn bad. Excuse me for breathing but I've got some serious down time coming and it doesn't include babysitting for the Barbie next door.

"Gretchen, can you tell me what it is that you want me to do?" She was either in shock or in tears, but whichever it was I needed to get her off the phone before I lost it totally. There was something about people who couldn't ask you a direct question or face their own problems that made me very anti-social.

"No, I don't think there's anything you can do. It's really my problem and it will all work out. I'm going to stop by your driveway on the way out and send Joe to your door with a package that was delivered here by mistake. It's addressed to you with a lot of forwarding addresses so I guess it's been around the system for a while. The USPS guy in Shaftsbury sent it to North Bennington, but they don't deliver out here and I said I would take it out."

Now I was hot. First she screws up my morning then she steals my mail?

"Are you saying you picked up my mail without my asking, or that the Post Office delivered mail to you by mistake?"

That stopped her for a minute. She seemed to be thinking of the right way to phrase her reply in order to get out of the deep hole she had just dug herself into.

"I went in to get my mail from the North Bennington Post Office last Friday. While I was at the counter getting stamps, the guy who works at the Shaftsbury Post Office was behind the counter talking with one of the guys sorting mail. He said they had this package for Agent Jill Benoit but they don't deliver mail out in the Hollow and didn't have a box for Benoit. This guy was asking if North Bennington had a box for Benoit. I told the clerk that I lived next door to you and would be glad to deliver it to you if they wanted me to. The Shaftsbury guy handed it to me and I brought it home. You were not here, and I forgot about it until this morning. I'm sorry if I have overstepped my bounds, but I thought I was being a good neighbor."

Now it was my turn to be silent. You spend years on your own, literally alone, being responsible for everyone and everything within a certain perimeter or jurisdiction and you develop a certain attitude or personality disorder. Some call it being a control freak. Others call it the need for dominance or always needing to be right, maybe even a self righteous attitude. What most don't understand is that alone you cannot control events that will happen but you can control how and to what you will react. It's your only salvation. If you wait for someone to shoot at you to see what you will do, you will almost certainly end up being carried by six. But, if you play act in your mind every time you are 'out there' by yourself what you will do if attacked, where you will seek cover, who you will radio, what you will say, what your location is, then you stand a chance of reacting in time to save your life thereby saving other people as well. At the end of the day, that's what you hired on to do – serve and protect.

Gretchen wasn't aware that her being a 'good neighbor' was in my world an intrusion, an attack of sorts. This was the unanticipated act of someone who didn't belong within my 'patrol area' and had taken something that didn't belong to her but belonged to me, out of it. Her motives didn't matter; her actions did. My best friend from childhood, Charlie, used to tell me all the time that good friends and relationships are the only things you can count on and things are disposable – let them go, don't get attached. Charlie is right about best friends being priceless but when you are alone on patrol with only yourself to rely on, you had better have the mental strength and agility to outthink the monsters of hell and the ego of Superman if you expect to survive the adrenaline rushes, the shakes, the fears, the doubts, the boredom, and the constant criticism from everyone over every little thing you do or don't do.

After 25 years of protecting the Gretchens and Charlies of my assignment areas by controlling everything, or trying to control, everything within them, it was not easy to let go and not be defensive when that space was violated. It didn't matter that the intent was to help. It didn't matter that the person was a neighbor or friend. What did matter were the intrusion and the fact that someone had 'slipped' by me and controlled something I should have known about. There was a malfunction in the environment and I hadn't seen it. I was asleep at my post.

The only thing I could do now was control my reaction which so far had been pretty rude. It was time for damage control.

"Please accept my apology, Gretchen. I got up way too early this morning and didn't get much sleep last night. That's no excuse for taking it out on you. I'd really appreciate your dropping off the package, and thanks for picking it up."

"I understand Jill. I've had a few of those days myself lately. We'll be leaving in about ten minutes. We'll just leave the box on the rail if that's okay with you."

"That's fine, and again, thanks. Let me know if you need anything while Joe Sr. is gone. I should be around all week."

"Oh, he should be back by 11 tonight. He said it wasn't an overnight trip. I expect all will be okay, but thanks."

With that, we both hung up.

As promised, the notorious Brinker SUV stopped at the driveway entrance not 15 minutes later and Joe Jr., delivery son extraordinaire, walked in his sharp military style, dressed in his wool BDUs or battle dress uniform style pants, tucked into his insulated jump-style trooper boots, to the porch rail and deposited my well-traveled brown box. His expression was one of disdain and amusement as I gave a quick wave of thanks at the kitchen sink window. He did an about-face and just as sharply marched back to the SUV, and off they went.

Fundy went out for a morning romp when I retrieved the box. I tossed it on the counter by the phone and poured another mug of coffee before looking at the list of addresses and postmarks on its face. The journey of mystery box started six months ago from Newport, Vermont and cycled through three or four USPS facilities before landing in Shaftsbury. It was hard to tell as the stamps were faded and on top of each other, plus the box wasn't that big. The addresses were interesting first going to Port Huron, Michigan, then Bellingham, Washington, on to Coleville, Washington and finally Richford, Vermont. It was rather curious that its journey through the

USPS should follow my journey through stations of the US Border Patrol. Was the postal service extremely slow or the anonymous sender very clever?

Being the cautious person I was, the package was flipped and analyzed from every angle for clues as to what was inside. It was doubtful that a bomb would survive the beating of six months in postal torture chambers from coast to coast, but I suppose someone could have dumped anthrax or some other deadly dirt or powder inside. The wrapping was traditional grocery store brown paper bag, and the tape was everyday over-the-counter packing tape. Using my Leatherman I cut the seams of the flap and carefully opened both ends, unraveling the paper enough to see the small green box inside. No strings or wires evident, and no powders or packets of white stuff set to spring open indicated that it was probably safe to unwrap in the conventional manner. Okay, so I was being a bit paranoid.

Paper was off and there sat the green box with the yellow lid. It was about 8x8x4 inches and sturdy enough to have held a gift of china or glassware, maybe those expensive figurines like Hummels. Lifting the lid I noticed the inside held crumpled newspapers to fill in space. They were carefully removed and placed on the outside wrapping. On the bottom of the box in the center lay a black square object that had obviously been exposed to the elements for some time as it had greenish mold covering parts of it along with a few pine needles, some reddish brown dirt and what appeared to be flakes or seeds of some wild flower or plant. The outside material was leather and a metallic object appeared to be inlaid on top although it was difficult to tell what it was exactly.

I had already put on a pair of disposable rubber gloves as a precaution and used my index finger to gently clear some of the crusted dirt from the edge of the metal. It didn't take long for me to identify the familiar outline and ridges of the United States Border Patrol badge. Detaching it from the carrier to determine the number on the other side was what I should have done, but I didn't. I never did remember that number anyhow and it wouldn't prove a thing. Radio call numbers were the only ones that meant anything to me or any other agent I ever worked with. They were our lifeline. Still, instinct told me this was probably my badge lost some 25 years ago.

The only time I could remember losing my ID was back in December of '78 when I was on patrol around the outskirts of Derby Line. I, Senior

Patrol Agent Metcalf, and another agent whose name I can't remember had run across a string of snowmobiles crossing the border with skids tied behind them. I'm the one who spotted them because I had taken a detour to catch up to Metcalf after using Mother Nature's facilities. Metcalf was pissed that I had slowed them down and he had gone ahead. He was more aggravated when I called in the caravan of four humping it across the frontier heading for the pine forest on the other side of the frozen lake. Once there, they could take three escape routes on manicured State trails and we'd be hard put to stop them all, if any. Our best bet was to get them on the ice before they hit the edge where cover wasn't as thick.

Metcalf and the other agent were two minutes to the left and I was directly behind and closing. I was ordered to stay behind and out of sight until they were ready to close in from the left, but I could see that our suspects would make landfall if I did that. So being the renegade and super agent that I was in those days, I turned up the throttle and cut an angle for the lead snowmobile to intercept.

As luck would have it, everything went south and fast. The last snowmobile had two riders, one of which had a 12 gauge that fired a very neat hole the size of a melon into the rear track of my machine. In my haste to catch number one, I had totally ignored the positions of everyone else. What happened after that is still a little fractured in my memory, but the report states that I flew some 50 feet through the air toward the edge of the lake and hit the ice, breaking through and landing in shallow water. The snowmobile was essentially destroyed. The four suspects got away. Metcalf showed up in time to pull me out of the water, call for medical assistance, and ream my ass. The second agent transferred out to someplace on the southern border as soon as he could. I heard a year later that he had been killed in a private plane accident.

My ID had been in my snowsuit inside pocket and I never understood why it had never been recovered. I had also lost one clip from my duty belt even though I carried two. Now figure that one out.

Someone had returned, at some expense and effort, something they had found. It must have been found at the lake somewhere around the edge judging by the dirt and green mold covering parts of the casing and badge. It didn't tell me when it was found or why it wasn't returned to the Border Patrol. They wanted me to know that it had been found and where it had been found, but why? The other thing that bothered me was how the person knew whose badge it was and where to mail it. IDs had badge numbers on the back for issue purposes but you had to have access to official files to know who was issued which numbered badge. Any written or photo information would have deteriorated in the water or muck. Uh, uh, someone sent this for a purpose other than idle curiosity at what I would do. Anyone with good intentions or trying to do the so-called right thing would have included a note of explanation or at least a name to contact for more information.

Maybe there's a clue in the packaging.

I spread out the papers that were used for packing and looked them over checking for dates, locations, and even read the news. Nothing was ringing any bells or making an impression. What did I expect from the New York Times Sports section of six months ago? The box was equally useless and provided no clues. Until such time as a new reason came up to think about this, it made more sense to put everything back together and set it on the dresser. Why worry about this now when I can stretch it out for a month of Sundays?

The light bulb was slow to come on, but come on it did. Was this in any way connected with Mr. Gloom and Doom Robinson? Did he have a case that was somehow connected to this incident? That couldn't be possible since they were never caught and no case existed. Metcalf made certain I never forgot that it was my fault that the whole thing went belly up. It wasn't his lack of speed, it was my over-zealousness and inability to follow orders that caused the escape. Who knows what was on those sleds? Who knows what was smuggled across the line? As far as Metcalf was concerned I was personally responsible for every explosion, robbery, and assassination for the next ten years, because I let those four sleds get through the line on purpose.

But regardless of Metcalf's personal opinion, there was no case and Robinson had no reason to research the incident as it was an internal Border Patrol matter. I doubt that some agent past or present would need a PI to investigate that snafu.

CHAPTER 3

The voice was coming from quite a distance and yet seemed very clear and distinctive. Each word clearly enunciated so as to remove any danger of mispronunciation or misunderstanding. Gradually the voice came closer and as if I were coming out of a drugged state of confusion, I began to understand how the words were forming together into a sequence of thought. Sentences began to connect and the sense of the speaker's intent became obvious to my somewhat befuddled mind.

"…ending a month-long search for the missing boat. In an unrelated story, the unidentified body of a man was found in the men's room of the Albany International Airport early this morning. Airport Police say maintenance personnel who discovered it shortly after 6:30 am found the man lying on the floor unconscious. He was taken to Albany Medical where he was pronounced dead on arrival. Police found no evidence of foul play but did not rule it out as a possibility. No identification was found on or near the body. An autopsy is being performed to determine cause of death. The victim is Caucasian, has brown hair and eyes, is 5'11", and weighs 180 lbs. Police are asking anyone with information who could help with the identification or were in the area between 5 and 7 am to contact the Albany Police Dept. at…"

Dead bodies at the airport had a way of ruining a good nap and sparking lousy memories at the same time. So far, retirement wasn't going as planned. I really didn't need to reflect on my career days on the southern border.

Discovering a dead body was never a pleasant experience, but some were nastier than others. I'm sure the maintenance personnel at the airport were duly mortified to find a corpse in whatever shape he was in, but nothing compared to the sight of 20 men, women and children packed liked sardines into a small box truck and left in the middle of a desert to bake and die. It was, and is, indescribable the length to which a human being will go to cross the southern border into this country. They will risk their lives, the lives of their families and children, and all of their worldly possessions to spend one month or, better yet, one year working in the fields for slave wages. It's better than what they have.

There are more than enough coyotes, or transporters, who are willing to take their money to smuggle them across in all kinds of life-threatening arrangements designed to fool the authorities and gain entry into remote areas. Any Border Patrol agent on the southern sector will not only catch aliens for deportation, but will also find those who were abandoned and died a gruesome death. All BP vehicles carry cases of water, all agents speak at least Spanish and ideally other languages, all agents can render first aid, and all agents have seen first hand what cruel and greedy bottom feeders can do to desperate, hopeless and naïve believers.

That wasn't all we dealt with. For every group of illegals we gathered and processed, there were always a percentage of them who turned out to be wanted terrorists, sex offenders, pedophiles, and sometimes kidnap victims turned up or the kidnappers. You just never knew who you had until the paperwork started to go through. After 9/11 no one wanted to let anyone slip through on their watch or their piece of the fence.

Still, finding a train boxcar crammed with illegals that had been sitting on a side track for days with no ventilation did not make for sweet dreams. Sometimes they were on the southern border but that didn't exclude other ports of entry as well. Illegals are smuggled into every entry point of the United States by every means available and left to the wolves while their transporters escape untouched. In those cases you called for the ambulance, unloaded the extra water and body bags, and prayed you could keep your food down while smelling the stench of death in the desert heat or mountain cold. Oh yeah, coyotes were real princes to immigrants and always kept their promise to get them to the US. The final destination wasn't always what they paid for or expected.

At least the guys in Albany had a whole body to look at and try to identify or so it appeared. It was neat and clean not in pieces or rat chewed or with half of him slightly softened by the sun and the other covered with ants and beetles.

Aren't we the cheerful one after a nap? Here it is 6:30 pm and I've managed to waste most of the day dwelling on the past and thinking of gruesome crime scenes. Well, at least Robinson hasn't called back. Wonder what the hell he wants? Maybe the day won't be so bad after all. I had read over all the files and paperwork that space and good judgment had allowed me to keep and there was nothing that jumped out at me as curious or worthy of an independent investigation. Most of the cases I had were fairly straight forward dealing with illegal entry or attempted smuggling. Gun running was the most serious along with illegal human trafficking, drugs, and money shipments.

The job was pretty basic and uncomplicated in comparison to many other enforcement agencies although strategically of great importance. You're on patrol and see something or someone unusual. You do an immigration check for papers, ask questions, and check containers, etc. if you have probable cause or reasonable suspicion depending on what you want to do. If you're lucky and good at what you do, you catch the bad guys and stop the drugs, illegal aliens, illegal imports, drug or counterfeit money, arrest the terrorist, or find the fugitive. It was all in a day's work.

Thinking about my first years on the southern border put me in the mood for dinner which Fundy and I did after taking care of the horses. Turned out they were as hungry as we were and twice as frisky. Cochise and Tracker pushed each other around playing the "I got here first" game which they did every night, while Nevada just stood there watching the boys be boys. She obviously understood that they were idiots to be tolerated because in the long run, both of them would rather die than let anything happen to her. Exactly what a good partnership should be like. She was a beautiful brown and white pinto mare and the geldings were both western mountain horses that had been raised wild but tamed and trained by a retired Border Patrol officer who had been injured in the line of duty. Tracker was all dark brown with black mane and tail. Cochise was more of a reddish brown with a light colored mane and tail. All three had been used extensively for patrols on the northern border and seen their share of search and rescue details along with long days and nights going up and down mountain after mountain chasing after what the sensors saw and the helicopters and snowmobiles couldn't quite reach or search out. Now they were with me for the same reason I was here, to retire and enjoy life without stress. Right.

The snow was still crunching underfoot but at least it had stopped falling and the temperature had moderated some. No lights were visible at the Brinkers', but that was normal. Gretchen must have hunkered down for the night after a harrowing day in town with hubby's SUV. Funny I hadn't seen her or the car return since early this morning. Must have missed them at nap time. Wonder why Fundy didn't bark?

I liked this time of day or night depending how you look at 6:50 pm in Vermont. Everything is still, white and clean with the new snow on the ground and the pine trees. You can see through the trees all the silhouettes of hardwood tree trunks standing like fence posts, and the stone fences surrounding the property have snow cover on top that looks like someone put too much frosting on a cake and it's dripping down the side. If you stand still you'll catch the motion on top of the snow of a mouse that skittered out from under the barn floor and thought it might find some grain that the horses forgot to eat. Like that's going to happen! Sometimes when the sky clears after a snowstorm, the stars and moon are so bright on the snow you can walk through the woods and see forever. It is breathtaking and gives me reason to appreciate winter.

Fundy began to move his ears forward the way he does when something of superb interest comes along. I listened for noise of car or beast but nothing reached my less than precisely tuned hearing. Then he began a very low rumbling growl as a sort of prelude to a full deep throated bark which never ceases to make me jump even when I know it's coming.

"What's up, boy?" I didn't really expect an answer, but it was one of those times I wished he were a Hollywood movie dog that was smarter than his owner. He tried to get up with the stealth of a mountain lion but it looked more like a labor of duress than skill. He bumped into a few chairs as he moved out from under the dining room table and moved the table enough to slosh the brandy in my half-empty glass. Still, I couldn't detect any reason for alarm, but recognizing that caution is usually a better way to go; I moved away from the table and turned off the light.

Within 30 seconds, Fundy was in full gear running for the opposite end of the house barking that deep "I know you're out there" warning that I was beginning to get accustomed to. Without hesitation, I turned on the outside floodlight on the south side between house and barn, flipped off the living room light switch, ducked through the bathroom which connected to the master bedroom and office, and picked up my 9mm lying under the pillow. As soon as Fundy sensed that both of us were on the same page, he settled into watch mode and stopped the noise, but maintained his alert status. Ears and eyes were intently focused on the window facing the barn area where I was cautiously looking through the insulated curtain with my back to the wall to avoid showing my silhouette.

The horses seemed to be alert but still standing around their respective piles of hay munching along as though not much was out of the ordinary. Of course it took several sticks of dynamite to get these guys moving away from food regardless of any outside threat. I never considered them a prime investment in my security system. Nevada was watching something in particular on the backside of the barn facing away from the house that was blocked from my view. Often times when the skies were bright like tonight and the snow had stopped falling, deer would cross over the stone walls at the back of the pasture and enter the woods on their way up the mountain to bedding areas. Sometimes they would stop by and sneak some hay from the guys and gal just to tide them over on the trip up. The horses didn't mind and neither did I as long as they didn't break my wire fencing on the way out. Usually the horses didn't perk up and the deer came right up to the barn within a few minutes. This was not happening.

Both the dog and I watched for a few minutes and nothing else seemed to be moving or making noise. Fundy's ears were starting to relax and my adrenaline was returning to normal levels as well. I tucked the gun into my belt at the small of my back, mostly from habit, and slowly moved away from the window towards the door where the switch for the outside spot was. My eyes were still moving from window to window and watching outside, but it was a pretty good bet that Fundy had miscued or eaten a bad biscuit. That thought brought a smile to my face and I turned to look at Fundy just in time to see his hackles go straight up as he leaped four feet off the floor and landed just short of the south door on the other side of the couch.

While I was deep in thought, he had walked around me and the bed, gone through the door where I was now standing and entered the living room which completed the circle of rooms on the first floor of the house. The couch formed a barrier from the bedroom door towards the opposite end of the house where the dining and kitchen area was. To the right of the couch was the living room, TV and the south door that lead to the screened porch and eventually to the barn access. It was at this door that Fundy was now standing tall and barking in all his glory. Me? I was pushing 5 shells into a 12 gauge pump and grabbing my binoculars while turning off the spotlight.

I double-timed it down the stairs to the finished basement and went into the middle room with the southern bay window that served as hobby room and library. The windows were at ground level and gave an unobstructed view of the barn, pasture, woods and driveway that stretched from the eastern to the western corners of the house in a straight line. If something was moving or out of place, I would see it unless it was on the roof or porch. The light was perfect. Good enough for normal vision which meant special night vision binoculars used in low light conditions were not required. Good thing, I didn't have any.

I glassed with the binoculars from left to right trying to move slowly so as not to miss anything, but afraid to move too slow and miss something on the other side. My ever-present and critical internal voice was saying, *Damn it, Jill. Are you ever going to be good enough for you?* Interesting thought at a time like this. Let's be scared and pontifical too. Hmmm, haven't heard that voice since I was a rookie. Can't say I've missed it either.

That's when it happened. Actually two things happened at the same time that added together equaled "bingo". There was an exchange of blows between Cochise and Tracker that sent a set of hooves solidly against the inside wall of the outside stalls where they stayed 90% of the time. Why the location of the stalls is important is because they are built U-shaped with the bottoms back to back, the openings facing east and west, and one common wall with the barn proper. When you whack the middle wall that separates the two stalls, on a cold winter night with two horse hooves flying with a ton or more of power behind them, you generate a sound that is the equivalent of any high powered gun you can imagine. Add to that the stillness of the night that's just been shattered, and if you are trying to sneak around the barn, you need to go home to change your tighty whities.

A fraction of a second following the horse volley, two figures moved from the right side of my field of vision and started to blend into the woods to the south. A third figure could just barely be seen on the far side of the stone wall about 150 yards beyond the pasture slipping behind a camp I had out there for kids when they came to visit. The movements had happened so quickly and at the extremes of my peripheral vision that I couldn't be certain of exactly where they had started from or what their description would be if someone asked. They were dressed in white camo for sure. Armed with rifles or shotguns was a guess since all I really saw was something that extended from the body. It could just as easily have been bows, arrows, javelins, or pogo sticks. Hell, it could have been kids having a paintball game.

After watching for another 20 or so minutes, I went upstairs and checked the view from there. It all looked clear and peaceful as if the entire evening had been uneventful. Even Fundy was sound asleep on the couch and the horses were back to munching on whatever they could find that had been overlooked from meals past. Reminded me of what one of my Field Training Officer's once told me about patrol work, "You'll spend seven hours and fifty-five minutes on patrol dying of boredom and then have five minutes of sheer terror." And they wonder why cops drink and can't have a decent relationship. Who can survive on adrenaline, criticism, and lousy pay?

Fundy's right, it's time to go to bed.

Next morning brought light and a new perspective on the events of the night before. Horses were fed as usual except for Cochise who only got half a ration of hay and no grain. He and I were going to take a little walk today. I went around the barn and grounds surrounding the house looking at the boot marks and noting that four, not three, persons had been in the area. The fourth had been further east, closer to Gretchen's house and had been out of my line of sight at all times. The boots appeared to be the type used by hunters and outdoorsmen with no particular markings making them outstanding. They were all pretty big in size, leading me to assume that they were more than likely men, although one could never take such things for granted. There were a couple of places next to trees that a mark was left in the snow which looked like it could have been left by the butt end of a rifle or shotgun. There were no traces of fabric, food, paper, or other material to indicate anyone had been there.

I decided to have a better look at my night visitors and their wanderings. Breakfast was solid since I intended to be out and about in the cold for a while. Protein, carbs and hot liquids were always a good way to go, so I scrambled up eggs with cheese slapped it between whole wheat bread, grabbed a bag of trail mix and a thermos of hot chocolate. At the barn I saddled up Cochise and checked his hooves to be certain the farrier had removed his shoes. Not knowing how far we'd be traveling, I threw on the saddle bags with grain and water for the horse, and emergency stuff just in case for me. I also strapped on the scabbard and threw in the 12 gauge. Fundy was going to have to stay.

CHAPTER

4

There are few times in my life when I feel at ease with myself and the universe, knowing that body and soul are in sync with everything in my surroundings. I feel the ebb and flow of motion, a calming effect in the touch of an animal or snowflake or gentle breeze. The skies and forests seem to blend into a comfortable home for both man and beast with no conflict or violence to cause discord with the music being played in the winds.

This morning was one of those times, as I stood just outside the sliding barn door and looked around at the snow covered landscape with its awakening population of winter residents. Little birds were dodging in and out of the plowed driveway area pecking at Lord knows what but seeming to enjoy it. Underground critters were running along the stone wall and would now and then duck under the snow, only to pop up 10 or 15 feet further away for a quick peek, and then down they would go again. I could see a couple of does over a shallow rise walking away from the shack out back. Bet they had a belly full of hay.

Cochise stood quietly to my side with breath clearly visible in light misty clouds at his muzzle that left little drops of moisture on his hair. His eyes were alert, soft and seemed to be saying, "Okay, we're all dressed up, do we have someplace to go?" His neck felt warm and strong to my hand as I stroked under his mane with my right hand and laid my cheek against him on the other side in a human-to-horse hug. "You have always been my patient one.

Just let me enjoy this another minute and we'll go do what you do best." As if in understanding, Cochise turned his head slightly to the left and looked at his friends on the other side of the paddock munching on breakfast. Guess it really was a bit unfair to keep him so near and yet so far from food. Let's mount up and enjoy the ride.

Once I was in the saddle, both Cochise and I fell into old routines. It mattered not that he had a winter coat of fur, that I had thermals, loose wool pants, a down parka and thermal riding boots. We didn't need the close contact most riders do when going out for a "Sunday drive". Cochise and I had a system of rein and verbal commands that had saved both of our lives on more than one occasion. Both of us had spent five years patrolling the miles of border with Canada from the Pasayten Wilderness in Washington, through the Idaho Rocky Mountains and on into Western Montana. That was rugged country covered with wildlife and beauty in addition to wildlife of a different sort.

Cochise had carried me up and down mountains on trails covered in rock that shifted at a moment's notice. We had climbed to elevations that changed from green to snow within a few feet. We had encountered everything from mountain lions to rattlesnakes, and snakes with two legs. Going up was never a problem for me, but coming down always made me wonder about updating my will, and if I had turned off the coffee pot before leaving the house. I was always very thankful that Cochise had been a tried and proven mountain horse before he became my mount.

Tracking fresh footprints in new snow on a clear day in the hills of Vermont was going to be a piece of cake compared to search and rescue in Washington. Fundy was happily curled up in front of the woodstove with his favorite chew toy and plenty of water. I had pulled a frozen beef soup bone out of the freezer and tied it to the beam where he eats, to gnaw on later if he felt the need. He was pretty good about staying home and guarding the joint when I went out for the day, and even for the occasional overnight. It wasn't his favorite thing to do, being the clingy type, but he'd put up with it rather than get kenneled or tied up in the barn. It's a wise dog that recognizes his master's limitations.

I really didn't want him tagging along and messing around with the tracks. Fundy loved to run with us when we rode in the woods. It was his idea of Nirvana to cruise out at a 45 degree tangent from the trail with hackles up, feet at full stride, barking at some imaginary prey until he would disappear from sight in the underbrush or over a hill top. Minutes later he would reappear from another direction and come galloping in with tongue hanging out the side of his mouth looking exhausted and ecstatic. Nevada was the only one who took exception to his behavior on trail and even she tolerated Fundy's enthusiasm – well, mostly tolerated. Fundy stayed away from her hind legs with a diligence he didn't show for much else. Nevada had made her point clear the first time that she did not appreciate surprise appearances. The vet said Fundy had been lucky not to have more than a concussion. I think Fundy agreed.

Instinct told me that sneaking around houses in early evening was probably not an accident, and whoever those guys were, they were not going to be easy to track. Having dog tracks all over the place was not going to help and Fundy was no bloodhound. I wished I had Mike Peterson's dog here. Turk could track fish through the Columbia River. Thinking of Turk reminded me of Mike and brought back a flash of memories that both angered and saddened in a way that only the pain of a deep personal loss could. I had Mike's horse, Cochise, but the two of us had forged a new relationship at Coleville that allowed me to push those memories into a corner of my mind that remained in the dark. Somewhere I didn't go and didn't want to go. It hurt then, it hurts now, and it will always hurt as long as it stays unresolved.

I spent half a second taking in the cold air, holding the breath, counting to ten and releasing slowly. I double checked my sidearm, food supply, first aid, and oversized-boot stirrups for foot placement. Speaking to no one in particular I said, "OK then. Let's go see where the yellow brick road goes."

I reined right and rode up the drive towards the private road not wanting Tracker and Nevada to get too antsy about being left home alone.

They didn't usually put up a fuss, but I didn't need a crowd today and certainly wasn't in the mood to go chasing after them. If my guess was right, I could head up towards Gretchen's house, cut between us and pick up at least one, if not more, of the tracks. Once I had one I would more than likely follow it to the other three.

My guessing paid off rather quickly and I had to move farther up the road to avoid riding back into my own pasture. "Crap, this jackass was closer to the house than I thought, fella. What have we gotten ourselves into here?"

About two thirds the distance up the road to her house, I cut in again and this time I cut the track heading towards her house plus a second coming in from the southwest most likely from the shack behind my house.

Cochise walked slowly through the woods until we could see the Brinker house and the surrounding open areas. A look with field glasses didn't show any movement at all either in or out of the house. That was very peculiar given that Joe's SUV was now in the garage with the door to the garage open. That meant that Gretchen must have returned home with Joe Jr. He was still in school to my knowledge. This being March, and today being Tuesday, and the hour being around seven, I would think at least the lights would be on in the kitchen at the front of the house.

Another look with the glasses at the tracks leading towards the house didn't show much at this distance. I would have to get a lot closer to be sure. It would be best if I went back out to the road and approached from there. At least if I woke her up, I could say I was out for a morning ride and was worried when I didn't see lights on, just doing a welfare check. It was the neighborly thing to do.

We rounded the corner and cautiously approached the house from the north while I scanned the yard and surrounding out buildings for any sign of life or activity. No one appeared to be home, and no lights came on or were left on indicating an earlier departure. I reined Cochise over to the garage on the northeast side of the house and dismounted putting myself and the horse out of view. I undid the safety strap on my 9mm and checked to be sure I had quick access if needed. This was just too weird for me.

Walking into the garage, I noticed that one set of tracks had entered, gone to the workbench in the back, removed something from a drawer or shelf, or perhaps had placed something there, and then left. I couldn't see that any dust had been disturbed anywhere so I opened the drawers. One drawer had files, chisels, hammers and a couple rusty screwdrivers in it. The next one held an assortment of hinges, door knobs, brackets, and miscellaneous hardware one would expect to find in a garage. The third of four held three hatchets of the camping variety two of which had broken wooden handles. The fiberglass handle had a significant amount of dark staining on the handle along with what appeared to be hairs or fur. A closer look at the wooden handles and broken off heads showed similar markings.

Without a warrant or probable cause, nothing I picked up here would ever count in court, but there's a lot to be said for satisfying one's curiosity, and sometimes you can work backwards if the need arises. I have never stacked a case or planted evidence in my entire career, but I've always believed in stacking the deck in one's favor when necessary. Bad guys never play by the rules. I see nothing wrong in pushing the envelope when needed.

With that in mind, I looked around and then remembered that I had brought some extra sandwich bags for garbage and placed them in the saddle bags. Grabbing two, I went back to the hatchet drawer and carefully removed two clumps of the hair or fur from the tools with a stick I had found outside and placed each in a separate corner of the bag. I broke off the tip of the stick with each clump and creased the bag lengthwise to keep the two separated. Next, I found a roll of electrical tape on the shelf, carefully closed the plastic bag being careful not to let the two samples touch, and taped the flap. There was an old Popsicle stick on the floor by a waste barrel where someone's aim had been a few inches short of the mark. *No two points for you.* This I placed midline between the two and taped it fast to the bag. Then I folded the bag over the stick and taped the bag to the stick on both sides.

Now all I had to do was roll the stick and the bag rolled itself up like a window shade with the two samples in their respective corners on top of each other, separated by plastic. I taped around the stick to keep it from unraveling, and went out to Cochise to place it in the saddle bags.

The fourth drawer proved to be a puzzle. This had to be the goal of the tracks from last night. Inside was a clear, dust-free 10x3 inch marking alongside another dust-free image that clearly outlined a hunting knife. Judging by its length, width, and design, I'd say it was a Bowie type possibly what they call a "gut hook". Lately, these had become popular especially with hunters as they made gutting game a bit easier and less messy if you maintained the cutting edges properly.

The design was your basic Jim Bowie knife complete with hand guard, thick back blade, strong handle (non-slip), and super sharp cutting edges on both sides at the tip. The tip is where the changes were made. There is a point on the outside but it also curves back in like a fish hook. The inside of that hook is also bladed, very sharp, and comes to its own point. The outside point at the end of the blade, while very sharp, tends to be more rounded, thus making it the perfect tool for skinning game.

When you skin game, you roll the skin fur side out and carefully separate the attaching membrane from the muscle of the animal. You want to be very careful not to cut hide or meat. You'll ruin the hide and get hair all over the meat which is awful to get off. When it comes to removing the entrails, you want to be able to slit the thin skin holding everything in place without touching or nicking internal organs.

You flip your gut hook over, place two fingers under the skin you want to cut, and lift. The hook slides between your fingers and follows the V formation as far as you want to go while the inside blade does the cutting. Once done, you can now dump out the insides and detach what needs to be for further dressing.

They make all sizes of these in various materials and colors. Some fold, some clip on your belt, and some machetes now have this type of hook on them. I would not like to meet the animal needing a machete gut hook to be field dressed.

Next to the empty spaces were two boxes of trash bags, a set of keys, and a note. Written in small block letters were three lines: **Training day 8:00 pm. Bring equipment. Don't be late.**

The empty space next to the knife outline and the size of the other boxes of bags looked to be identical. That box of bags must have been removed along with the knife, perhaps to assist with something nasty? I picked up the keys and looked at them trying to identify what they might unlock. One said Schlage, which might open the house or possibly the garage door. I'd check on the way out. Two were for Master locks and could be anything. One was a Ford and probably went to the SUV here in the garage.

I opened the SUV door with the Ford key, first checking for anything out of the ordinary. Looked okay outside of the fact that Gretchen wasn't home, and Joe's SUV was here locked up with the garage door open, and people were sneaking around her house at night with camo and guns. When all those thoughts collided together in my head, I decided it was time to go directly to the house. There were too many details not fitting together, and several indicators that Gretchen may be in harm's way along with Joey. I'd call the State Police if it seemed appropriate depending on what came of my call at the house.

On the way past the garage door, I checked the doors for locks. The doors were wooden with small glass panes in a series of four squares making one large square in each door. The window washer hadn't done his job here in quite some time and the odds of being able to see anything other than shadows through either door glass were zero to none. One door was almost closed but came short of its mark by two feet or so due to the sod having heaved with frost and ice build-up from melting roof snow. The second door was fully extended open and flattened against the other side of the garage wall. I checked the partially opened door first and found what I was looking for. Hanging off the handle was a Master lock looped through a piece of chain about 28 inches long.

The chain was the sort used for light-duty hauling around the yard as in large tree branches and such, or safety chains on hitches. There was also a deadbolt lock in the door that had seen better days. It appeared to have been assaulted by the business end of a chisel or small crowbar, and the wood around it had been damaged indicating someone seriously wanted said lock out of the door. I did notice the stamp on the lock read Schlage.

Jumping to conclusions, I assumed someone had tried to break in to Joe Brinker's garage but was either caught and ran off or gave up. Or my second choice - Joe or Gretchen had lost their key and tried to break in to get their car and failed. Either way the attempted break-in was discovered. Rather than replace the lock, Joe (most probably) finds a length of chain and padlock to secure the garage doors.

Cochise, who was patiently standing next to me listening, brushed his muzzle against my shoulder ever so gently as if to say, "Nice work, partner." Then he lifted his head and turned slightly to the right to catch sight of a blue jay landing on a pine bough a few yards ahead. That singular motion managed to push my shoulder way beyond my center of balance and started both feet in a not- so-graceful slide towards the opposite snowbank. Rather than land on my back, I managed to turn and slide into the snow like a ball player stealing third base. I rolled over onto my back and looked up into the loving eyes of my brave horse who just stood there wondering what I was doing on the ground.

I started laughing at myself and grabbed his reins expecting him to pull me up when I saw them. There was no other position a person could spot them from, except from the ground and upside down. Unless of course you were the one who put them there. I might need the State Police for a house entry but this was definitely Department of Fish and Game violation territory.

Now it was time to call Gus.

CHAPTER

5

The one thing I could always count on was a quick answer when I dialed the Vermont State Police dispatch line. For Mom it was death and taxes, but for me, this was it.

"State Police, Dispatcher Bevins. How can I help you?"

"Hey, Angie. It's Jill Benoit out in the Hollow. Who's covering major game crimes in these parts today?"

"Jill? Haven't heard from you since Ricardo's retirement party.

What kind of trouble are you into now?"

"Well, you know how it is with me and the neighbors, one minute they behave and the next all hell breaks loose. Actually, I don't really know for sure what's going on except that it's something for either the State or Fish and Game to high-tail it out here and take a look at ASAP."

"Hang on, Jill, Gus just walked in. I'll put him on the other line." There was a pause of a few minutes and then Gus cut in with his unmistakable voice that sounded like a bull moose in pain. "What the hell have you got into now, Benoit? Haven't I got enough problems without you messing things up?"

"Gus, I miss you too. Stop being such a charmer and haul ass out here to my place. Last night four guys in camo with guns were sneaking around my house and barn. When I started to check out their paths and back track them this morning, I found what I think may be nine carcasses hanging in the pine trees at my neighbor's house. My neighbor should be home with at least one of her kids, but doesn't seem to be. Her car is here, the house is dark, and the son should be in school, as this is a school day, but no one is stirring. I haven't checked the house yet since I don't have probable cause or back up. Anything else you want to know?"

After a long pause, I heard Gus mumble something to Angie, and she cut back into the line.

"Jill, Gus is contacting one of the troopers just south of you returning from a call in Pownal. His ETA should be 20 minutes or so. We'll log this in under inter-agency call with Fish & Game taking the lead unless something else develops concerning your neighbor. Gus will pick up additional assistants on his way out and should be at your house in 15. He asked that you wait before checking the house, okay?"

"Got it, Angie, and thanks. Give my best to your better half." I closed the cell phone and stuck it back into my inside jacket pocket. Well, guess it was time to get up off the ground.

That was more co-operation than I had expected given the time of day and the fact that the State Police, or VSP, and I were not the best of pals. It wasn't personal, it was traditional. The age- old classic distrust of one law enforcement agency for another based on what only the ghosts and goblins knew. I suspect it had to do with "mine's bigger than yours" more than anything else, and the unending need for men to beat each other to the punch or get the gold star.

I remember after 9/11 when Bush decided to create Homeland Security for purposes of sharing intelligence information to combat terrorism, I said to anyone who would listen it wouldn't work. Why? Because law enforcement agencies are territorial and protective of their "stuff" to the extreme and do not share anything. They protect their own at all costs, including information. Any officer will die in defense of or to protect another officer from a bad guy, but he or she will be damned if they will help another agency get the "glory of the collar" or the bust or the arrest, or any other end result of days, months, even years of back-breaking, ball-busting investigation.

We've all heard of inter-agency cooperation and think that HLS is this big happy family of FBI, CIA, DEA, NSA and all the other Federal acronyms. Supposedly they're having these nice meetings in closed rooms with coffee and doughnuts discussing their latest intelligence about international bad guys and what to do about it. Bullshit. Before these guys sit down, if they sit down at all, they've had their own individual internal meetings with their own people and decided what they are going to divulge and what they will hold back to pursue on their own. They spy on each other and use each other almost as much as they do the bad guys. When someone gets dead, or an attack on a domestic target almost happens or worse yet, a terrorist escapes back to his private hell hole, each agency feels free to blame everyone else for not sharing and playing nice with the team, knowing full well they are just as guilty and responsible for the snafu. It wasn't unusual to have officers quit their respective services or special task forces because they just couldn't take the double dealing among their own. It wasn't about the enemy anymore, it was about gaming and one-up-man-ship.

In the end, it's about money. The agency with the biggest coup, the most arrests, the highest profile cases, gets the largest piece of the pie as we all called Congressional funding or the State allocations from the budget. You don't make the case for more funds if you do all work, tell your friends in another agency what your informants have developed, and share all your hard earned insights. Because just as sure as the sun will set on your retirement, that other agency will take that information and put it together with their information and "surprise, surprise!" they just happen to be the team that's coincidently on the tarmac when the plane lands with Mr. X, his false passport, and an encrypted message from Ali Chazzan. You snooze, you lose. There may be no honor among thieves, but there isn't much more among cops when it comes to sharing information.

There were exceptions that existed with agencies working hard to cooperate with each other and back each other on a daily basis. The Spokane Sector of the Border Patrol for one, and several other Sectors, were spending a lot of time and energy along with personnel from enforcement agencies in other departments to provide information and back up whenever and wherever possible. It made the jobs of all easier and a lot more efficient when it came to finding bad guys and slowing the flow of contraband and aliens across the frontier. It also helped tremendously to effect rescues and provide for an officer's safety when on duty. I guess it wasn't all bad. Maybe I was getting prejudiced in my old age.

Gus pulled into the yard in his Dodge truck, followed by two other Vermont State official 4x4s. Gus's truck and the smaller Jeep were green with Vermont Fish & Game insignias, light bars, radios and all the other bells and whistles that go with enforcement of laws in Vermont. I was a great supporter of arming wardens and was amazed to learn that they hadn't always had enforcement powers equal to other officers in this state. As far as I was concerned, theirs was a far more dangerous job than anyone else's. They always faced people with guns and usually in places where being hidden was easy. The odds of a Game Warden being ambushed and killed were far greater than mine; and they always worked alone during the most dangerous time of year, hunting season. Nope, you'd never get me to be Game Warden in any state.

The third truck was white and had a trailer behind it with three snowmobiles. All three machines had State Police logos and colors. The driver was a young man maybe in his late twenties with the military cut of a new recruit and the all business attitude of someone trying to impress. *Oh Crap! Dudley Do Right in the flesh.*

We introduced ourselves all around. As it turned out, Dudley was really Trooper John Filbert, a newly graduated recruit from the last academy class. The Deputy Warden was Abigail Buskirk from North County. We had met once or twice before but neither of us ran in the same circles. She seemed okay to me and after noting that she preferred to be called Gail, we got down to business. Vehicles were moved into an arrangement that allowed the Jeep and Dodge to move out as needed, and the snowmobiles to be unloaded at a later time if requested. The trooper from Pownal had space to pull in and turn around when he arrived, which we expected momentarily. Meanwhile, I brought Cochise to the barn and put his tack away, making sure he was brushed out and his feet were cleaned of snow clumps. Tracker and Nevada were glad to see their pal back, mostly because they knew he would get a little hay for being a good boy and, of course, they would too. I threw the saddlebags over my shoulder, grabbed the shotgun and walked up to the house just as the cruiser drove in.

Captain Richard Dugan stepped out of his cruiser and walked with the ease of someone who had been on the job for more than a month or two. He had that smile of recognition that said he was pleased to have been sent and curious about the reason.

"Jill Benoit, you're looking a little less than retired to me. You aiming to use that door buster, or just mad at Gus again?"

We weren't much for the "no touchy" laws between males and females in the work place and all that other stuff, so I just leaned the shotgun against the porch rail, dropped the saddlebags, and gave Rick a hug.

"Hell, Angie didn't say it was you coming up. I would have yelled sooner."

Rick and I had a history that went back a few years to 1966- 71 when I worked part-time as a security guard for the US Forest Service in their campgrounds. Short version was that I got into trouble and he bailed me out. We've been friends since. He's saved my bacon several times, my daughter's once, and I have returned the favor whenever possible. They don't come any better than Rick Dugan.

The five of us were standing around outside when I heard the unmistakable bark of Fundy on the other side of the front door.

Crap, if I didn't let him out, not only would the door crumble but his "deposits" would be all over the place.

"Folks, I have to let my dog out. Anyone have a problem with dogs?"

No one seemed to, so I went up the stairs to the porch, opened the front door and was immediately run over by a yellow furball that quickly jumped the rail and ran for his favorite pine tree. After a very long time, in dog terms, Fundy ran another 15 yards or so over the other side of the drive and completed his quest for relief. Back he came, bounding over snowbanks and bushes until he spotted Rick and immediately made a beeline for him. Rick saw the monster approaching and was prepared for the paws which he took in both hands and allowed Fundy to give him a huge slurp of the tongue before setting him down. Now there was a happy dog.

I spent the next 15 minutes explaining to the group what had started the night before at about 8:30 pm up to my call to Angie at 7:15 am. I was still debating if I should mention the fur samples I had in the saddlebags. There was stuff still left on the tools to be sure, and I didn't think they would need to attach each tool to each hide. I thought I'd wait and see how it played out for a bit. I could always come clean later.

I did mention that I was concerned for Gretchen since her husband had not returned as expected yesterday afternoon, and she had not contacted me as she usually does when stuff doesn't go as planned. I had also seen no signs of activity at the house at all, but had seen one set of tracks from the four intruders leading directly to one of the windows. She had two children, one at home the other in college, and there was no sign of them either. It was now almost 8:10 am and I didn't think time was our friend.

Rick agreed that Gus should take the lead since game violations were the probable cause and called-in complaint. I would go with Gus in his truck and Gail would take young John with her in the Jeep. Rick would take his cruiser and go directly to the house using a welfare check as his probable cause with me as the concerned neighbor calling it in.

Welfare checks were not uncommon. All agencies do them on request without requiring an act of Congress for action. Any officer on duty will stop by, or even stop a car with a given plate number to check on the welfare of the occupant and/or driver at the request of someone who gives a reasonable explanation as to why they think that person may have a problem. It can be health related, medical, mental, or suspicion of criminal activity such as a runaway, hostage etc.

A wel-check gave Rick what he needed and everyone was covered case wise plus back up. Fundy was left on guard duty once again but this time he wasn't as happy about it. "Sorry, my friend, but this just isn't the time or the place for fun and games. I'll make it up to you tonight, maybe."

Gus pulled his truck straight into the garage space facing the half open door, and Gail parked her Jeep three car lengths back. She and John got out as Rick came up the drive, continued past towards the house, and entered the small driveway. John walked up the road the short distance and entered the exit of the semicircle to back him up. Both officers had radios and were armed, although only Rick was in full uniform. John had his badge on a chain around his neck, fully visible.

Meanwhile, Gail had opened the back of the Jeep where she retrieved a camera and field kit for collection of evidence. I walked down to see if I could assist and she handed me several cases to carry. Gus had removed a ladder from his truck and was in the process of setting it up under one of the evergreens where I had pointed out the trash bags suspended underneath the massive boughs overhead. He took a large coil of nylon climbing rope and a four inch pulley with a clipping system that looked like a piece of rubber coated chain held together with a link repair clip.

"I'm going to throw one end of this rope down to you when I get it set up to lower those bags. Take it around that small tree over there twice and hold it tight until I tell you to lower the weight. We don't know how heavy or light these things are and I don't want to drop anything twenty feet down to splatter in my truck bed. Got that, Benoit?"

"Yes, sir!" I fired off with enthusiasm. "I'll try not to disappoint you, sir."

"You're such a jackass."

"Stop treating me like an idiot." Like that was ever going to happen. After a few seconds of mutual glaring, Gus went back to work and I waited for the rope to come down.

Gail took several shots of the suspended bags with the zoom lens and then backed up to take several more of the garage in relation to the tree. She searched the area for prints, found the tracks and took pictures with a filter to cut glare and sharpen the outlines. It was obvious by the way she carefully walked around the area, moving slowly, lifting objects trying not to disturb but needing to see underneath, and photographing only those things that were pertinent to this situation, that Deputy Warden Buskirk was very good at her job. I was impressed.

Gus was now at the top of the ladder securing the pulley to the branch above the first bag, and stringing the nylon rope through the top of the pulley and down towards the bag. The rest of the coil he tossed on the other side and down to me where I picked it up and shook it loose to make sure it did not knot up. Then twice around the tree it went until Gus was satisfied that the slack was out and he could proceed and tie off the first bag. That being done, he cut the older rope and the nylon rig went taught.

The first bag came down easily and settled on the ground. Gus came down and Gail came over from the Jeep where she had picked up another roll of film and reloaded her camera. Pictures were taken of the outside of the bag which really didn't show much detail. It looked to me as if two bags had been used and both were the type used in construction sites for waste. There were a few hairs here and there, which appeared to be fur in nature, stuck to the plastic with a gooey substance that was probably blood. Gail took a swab and swiped both off and placed them into a container to be labeled and dated. Next, Gus untied the ropes and the bags. With his belt light, he looked inside and made a face that looked even worse than the one he usually had.

"Son of a bitch, I really hate poachers."

Gail took over the rope detail and I left the two of them to whatever it was that they do when you have nine bags of chopped up deer meat. It was a bit more than I was willing to get involved in at 9:00 in the morning. Why any of the Brinker's would be involved in poaching activities was way beyond me, but I certainly didn't appreciate being brought into it by having people with guns running around my house at night. The Brinkers knew I was retired Border Patrol. They knew I had a lot of cop friends who popped in and out of the house at all hours of the day and night. Hell that was one of the reasons Gretchen said she liked living next door and felt safe. So why take a chance and run a poaching operation out of your garage? Better still, why get me involved by sneaking around my house and getting my dander up? It just didn't make any sense to me, assuming there was a connection between the two.

I walked around the garage and hiked through the snow to the side of the house and jumped a small snow bank to the semicircle drive to check on Rick and John. The cruiser was still there, but neither man was in sight. I walked to the front door which was closed and kept going to the other side of the house to look around the corner.

There I saw Rick and John about 160 yards out in the woods walking back in towards the house. Looking down at the snow near the window, I could see where both men had started to follow the tracks of my night visitor out to the woods. I wonder how far they went and what they found. The window itself was closed, although from where I was it was impossible to say if it was locked. At least the glass wasn't broken. Rick walked into the shoveled area of the drive and stamped the snow off his boots.

I didn't wait long to ask, "What did you find out?"

He looked at me with a bit of concern and shook his head from side to side.

"I'm afraid not much of anything concrete. The doors are locked and so are the windows. We can't see anything inside to indicate trouble or foul play and there is no sign that anyone is home. John and I followed the tracks for maybe half a mile. They zigzagged all over the place and met up with two, maybe three, others half-way up the mountain when we quit and came back. I'm not really dressed for this and it's probably a game thing anyhow.

"Unless you have reason to believe that this is an abduction or other crime against persons, I'm inclined to think your friend was picked up by someone else and hasn't returned home yet. Were you gone yesterday or could you have missed her husband coming home and picking her and the kids up?"

"Sure, it's possible. I wasn't out of the Hollow, but I was searching my old files in the attic and downstairs which is sort of a buffer zone when it comes to road sound. Fundy usually barks at cars going by, but not necessarily if he recognizes them like Joe's or Gretchen's. I'm still uncomfortable with the fact that school is in session and she is adamant about their attendance. Why would she take off with the kids on a school day?"

"Maybe she didn't. Maybe she has someone taking care of them elsewhere and she is taking a time out with hubby. A second honeymoon to recharge the marriage batteries sort of speak."

There were a lot of possibilities, but none of them made me feel any better. I like change as much as the next guy but this wasn't change. This was weird.

The three of us walked back to where Gus and Gail were just picking up the last of their gear. All nine bags were in the bed of the truck along with all the ropes used to suspend them.

"Did you look inside the garage?" I asked Gus.

"Not in any detail, did you?" His voice grated like a York rake on an old dirt road that didn't want to be fixed. He was just itching for a fight, something to stick me with.

"I think it would be worth your while since you have pc and all that. You know, probable cause, pc, that stuff they taught you at the academy you needed to do a lawful search? They did teach you that kind of stuff way back then didn't they?"

"You didn't leave fingerprints or any shit like that, when you went in without pc, did you?"

That did it. Now I was not only a jerk for doing an illegal search but incompetent at it too. It was hard to decide which I wanted to do more, beat the shit out of Gus, or just shoot him and get it over with. He was such an arrogant, insufferable ass. "Just what is it about me that bothers you so much, the fact that I know how to do the job or the fact that I have to tell you how to do yours?"

Rick stepped in between the two of us and looked at Gus. "I think in the interests of both our cases, it wouldn't hurt to look inside to make sure we have everything you need to make a case for poaching. It will also make it easier for me to complete my report for the welfare check on Mrs. Brinker and her son. Jill can wait out here and help Gail pack up; John can walk up and bring the cruiser down."

Gus shifted his glare from me to Rick and back to me. Mine never left his face. I had had enough of his insults to last me a lifetime. The chauvinist attitude was really old and really annoying, and it just wasn't going to fly anymore. I wasn't in uniform and, by God, I didn't have to put up with this. That sentiment must have traveled through the air and hit Gus somewhere between the eyes because the next move he made was towards the garage with gloves in hand and flashlight out.

Rick motioned for me to join Gail and told John to get the cruiser. Five minutes later, Rick came out and asked Gail to bring evidence bags and the camera into the garage, and I stayed put at the Jeep. A little while later Gail came out the bags filled with hatchets, the note, boxes of trash bags, coils of rope, a pair of boots, a pair of camo pants, and a ledger. Everything was packed into Gail's Jeep or Gus' truck and the two of them left.

John, Rick and I went back to my house where I made coffee and found some day-old Danishes that passed for edible food. We sat around the table and talked about the stuff found inside the garage. The ledger looked like an order book for venison with cuts desired, amounts, prices and delivery dates. There were names and addresses with contact numbers but no check numbers or other financial information to trace. My guess was they were paying the price by direct deposit to an account that was blind. I had seen this before in a smuggling operation out west. More sophisticated of course, but the end result was the same. You had to catch each individual purchaser before you got the dealer unless you could run a sting, and that wasn't easy.

Gus didn't know it, but he had just landed the break of his career. He had caught a dealer by chance. Had it not been for last night's fluke and my curiosity, this ring would have gone on until the dealer decided to stop or change product. Come to think of it, there might have been another product included.

"Did Gus check to see if there were drugs in the meat?"

Rick looked serious and John nearly fell off the chair. "Why do you think there were drugs in the meat?" Rick asked.

"I don't know that there were. I just know that often times on the border smugglers use one kind of contraband to smuggle in another type of riskier stuff. They figure if an inspector or customs guy can be bribed not to look for a little thing, they can get a nastier thing through and he won't bother to check."

John was all ears and eyes now, practically drooling in his coffee. You could see the "kick ass and take names" look come across his face. I didn't know if I should laugh or cry.

John asked, "Did you really catch smugglers?"

"That's what Border Patrol does, when they can."

Rick wasn't about to let the conversation deteriorate into a war story fest which he knew I deplored.

"How much do you know about your neighbor?"

"Not a whole lot, at least from an investigative point of view. Joe Sr. is an attorney. He's out of town now and then, but I don't know why. Gretchen is okay and minds her own business except when Joe leaves, and then she gets paranoid about everything. She calls me about every noise, shadow, movement and bump in the night. When Joe left this time she called upset because he took her car and left the SUV. It seems that the news had stories about SUVs being blown up in California for being gas guzzlers, and she thought if she went into downtown Bennington someone would toss a fire bomb at her.

"They have a daughter, Tracey, who's 19 and in college. A freshman at Southern Vermont and doing pretty well, I understand. The son, Joseph Jr. is 15 and gives me the creeps. He's tall for his age and works out a lot, judging by his build. He looks like he should be an all-American boy, but my feeling is he's into something else. He dresses like one of Hitler's Brown Shirts and never talks to anyone or has any friends over. The kid scares me."

"Ever see anyone go to the house?" asked Rick.

"I've seen delivery trucks and that sort of thing, but no private vehicles. If they have local friends and family, they go out to meet them."

"How long have they lived here?"

"Eight, maybe ten years."

"That's a long time to live somewhere and not have people visit. Are you sure of your facts?"

"Rick, all I can tell you is what I do or don't see or hear. I'm not always here and I'm not always awake. The next residence is half a mile west of here on the Hollow Road, and then you'd better have transport if you want to find another house. I live here because I like being alone. I'm not sure I even like being close to the Brinkers or their being around me. I was here first. You'll have to ask them why they live here and why they live the way they do.

"And as for Gus, I expect he will deal with the poachers and I won't have to shoot someone in my backyard for threatening my animals or my safety."

Rick grinned, drained his coffee mug and nudged John to his feet. "Nice to see you haven't changed your soft style and gentle touch. Don't want you getting old before I do." With that he patted Fundy on the head and opened the door to leave. John went out first and headed for his truck. It would take him a few minutes to turn the trailer around and head out so Rick partially closed the door to keep the heat in and turned around.

"You know, you might cut Gus a little slack. He's been having a rough time lately."

"I'd be happy to give him slack if he would be so kind as to acknowledge me as a human being with an IQ higher than one."

"Did you know his daughter, Irene, the one who was in Desert Storm?"

"Yeah, we went to high school together. She joined the Marine Corps just after I left the security post at Somerset. We kept in touch for a while. But I lost track after she went to Camp Pendleton. Last I heard she made Major or Colonel or some other high rank."

"She died a year ago, two weeks before her retirement. Her vehicle was involved in an off-base accident that killed her and another officer on their way to testify before a Senate sub- committee. Gus thinks there's some kind of cover up going on and his daughter was sacrificed for the glory of the Corps. He's been poking around, and the boys from the Pentagon have told him to back off. It makes him a little grumpy especially when he and his wife are stuck with raising her 14 year-old step-child."

"How the hell did they get stuck with that?"

"That's a story for another weekend. Let's just say Irene didn't always make good decisions and Gus usually cleaned up after her. It makes him a hard man and a hard personality. Try not to take his attitude too personally."

I looked at Rick for a long time not knowing what to say. Mom always told me to say nothing when in doubt. But this wasn't doubt, it was confusion.

"You have me at a loss for words. No one deserves to lose a daughter like that, including Gus. All families are messy when you come right down to it. Mine is no exception, as I'm sure yours isn't either. But using our misfortunes as an excuse to put other people down or a reason to be unprofessional is bullshit. Life sucks sometimes, and you deal with it on your own time. Gus is a Game Warden and the best one this county has seen for some time. He needs to act like a professional officer when he's in uniform not a father who's in pain, even if he is both at the same time."

"Your point is well taken, but hard to live by. We are not perfect and sometimes the pain is more than the uniform can carry."

"I would buy that if Gus was capable of treating me with respect some of the time. Unfortunately, with me it's all the time. Either he dislikes me personally, or he dislikes working with women. Since he works with Gail, I have to assume it's me."

The look in Rick's eyes and the silence were more than enough to support my conclusions. With a voice that conveyed both understanding and some sadness, Rick said, "Well, I can't spend the whole day arguing with you. I'll be in touch with any news concerning your neighbors, and keep me posted if they return. I want to talk to them as soon as possible. Call the barracks if any more camo guys come around tonight. Try not to shoot anyone." With a quick peck on the cheek, Rick was out the door and down the drive.

Locking the doors out of habit, I headed for the couch and a short nap. Fundy was already curled up on the rug anticipating my move. All this outdoor stuff was exhausting. Sleep came along with dreams of invaders in white pajamas and bags of bunny rabbits carrying rifles being chased by Fundy. That's what day old Danish will do to you.

CHAPTER

6

Bill Robinson knew when he saw the dark brown hair pulled straight back in a tight French twist and those piercing brown eyes that never wavered from his, this woman was going to bring him nothing but grief. It wasn't that he hadn't known grief already in his ten or so years as a private investigator, but this was going to be grief of the worst kind. She looked dedicated, driven, and clothed in the armor of a self-righteous cause that would sustain her until hell froze over.

Stephanie Kincaid was not unattractive in her very expensive green heather suit with matching coat and small golden hoop earrings. Anyone passing by his office at that moment would have said she was there for a photo shoot had they looked through the solid oak wood door that separated private office from hallway. She spoke quietly but with a tonal quality that said, "Listen carefully, I'm not kidding around and I want action." The expression in her eyes kept Bill fixed and concentrating on every word as she chronicled the story of her father Robert, his trip to the First National Bank in Island Pond, Vermont, his death as a hostage, and her need to know who gave the order.

As Bill's USAir flight droned ever closer to Albany, New York, he went over the last few days and tried to make sense of what seemed to be an endless list of details that were just flying in the wind like the airplane. Although his plane would land in an hour or so, he wouldn't be as lucky with this case. *Let that be a lesson for you, dummy, don't pick up cases just because you see a challenge and a pretty face.*

Professor Robert Kincaid was a most beloved father and faculty member at Lynden State College, living just south of Island Pond with his wife, daughter, and two dogs in 1971. One day he goes to the First National Bank to make a deposit when a robbery occurs and he's taken hostage along with others. Vermont State Police respond, start to negotiate, place sharpshooters around the place with a "don't shoot unless command gives green light" order. The day goes into night, and into next day. People are tired and the robbers are starting to say they will let some people go if VSP will send in food. At one point, a sharpshooter says he has a clear shot at one of the suspects, a second one says he also has a shot, but the Commander has a poor radio contact and claims he gives a DON'T SHOOT order. The first officer shoots anyhow and he thinks his bad guy goes down. All hell breaks loose after the first shot, leaving two hostages dead and two robbers in custody.

Robert was the "bad guy" shot by the police but all hostages agree he was **not** one of the robbers but one of the hostages. The second victim, Samuel "Dutch" Donaldson, was killed by the second VSP officer with a rifle slug from the second position. According to the VSP report, the witnesses/hostages were unsure if there were two or three robbers in the bank and some thought there might be more. They all agreed that being separated and confined for such a long period left them very confused. The count of bad guys was based on conversations overheard by some, and different first names they called each other. Prints proved to be useless as all suspects wore leather gloves.

At first blush this didn't seem to add up to a great case. It was more than a cold case, it was downright frigid! How in hell could he figure out who had given a green light to shoot 32 years after the fact? Was anyone still around who even remembered the event? He was ten years old at the time, living in Burlington, Vermont, and he didn't remember. Stephanie had been convincing in her belief that dad was intentionally taken out for reasons unknown and she wanted to know why, but Bill was having serious doubts about his judgment in taking the case. After 12 years of working for the Burlington Police and ten years of private investigating, he had seen a lot of VSP investigations. They weren't perfect, but they weren't the mafia either. He just couldn't picture a conspiracy or plot where an officer in green and gold planted a scope on Kincaid and blew the top of his head into the marble wall. This was Vermont, for Pete's sake.

Looking out the side window at the ground far below Bill realized it wasn't so far below anymore. Just then the intercom made its singular tone and it was announced that the approach to Albany had begun. Time had passed more quickly than anticipated which pleased him since all he really wanted was to get this over and done with. Kincaid was beginning to feel like the kiss of death. There was no luggage to claim and a car had been already reserved which made clearing out of the airport a cinch. It wasn't, however, pleasant to note the crime scene tape next to the boarding gates. Two officers were guarding the entry to the men's room. He knew what that was about. Who was that guy early this morning, and why didn't he have any identification on his person?

As he walked towards the rental counter, his mind retraced the incident before boarding for his flight to Los Angeles earlier. It was like something out of a movie when the shadow in the mirrored finish of the towel rack came up behind him. Instinct and training had taken over as he stepped quickly sideways and turned into his attacker with his left arm up deflecting the slightly raised right arm of the man with the ice pick. It only took two more moves to twist the arm, grab the wrist and remove the weapon. What Bill didn't count on was the slick floor from maintenance having washed it a few minutes before and the assailant going down like a stone when slugged in the jaw. The attacker cracking his skull on the tile flooring was one hundred percent accident. That it was an accident wouldn't matter to the police, and it wouldn't matter that it was self defense. It would still take a month of Sundays to get himself out of this, and get back on track with the case. And to make matters worse, Bill couldn't find one tiny itsy bitsy bit of ID on him. How weird was that? Weird enough to make him decide to leave the body and take his flight to LA. Let the cops figure out who the mystery guy was.

It was downright hinky this business of having crime scenes and bodies turning up everywhere he went with this case. Still it didn't feel right putting the ice pick into the space between the partition and the vending machine after wiping off his prints. But, what was Bill supposed to do, leave it with the guy? Take it on the plane?

The voice shook Bill out of his thoughts. "Your Crown Victoria is the third car from the left, sir. Just sign where indicated at the bottom... here and here...Thank you and have a safe trip, Mr. Robinson."

Placing a call to Agent Benoit crossed Bill's mind briefly, but was filed under the "maybe later" tab. Instead, he started the long haul towards Route 7 east. Traffic was heavy, making it difficult to maneuver into the lanes necessary to be in the right place at the right time. There were a few angry horns blaring but no fender crunch which, after all, was the main point. Fifteen minutes later Bill was making his way eastward and wondering how he was going to convince Jill Benoit to help him. Based on his knowledge to date, she was becoming more central and necessary to the case even though proving it to her was not going to be easy.

Traffic really thinned out once he passed the Tamhamnock Reservoir and he was relaxing a little thinking about food for a change. There hadn't been much time in California and somehow USAir snacks were a little short on the fill me up stuff. Having driven this road more than a few times, he knew The Man from Kent Bar and Grill wasn't far off. He glanced in the rear view out of habit and noticed a car off in the distance coming up rather rapidly. The cruise control was set five miles above the limit, which was what New York tolerated before they jerked you over and started writing tickets. He clicked it off just to be cautious. No sense taking a chance today. With his foot on the accelerator maintaining the limit exactly, he continued and watched as the approaching vehicle came up to within two car lengths. Oncoming traffic prevented the car from passing him, but at the same time gave enough illumination for him to see that it wasn't a police cruiser.

After having plenty of opportunity to pass, it remained behind until Bill signaled to pull into the Grill's parking lot. There was a turn off a few hundred feet to the right before the Grill and the car behind him turned and disappeared down the road. He saw the side and rear of the car enough to determine that it was a late model SUV, black with silver panels on the bottom to protect it from road damage. Best guess at make and model was a Jeep Cherokee although the other driver took the turn so fast it was hard to see an emblem. The shape and design were the only distinctive clues. Bill had always been good at catching plate numbers and he didn't miss this one either...125CXJ Vermont. He'd bet his life on that. One person was visible in the car as driver but no passenger.

Before the other car had a chance to return Bill's lights were off and slowly his Vic rolled to the other end of the parking lot. At the far end away from the turn off, there was a pick-up truck parked at an angle to the bar that blocked the view from the highway. If he could squeeze between it and the bushes near the edge of the lot, perhaps he could escape detection. Bill didn't want to use the brakes as the lights would give away his position if the other car returned to the intersection. With a great deal more patience than he wanted to use, he put the car into first gear, lined her up straight, and gently touched the gas easing the car forward. Forward it went at a crawl coming ever so close to the pick-up and bending the branches of the forsythias. Hertz wasn't going to appreciate the new look on their brand new Crown Vic.

When he had the car as far as it could go without denting the front grill, he shifted into park quickly hoping the reverse light wouldn't glow too long or too bright and give away his position. Within a millisecond of the action, he caught sight of his presumed tracker turning into the lot. His only chance depended on sheer luck. Maybe the car wouldn't be seen and the driver would go further on to wait or call someone for instructions. Or, he'd go inside to look for Bill without blocking his exit so he could sneak out and go down the highway. And if wishes were fishes we'd all be throwing nets.

Bill carefully eased himself through the divided front seats, keeping his body mass below the windows to avoid detection. Now he was crouching on the floor in the back of the Crown Vic waiting for something to make a decision for him. The ball wasn't really in his court. New York hated to have PI's carry weapons and the airlines were not fond of it either so it was with great regret that his Glock was sitting in his office locked up tight in the safe. He figured if Mr. Jerky in the Jeep wanted to check the car, he would look in the front seat. Maybe he would miss the back seat floor and wouldn't risk pulling on the handles to open the door for fear of setting off the panic alarm. Hey, it was worth a try.

He could hear the car crunching the gravel on the other side of the truck but it seemed to be closer to the highway than it was to the truck. He wasn't sure if it was the same car. Next, he heard a car door slam and a voice. The voice started to move and get louder although he suspected it was more to override the traffic noise than anything else. His guess was a cell phone conversation and it definitely was his friend Mr. Jerky.

"I'm telling you he's halfway to Burlington by now. He's a PI and not a dumb one or he wouldn't have gotten as far as he has, so get off my case." There was an extended silence. "Fine, you do it. I'm not doing your dirty work tonight. And don't threaten me with that. You know as well as I do that if I turn up dead or get caught, Dugan will put two and two together and come up with you. I'm leaving now and heading for your place." He could hear the snapping shut of a cell phone followed a few seconds later by the slamming of a car door and the spitting of gravel as Mr. Jerky spun out of the lot and headed east on Route 7 for parts unknown. Bill climbed back into the front seat and started the car.

After backing out of hiding, he parked in a better spot although a bit hidden and facing the highway. Okay, so it wasn't a total concealment. He was hungry and tired and had just been threatened for the umpteenth time. What did you expect?

He went inside the bar, had something to eat, and a much needed JD on ice. After that Bill called Jill Benoit and left a message asking for a meet at the K-Mart shopping mall in one hour. If she had doubts about his character or motivations, she should contact Charlie in Los Angeles. She needed her help.

After that he drove carefully and alert to Bennington where he awaited Jill Benoit. This was going to make or break this case. If she didn't have the missing parts, there was no solution.

CHAPTER

7

The headlights caught the tail end of one scared bunny rabbit when it suddenly did a freeze-frame, turned left, ran back and forth in front of Jill's car and dodged off to the right side of the road in time to save his sorry butt. *Rabbit number one thousand four hundred and thirty-five has crossed my path successfully. If it wasn't for the wildlife on Vermont roads, driving would be plumb boring.*

Jill continued with her thoughts as she headed south out of the Hollow. Fifteen minutes later she hit the outskirts of Bennington. When it came right down to it, Bennington wasn't a complicated town to drive through once you got the hang of it.

Development of traffic patterns and major highways pretty much followed the compass and businesses adjusted to the road configurations. Industries had come and gone in stages bringing boom times and depressions as most small towns in Vermont experienced. Bennington had survived and bounced back better than some. Present population was somewhere between 15 and 17,000, and the average income was good for this neck of the woods. Unemployment was in the three to four percent range meaning there were jobs available out there at minimum wage, but you couldn't afford to take them; your income would never cover your cost of living. Housing and food costs were high while transportation was a must if you expected to have a life.

Pownal, Shaftsbury and Woodford surrounded Bennington and contained smaller businesses unique to themselves and the communities they served. Their survival improved considerably if the flow of tourists was good. Corner Mom and Pops, animal clinics, multiple antique shops, organic farms and flower shops, and all manner of arts and crafts, stores were scattered up and down the roads traveling north, south, east, and west between these towns and Bennington. It was heaven for tourists, leaf peepers, skiers and the notorious Flat-Lander, defined as anyone from out of state – particularly Connecticut, New Jersey, Rhode Island, Massachusetts, and all but northern New York.

Reminiscing about the local evolution had occupied my thoughts for the 15 minute ride to town. Mr. Robinson had requested the meet and here I was. Pulling my dark green Subaru Forrester into the K-Mart parking lot, I circled wide towards Staples and the back. This was one of two strip malls in Bennington, but the only one with a K-Mart and the smaller of the two. Why had Robinson picked this one? Again the annoyance that came with his message and reference to Charlie set my blood pressure up a notch. I truly dislike people who intrude into personal lives for their own selfish reasons particularly when they pick on my life and my best friend. *This damn well better be a case of life or death, Mr. Robinson, or you are going to wish you had never heard of Charlie or me.*

After driving to the furthermost corner of the mall more than 190 degrees from where I had entered, my Subaru was parked between two box trailers that had been detached for layover pending deliveries. My .45 was tucked inside the pocket of my jacket along with ID which classified me as a retired Border Patrol Agent and the pertinent information needed. Trust? Oh yeah, I had trust. Trust in my judgment and trust that I was not about to take Mr. Bill Robinson's word for anything without proof.

Waiting for a few minutes proved to be fruitful as the eighteen- wheeler that had been idling at the back by JCPenny's started to move slowly and make its way around the corner of the buildings to the front of the mall. Having driven by the lot several times in the previous hour, I had already spotted the Hertz rental parked at the opposite corner directly across from where I was now standing. The car was facing the stores allowing full view of anyone approaching the vehicle, but didn't prevent someone from seeing the New York plate and Hertz sticker from the highway. Plus I had already called Airport Security and given them his name along with a request for any info they could come up with. It wasn't much, but it did include his plate number. Nice to have friends scattered around.

Walking with the truck and making sure it stayed between the car and me, I made my way through the parking lot to the dumpsters and using other vehicles for cover, managed to come up to Bill's vehicle from behind. A quick check of back and front seats showed no weapons or other persons to worry about immediately. With a gloved hand on the .45 inside the pocket, and standing just behind the opening swing area of the passenger door, I knocked on the window twice.

"Holy shit!" Bill jumped and swung around to face the door with one hand on the wheel and one hand on the gear shift. The car had been in idle and he was ready to bolt.

I replied with a cool and hard tone, "You called me. I didn't call you."

He seemed confused and not sure what to do. I backed up a little thinking he might not be able to see my face and then it occurred to me that he might not know what I look like. *This is getting really stupid.* "Let's both dig up some ID, okay?"

This he seemed to grasp and started to fumble inside his overcoat.

"Let's be slow and careful if you don't mind," I reminded him.

He slowed down and came out with a leather ID wallet that he flipped open and held up for inspection after lowering the side passenger window. His left hand he left on the steering wheel where I could see it. I took my ID out and did the same while leaning on the door frame.

"Well, now that we're the best of friends, what can I do for you and why?"

Bill looked very uncomfortable sitting out in the open and said he had way too much to discuss for a parking lot.

"I need to speak with you about matters having to do with an old bank robbery, a possible murder, smuggling, and it could take a while. I think it may involve the State Police, maybe the Border Patrol, maybe your friend in LA, and maybe you have the key to all of it. I am being followed, someone tried to kill me two weeks ago, and today, and people keep dying around me. That's it. That's my speech. That's what I didn't want to tell you on the phone from the airport because I was being watched."

Wow, that certainly was a mouthful. After a few minutes of quick assessment I asked, "Were you followed in this car?"

"Yes. Someone followed from the airport, I think, although I didn't pick up the tail until Hoosick Falls. I pulled into the Man from Kent Bar and ditched him there. What makes me jittery is I overheard a cell conversation he had claiming I was halfway to Burlington. That means they know who I am and where I'm from. That's a lot of information to have about a PI working on a cold case. He also added something about not wanting to do the other guy's dirty work. Where I come from that usually means I'm a target for a hit. Lately everyone seems to know where I'm going before I do and show up just as soon as I get there."

Plan A was beginning to take shape in my head. "You probably should dump this rental for now and get a different set of wheels. I have a friend in town that does favors for me now and then, and has a lot of free garage space. We can leave it there until alternative transportation can be arranged." *And then what do I do with you?*

That would have to wait right now. We needed to get out of sight before both of us were spotted and I became associated with whatever Mr. Robinson was involved in.

Taking out my cell phone I called to make arrangements for the rental. Bill was not certain that this was a good idea, but not having that Crown Vic hanging around like a huge target on his back was rather comforting to both of us. Soon, in its place he had the keys to a Chevy Tahoe, white, fully loaded, complete with a full gas tank. He was expected to return it with a full tank and in one piece, or as my friend had stated, "In pristine condition." Tomorrow my friend would return Bill's car to Hertz in Pittsfield, Massachusetts along with an appropriate story and the cash to cover extra charges. This was to dodge anyone watching the airport or the Hertz rental in Burlington waiting for Bill.

While all this mad trading and maneuvering was going on, a sumptuous dinner of burgers, fries, and shakes was consumed with little conversation about anything. We ate outside by the Tahoe which prompted a visit from several Bennington officers as they drifted through the parking lot on their daily rounds or stopped by the Burger King for a break. All were friends of mine who traded smart remarks and friendly hellos while I kept my fingers crossed that none would question too closely what I was doing there eating "crap food" as I called it. Rick was right, my smart mouth was going to come back and bite me in the ass some day. I was really hoping today wasn't that day.

The friend who had loaned Bill the Tahoe stopped by forty- five minutes later and told me that he had negotiated for a late model Honda Accord with good snow tires and low mileage for Bill to use. It was a better vehicle to drive around in than the SUV, but wouldn't be available until Thursday afternoon, a day and a half from now. After a quick side conversation with Bill, I told him to leave the Honda in the Price Chopper parking lot when it was available on Thursday behind the New Englander Motel. He was to leave the keys at the desk of the motel. The Tahoe he could pick up at the Bennington District Court House parking lot on the side near the lock-up cells next to the sheriff's slot. There was no doubt he knew where that was. He was to bring a spare key as I would lock it up with the keys inside.

I made a call to Jean Dugan, Rick's wife, to see if he was around or on duty. Rick had been called to Montpelier for some sort of meeting and then had to report to the Academy in Pittsford for a class he had to teach on Friday. He wouldn't be home until late Friday afternoon. I explained that I needed a quiet, secluded place that was reasonably secure to talk with a PI about one of his cases, and asked if I could use Rick's old office. They lived on a defunct sheep farm on the east side of old Route 7 and it was ideal for this kind of thing. Rick had converted some space in an old barn out back into an office that was secluded and very private. Jean was more than pleased and said that Rick wouldn't mind. She was sure of it.

Thirty minutes later we were in Rick's office pouring coffee into the mugs that Jean had set out for us.

"How long were you with the Border Patrol?" Bill asked.

"I put in 25 years."

"Do you miss it?"

I had to think a little about that. "That's not as easy to answer as it would seem. Do I miss being a police officer doing the job? Yes, I do, very much so. Do I miss the double standard, the doing twice as much for half the recognition, the being passed over for younger men? No, not one fucking bit."

He looked a little surprised at the sudden change in voice. There was no missing the anger and bitterness that came with the last statement. He continued, "Are you saying there's discrimination on the Federal level of law enforcement?"

I had to laugh and shook my head with little amusement. "You guys will never get it, not because you don't want to but because you can't imagine it. It's like trying to explain to you what it's like to give birth. I could sit here and explain every little detail of pregnancy, labor, delivery and the birthing process and you would never really understand what it feels like. Equality isn't reached because the requirements for the Academy are the same for men and women, or the pay is the same, or the issued equipment for duty is the same for both. Discrimination between the sexes exists when one officer doubts that another will back them because their gender makes them weaker in that officer's mind. There is no law that can cover that. Women see that in their partner's eyes, feel it intuitively, and hear the whispers and rumors. It wears you down after a while."

Robinson shook his head and looked at me with curiosity. "Are you saying that guys are deliberately plotting to keep women in their place and robbing them of rank on the force just because we're afraid you won't take a bullet for us? That's a pretty broad swipe against men and petty prejudice if you ask me."

I knew this was not the time or place for a discussion on women's rights or gender discrimination. So why continue the conversation? Truth be told, this was the raw nerve that always brought my blood pressure into the danger zone. This business of women in uniform in male dominated professions had for my entire life been an elusive and problematic questioning that never seemed to have a clear answer. At least it didn't have an answer that satisfied everyone, including myself.

"No, I don't think plotting is a good word because I don't believe men spend a lot of time thinking about it to be truthful. Why should they? They have nothing to gain or lose. Whether women serve and protect is irrelevant to men because they get to fulfill their life's dream. Women, on the other hand, will never get an even break until men understand that the fire burns just as hot in our blood to be cops as it does in theirs. We just have a different way of doing things. Some of us can be just as physical as you, but we don't have to. No one questions that it is fact a man can bench press more weight than a woman and can chase a felon down an alley, leap higher, tackle him harder, and beat him to a bloody pulp. His female partner probably can't do his job just like that, but is that the way the job should be done? Equality is supposed to mean equal access not sameness. The whole point of equality is if you drop the E you end up with quality. But, until females are accepted as good officers instead of equal officers, we will always be doing twice as much and get half as much in return."

Bill looked thoughtful for a moment as if he had a lot to say but was afraid to say it. When he did speak, it was carefully and painfully. "I spent 15 years on the Burlington force fighting a battle that I knew no one else understood or cared about. My brother, my older brother by five years, had been a cop before me and made a big name for himself as an undercover guy kicking ass and taking names in the dumps and back allies of the worst dives on the lake. Man, he was the best narco sting man Burlington had seen in a decade. Sometimes when you think you're too good to die, that's exactly what happens...you die. Jerry got the hero's burial, Mom got the flag, and the papers played it up big. I swore I'd join the force and get the scum bags who shot and murdered my big brother.

"It didn't take long before I started finding out that Jerry the hero was a little tarnished. At first it was his own idea to take a little hit, but then his partner thought it would help with the busts if he was "really" on the inside of the drug business. Guess they figured he had to be a drug addict to catch them. Jerry was actually killed in the process of a drug deal gone bad – his drug deal. His own team shot and killed him.

"I couldn't believe it and dug deeper into the whole process Burlington used for drug enforcement. I didn't find anything like Jerry's case but there were other similar stories. This was the thirteenth time in twenty years that a cop had become an addict and either died or got fired for being unable to report for duty drug free. In other words, they were addicted to drugs and couldn't clean up. No effort was being put into rehabilitating these guys and gals or finding another way to fight the drug culture. After my third disciplinary hearing for "inappropriate investigation" into matters that were above my pay grade, I quit. I was going to go public with what I knew or thought I knew, but Mom told me to think of the families and kids I would hurt if I did that. They didn't deserve to have their hearts broken and memories blown to hell just because the system was up to its armpits in shit. She was right. I think her point was, some injustices just are."

Both of us looked into our mugs of coffee without saying anything, each lost inside private worlds of struggle and pain searching for that elusive concept that would clarify everything. He was looking to find the answer to why The Brotherhood had abandoned his brother and so many others who had given everything including their integrity and life. I was struggling to understand why it remained that... The Brotherhood... and would never include a female component without sounding queer even to my ears.

Eventually I broke the silence, "I can certainly empathize with your feelings concerning change in a system that is fixed in bureaucratic red tape and old style tactics. And I really am sorry about your brother. Border Patrol is not immune to its loss of fine agents to the dark side either. But I'm not sure we are talking about the same thing. Both of us are trying to find reason and answers to personal pain and struggle related to law enforcement and its entrenched workings, for lack of a better way of putting it. You, however, are looking at one set of circumstances and one department's responsibility for those officers involved.

"Gender discrimination and its effects are pervasive to all women in all uniforms. It's much harder to define, harder to evaluate, and almost impossible to fix because everyone is involved. When everyone is involved they all have an opinion and it ends up being a cluster."

Bill looked at his watch and was shocked to see it was 10:30. "I think we'd better leave this for another time. I have to get some sleep before heading north tomorrow and we still have a lot to talk about."

"Fine with me, I get tired of the old fight anyhow. It was one of the really nice things about retirement that I fully enjoyed, not having to discuss the role of women in law enforcement."

With that we both grabbed one of the sandwiches that Jean had left for us and a fresh cup of coffee. We parked ourselves at the conference table on the other side of the office, away from Rick's massive oak desk and the comfy stuffed chairs that would put both of us to sleep. There was plenty of light overhead and the insulated curtains were keeping the cold outside the huge windows in the corner. With the woodstove going and the smell of good coffee, it was hard to tell this was a business meeting.

"Okay, Mr. Robinson, what have you gotten me into?"

It was well past 3:00 am on Wednesday when I finally made my way through the quiet back roads of North Bennington and headed farther north to the Hollow. I had guided Bill Robinson south towards Bennington and suggested he find a quiet out of the way motel to spend the next day. I was going back to my house to take care of the animals, and get some rest, after which I would do some research on my own with the information at hand. Information at hand, now that was a stretch, it was more like a bunch of stories and facts without a home.

I went over the evening's conversation again, trying to see any connection within itself or see any blank spot where I could fill the void with my own facts. First, there was the cold case Bill was using as ground zero. The National Bank robbery and hostage casualties had been big news in '71. It had made the national media and anyone with any interest in law enforcement made it a point to study the case to death. When I was a student at the University of Vermont for both my criminology and psychology classes it was often a case study, although used for different reasons to make different points. At the Academy later on, it was also brought up in training for hostage situations and negotiating with armed suspects. Usually they used it to point out what **not** to do although instructors were quick to add that any situation could go south at any second no matter how good you were. It was the nature of the beast, and the truth of the matter was bad guys may not be in control, but they usually knew more about the situation than the good guys did. Hostage situations are more like a game of checkers than chess – a game that can't really be won but ends in a draw unless someone makes a mistake. You always work the situation hoping for the bad guys to make the mistake and the good guys to win.

Essentially, Robert Kincaid walked into the bank to make a deposit and was taken hostage along with three others. One of the tellers managed to hit the silent alarm which brought the Vermont State and local police to the scene. There were two confirmed suspects in the bank wearing ski masks and tokes, or knitted caps worn tight to the skull by outdoors men, armed with hand guns making demands for land transportation out. They would take one hostage with them and release once they crossed the Canadian border.

Police had placed several officers around the bank and sharpshooters were positioned on two sides of the bank that had windows with unobstructed views of the interior where the suspects and hostages were thought to be. One suspect was identified as such because he was on a phone when negotiators were talking to the suspect, and clothing color, hat, height, etc. were noted. It appeared likely that the figure seen in the window talking on the phone was a suspect not a hostage. Another similarly clothed person was seen frequently next to this person on various occasions, but no one else was ever seen in proximity to the windows or wandering around inside the bank. At least no one was observed to the extent that could be seen from the street or rooftops. The standing order to all officers was to hold fire. They were to keep their scopes on all open fields and tell the command post if a kill shot presented itself at any point in time, but they were **not** to shoot unless given the green light by the Commander.

Late on the second day, with everyone pretty tired and strung out, it appeared that a settlement was going to be reached with the suspects. According to one officer's report, he saw the suspect with the phone step into his line of fire and called Command saying he had a clear kill shot and was asking for a green light. At the same time, a second officer called Command asking for the same. The assumption was that the second call cancelled the Command's reply to the first officer's request with a **no shoot** order. In any event the first shot was fired and the second soon followed.

One VSP officer, a Corporal Jerome Metcalf, was very close to the bank entrance, and he breached the front doors without back up. Within moments there were several shots fired inside the bank followed by half a dozen officers storming the bank after him. Moments after that, Metcalf opened the doors and the hostages were led out along with other officers leading two men in handcuffs. Newspapers across the country carried photos of Corporal Metcalf holding a hysterical Janice Beemer as he escorted her across the street to a waiting ambulance. He was a hero.

Then the proverbial shit hit the fan. According to the hostage debriefing, the two men they had in custody were the men who attempted to rob the bank …the only men who tried to rob the bank. Robert Kincaid was a customer and a very nice man, nothing else. When the suspects first came into the bank without being seen and took over, they had separated all of them and placed them in individual rooms. No one knew where the others were or what went on. No one was in the front of the bank when the shooting started. No one had any previous knowledge of Zeke Faraday or Maxwell Johnson, the two suspects arrested for attempted bank robbery. In other words, nothing made any sense.

Samuel Donaldson was killed by the second sniper as the "suspect #2" standing near the window. Robert Kincaid was shot as "suspect #1". Samuel "Dutch" Donaldson had worked at the bank for 15 years as a teller and was the shift supervisor. He was married with two grown children both of whom had married and were living on the west coast. His wife worked at the local hospital as a nurse's aid. Kincaid was damn near a legend and it was his daughter who was looking for answers. There were no explanations given in the file why Kincaid was on the phone or said to be on the phone when seen in the windows. No phone records were included in the file.

The other thing that tugged at my "something's ugly" strings was Jerome Metcalf and his rescue. What were the shots about? No one came out injured including the suspects, and no ballistics had been in the file so what kind of acting was that all about? Bill mentioned that his sources reported a lot of discontent between Metcalf and his peers at the time. His reputation was pretty bad and no one wanted him on their shift. They didn't trust him to cover their back and thought he spent too much time sucking up to the brass. Maybe the shots inside were part of a show to impress the media. He did end up with national recognition. I think the Governor even gave him a medal or something. I wonder if he knew more about the hit and knew it was safe to go in.

My thoughts were temporarily interrupted as I turned into the driveway and made my way to the barn to check on the horses. Fundy was frantic and jumping himself into the next generation at the sight of his master finally returning home. "What a jerk. It's not as if I don't leave you with enough food and water to last a week. You're worse than the horses."

After letting him jump into the back of the car, I checked feed, hay, and water, and closed the gates to the out pastures. Walking back into the barn, I checked the doors on the opposite side to be sure they were latched and glanced at the small window facing the house. That's when I saw the light. Without missing a beat, I drew my cell from my inside pocket and hit the 'I' on the ICE numbers which directly connected to State Police dispatch.

"State Police Dispatcher Rogers, how can I help you?"

"This is Jill Benoit in Shaftsbury Hollow number 132. I've got an intruder in my house downstairs, basement level. I am outside in the barn and armed. I'm retired law enforcement and need to know what the closest back up to my location is."

"Please hold." Several minutes passed as I watched the tiny light move in and out of the two downstairs rooms sometimes disappearing entirely.

"Hello? Ms. Benoit?"

"Go ahead."

"Both troopers are on calls that put them out at least an hour or two from you. One is in Rutland on a domestic assist turned stand off and the other is in Readsboro on a three car fatal." Great, this really wasn't the time for heroics.

"Are there any deputy sheriffs on or other VSP on call close by?" I was getting desperate. If Rick had been home, I would have called him. I'd call Bill Robinson, but had no clue where he was staying for the night.

"I've got a deputy warden out back having coffee. Want to talk with Gail?"

That wasn't a bad idea, come to think of it.

"Yeah, put her on." A few more seconds went by as I watched the mini-flashlight recede out the doorway of the middle room downstairs and disappear.

"Jill? This is Gail. How can I help?" I wondered that myself as I saw the small light emerge at the top of the staircase on the first floor and watched as the figure holding the light made its way to the door facing the barn obviously intending to exit the house. Whoever it was would see my car any second now and would know I was in the barn. Whether they choose to continue this exit, stay inside and wait for me to come in, or go out the other door remained to be seen.

"Gail, I have some guy in my house who I think just figured out I'm in the barn. He's heading for the door facing me and I'm waiting to see what he's going to do. Hang on a minute."

The light went out and I couldn't see much movement. There was a floodlight on the other side of the house that illuminated the inside of the house through the windows where the drapes were open, but I kept most of them closed at night to keep heat in and cold out. Only the small kitchen window by the other door and the dining room window by the wood stove on the opposing wall were open. Still, tonight there was almost a full moon and the inside of the house showed up a little.

Gail asked if I was still there and I responded in the affirmative.

"Look, I think it's a bad idea for me to tie up the line like this. I can't think and you can't help if you're in the barracks. Can you back me up out here?"

"Sure can. I should be there in twelve to fifteen. Want me at your house?"

"That would be good, and don't use lights or siren when you get close if at all. I don't know what's up here. I have my .45 but everything else is in the house. Whoever this is they were searching in… shit, gotta go, he's out the other door."

With a quick check of the car to be sure Fundy was closed in, I pulled the .45, checked the magazine, and slid a round into the chamber. All of this was done with eyes watching the house on both sides for movement from either corner, whether towards or away from the barn. I didn't need to look at my hands to know how. It was second nature and came from years of practice.

Off to the right I saw a shadow move slowly through the pine trees circling towards the far stone wall on the south side of the pasture. Once he made that wall he had good cover and I'd never catch up. But, between here and the pines there was nothing but clear ground with two big oaks maybe 60 feet apart to the left and right of the yard. The only other thing I could do involved going behind the barn away from him, and ducking behind the other stone wall that ran perpendicular to the southern wall. If I could beat him to his goal, I might have the element of surprise and get the drop.

Since that was the only sensible thing to do, I backed my way out of the barn and edged under the horse fence and through the paddock being careful not to excite the horses and give my strategy away. After what seemed to be an eternity of placating Tracker, who always needed more attention than the others to be quiet, I was able to reach the stone wall and stepped over the top rocks. After lowering myself to the ground, I immediately started to crawl through the snow towards the far corner. As I advanced to the south of the wall and cleared the barn corner, I carefully edged up enough to look across, hoping to spot my quarry. There was some small movement off in the distance, but it was hard to tell if it was a man sized shadow or some other creature moving pine branches.

Continuing with as much speed and silence as possible, I advanced towards the intersection of walls hoping to be the winner of the race. At the corner I stopped and again drew the .45. Here there were several small saplings without leaves and small pine scrub trees that afforded limited cover. I was able to come up into a crouching stance and get a better view and some solid footing should I have to stand quickly or run. My eyes scanned the woods from house to wall checking every tree trunk, tall stump, large log, heavy snow bank and hill for a shape or movement out of the ordinary. It didn't surprise me that he had beaten me out to the wall and beyond, but it sure as hell disappointed me and in addition made me boiling mad.

The rage I felt at having someone in my house going through my things was probably why I didn't see the gloved hand come around the corner of the shack on my right. It was only 80 feet from me and certainly worthy of my attention as a possible hiding place, a place where someone would lie in wait for me. A place any smart cop with half a brain would have been wary of. But I didn't, and when the bullet burned a hole through my left arm, it was too late.

The instant pain and overwhelming urge to scream was so intense it froze me in place for a second. Then I had the presence of mind to roll back and against the wall I had come from which took me out of view from the shack. Thinking quickly, I rolled on my belly and slid in the snow down and away from the wall across an open space towards a pile of big rocks that had been thrown into some briars at the edge of the pasture. It wasn't much of a mound for cover, but I figured if this asshole was going to check to see if I were dead, he'd be looking where I was last seen, not 20 feet away. Plus, for him to come up from the shack he had to walk up a small rise to the wall and turn the corner around the trees. That would put him in the open at least for a little bit. It would be enough for me to squeeze off a shot if the burning pain in my arm didn't make me pass out first. Damn, that hurt!

It seemed like an eternity before the sound of dead leaves crunching under snow gave away his movements. My eyes were watering from the cold or maybe from the pain, but in either case, I was finding it hard to see clearly. The top of the walls were blurry as I tried to focus to see any kind of movement. Suddenly the thought crossed my mind that I might not have removed the safety on the .45. I struggled to remove my glove to feel for the familiar lever only to realize this was not my Smith & Wesson, but a different gun that had a different safety system. This was not the time to start losing my mind or ability to think clearly.

That's what I was thinking when a figure rounded the corner with a flashlight in one hand and a weapon in the other. Thoughts were beginning to freeze frame in my mind as I tried to make my head clear from the continuous pain and burning that was now engulfing my entire upper body and neck. It was hard to breathe quietly and even harder not to moan with the waves of pain that came with each tiny move I made to adjust my position in an attempt to remain concealed. It wasn't only my vision that was blurry, but now I was feeling dizzy and a little nauseous. All I needed was to vomit and give my position away. Wouldn't that look great as a headline, **Ex-cop killed while barfing from fear**. Somehow I managed to hold it together long enough to at least have a firm grip and fair target picture before he knew where I was.

* * *

He quickly saw that Jill was not where he had expected and immediately started to pan the snow where she had left a blood trail until his light landed on her. He felt the pain of her bullet smashing into his left forearm just below the elbow before he heard the gun go off. Still he managed to fire off another round that creased her hairline just above the right ear bringing a blinding light and immediate darkness to Jill. She slumped forward slightly and was very still, never hearing the next two shots fired in rapid succession.

The Hollow was once again at peace, silent as a blanket of rolled cotton except for the distant muffled echoes of a shadowy figure trekking through the crusted snow far up the slope of the mountain out of sight from the barn. The lone man with a long ponytail and grey beard was dressed in white camouflage and carried a rifle with a sniper's scope and night vision capabilities. On his cell phone he made a call as he walked over into the next town advising that the search had turned up nothing, JB was presumed dead, and ZF was no longer an issue.

CHAPTER

9

"Shit, gotta go, he's out the other door," was the last Gail heard from Jill.

Those words kept echoing in the back of her mind as she took the hard right up Twitchell Hill and prepared to slide left onto Horton Hill Road. Town crews had dumped an adequate supply of salted sand on paved roads, but Gail wasn't sure it would be enough to help once she hit the dirt that would continue from here on out to Jill's place. The Jeep was good in snow and carried plenty of weight from equipment in the back. That plus good mud and snows and four wheel drive made the Jeep a Mean Machine. Of course all bets were off once you started to use this thing like a cruiser and stepped on the gas like she was doing now, blowing through the intersection of Meyers and Tinkham.

Jill needn't have worried about her using lights or siren as the need wasn't there at this hour of the morning. Gail hadn't seen one car or even a house light since leaving the barracks. The dash clock showed 3:32 am or eight minutes since departure. That was pretty good time considering road conditions. The intersection at Cross Hill didn't go as planned and loose sand gave way putting the right side of the Jeep in the culvert. Luckily, she was used to impromptu adjustments on slippery back roads, and rather than hit the breaks in panic, she just eased up on the gas and straightened the steering to follow the culvert. Once the vehicle was at a slow roll, Gail hit the 4X4 button and with a little gas drove out onto the road's surface again. Once on the road, off came the 4X4 and up came the speed to a prudent level… no sweat.

Her stomach did a little tumble and felt nauseous after the close encounter of the snow kind, but that wasn't the only reason she was having indigestion. Gail was scared. No ifs, ands, or buts about it. She had backed up law enforcement before with Gus but never alone and never at three in the morning. Funny but the thought of someone shooting at her in the woods over poaching deer or hiding a hunting accident didn't bother her. She supposed because most of them didn't have intent or motive in their black little souls at least until caught. The majority were just shooting out of fear of being caught and they couldn't aim worth a damn at another human being anyway. It's one thing to kill an animal out of season for meat to feed your family when you're out of a job or don't earn enough to feed them. It's another to kill a person for a deer. Most guys don't have it in them.

Accidental shootings were another matter and a little trickier, but for the most part the same applied. Once a hunter discovered that their shot found its way into another hunter and killed him or her they usually panicked. Were they going to compound that error by killing another human being? No, probably not. The most likely reaction would be to run like hell before being caught or until some game warden stopped them. They might fire in your general direction trying to scare you off hoping to escape capture, but when you yell, "Stop, or I'll shoot!" they usually figure the jig is up and call it a day. Of course you can't actually shoot someone if they don't stop. Vermont has this thing about shooting fleeing felons... you can't do it legally.

Backing up Jill was not going to be a romp in the park. First of all, she wasn't active law enforcement which meant the whole legal status would be on her shoulders as back up. The second thing that bothered Gail was the incident at the Brinkers' and what Gus had told her last night about the findings so far. This so called poaching ring was more involved than Jill knew and Gail wasn't at liberty to share that information. What if this intruder was connected to the case? What if Jill was in danger, serious danger, and Gus was keeping her in the dark deliberately using her as bait?

Or worse, not giving a shit for personal reasons? He certainly hadn't shown any warmth on Tuesday and had made it clear he didn't want to talk about it later on in the office. Whatever the reasons might be, the reality was that a serious situation had developed and Jill had need of back up. This was more than adequate cause for an upset stomach.

Finally, up ahead was the right onto Shaftsbury Hollow Road and with 11 minutes gone and counting, it was still a race with a handicap. The Hollow was legendary with its Dew Drop Inn on the corner, its once large and plentiful herds of deer and black bear, and recreational hunting that pulled in hunters from a tri-state area and beyond. The Hollow Road forked to the right and ended in a cul de sac that was more of a dead end for vehicular traffic. The unique property of the Hollow, other than its beauty, was the magnification of sound.

Within a few hundred feet of the right turn, the mountains on both sides began to close in on the small and narrow road that wound its way for three miles to its dead end. It was a perfect echo chamber especially in winter time when the leaves were off the trees, for sound to travel down and out to the open end of the road. Shots and shouts could be heard for miles. You couldn't tell where it came from exactly, but you sure as hell could hear them. Sound is exactly what Gail heard as she barreled up the road, the sound of a loud sharp crack. It could have been a large tree branch snapping from snow or ice build up and finally breaking, but she had a hunch this was not her lucky day. She grabbed the radio and told dispatch shots were fired and asked for back up from White Creek if available knowing VSP was not. The dispatcher had already anticipated that maybe something might be needed and he had called the New York sheriff's on a land line to see if they had a unit nearby in Cambridge. The New York border was five minutes from the Hollow and New York enforcement agencies often assisted VSP and other law enforcement officers, or LEOs for short, on calls. Dispatch informed her that two sheriff's units were already on the Hollow Road and should be visible soon. Right on queue they appeared in her rear view with lights flashing. Gail radioed to dispatch that the units were in view and switched to sheriff's frequency to contact the New York cruisers. Both deputies responded to Gail and followed her lead.

Jill's private drive came up and all bar lights went off as they ascended the hairpin turns. Rounding the last turn, she saw two muzzle flashes almost simultaneously out to the right and back by the end of the closest pasture. Gail was watching a dark figure standing a little bent over while trying to negotiate the narrow drive at the same time aware that being in the lead was impairing the other two cruisers from reaching the house and barn. This was after all a shooting situation and more up their alley than hers. Then they heard the volley of two shots as they drove down to the barn and stopped behind Jill's car. No doubt about that sound. Gail had practiced enough with an AR-15 to know what it was. The figure that had been standing out back staggered backwards away from them and fell motionless. The horses in the paddock were prancing around almost in panic. But no one saw muzzle flashes or movement to warrant a foot chase.

The last deputy in line stopped very briefly at the house, seeing no sign of an intruder or need to remain there, he went immediately to the barn. While he was securing the house, Gail and the first deputy had seen Fundy in the car and decided he was better off staying there. Fundy didn't agree with that decision and barked his disagreement loudly, but the decision was firm. Without wasting a lot of time, and with guns drawn, Gail and the deputy searched the barn for Jill or any suspects and came up empty. Gail had expected as much but still hoped the muzzle flashes had belonged to someone else.

With help from assorted pieces of rope and scattered equipment around the hay barn, the three of them barricaded the paddock where Cochise, Tracker, and Nevada had gathered. They were panicked to say the least. It was clear from the prancing and quick bursts of runs with abrupt stops, that the gunfire had shattered their sense of safety. They wanted out. Unfortunately, out meant going where the shooting had occurred and the officers agreed that wasn't going to happen.

Gail turned to one of the deputies and asked, "Could you open the back of my vehicle and grab the medical blue bags? I have a feeling we are going to need them." Before she could turn and start down towards the end of the wall where the other deputy had already made his way, she heard him yell back to her.

"Hey, you have a camera with you?"

Gail wasn't sure she heard right, "Do I have a camera?"

He yelled back, "Yeah, you have a dead body and I think a live one, but you'd better bring both medical and camera."

Gail's stomach went sour and her mind went blank. The motion of the deputy tossing the blue bags at her feet snapped her back into focus. The deputy asked, "Do you want me to get a camera?"

"No, I'll get it. Run these bags down there. I'll find it faster and be right behind you."

As she went to retrieve the gear, the dread of finding out which body was dead and which was alive seemed to slow her movements. She didn't want to find out that Jill was dead and Gail had to rescue, or at least try to save, the person responsible. On the other hand, standing here and ducking the issue wasn't in Jill's best interests if she was the one wounded. That brought the sense of urgency back into her blood and hustled the camera out to the scene.

When Gail reached the corner of the walls, she tossed the camera to the closest deputy and said, "Take all the photos you can of this mess. What's the story?"

"Closest I can figure, this guy on the corner got himself killed with two in the chest after your friend over there hit him in the arm with her .45. She's in bad shape. Don't figure she'll make it, but maybe."

There were two bodies lying in the snow, one male on his back towards the south corner with two obvious gunshot wounds in his chest and a bloodied left arm. The second body was hard to see at first. There were several large boulders behind some briers and down a slight incline. Over the top of the boulders you could see an arm hanging over, loosely holding a gun that was half buried in the snow.

Gail went towards Jill's position, "get those medical bags down by her feet where I can work on her. One of you get emergency services out here. Start your photos over here." She must have said this with the right tone or authority because both officers immediately went to work and things began to happen.

When Gail reached Jill, she was lying face down. Turning her over revealed a face covered in blood. The toke she had been wearing was cocked to the side as if she had scratched an itch and forgotten to adjust her hat. Gail placed her fingers on Jill's carotid artery and found a pulse but it was faint and hardly worth mentioning. After rolling her over and opening her parka, the upper arm wound was obvious as it continued to seep blood steadily in a flow that said one thing… hit to major artery. Even if it was only a nick, it was serious given the amount of time between the shot and now. There was no way of knowing how much blood she had lost. The face injury turned out to be a head wound that may or may not be critical. It too would have to be tended to by someone smarter than her. It looked like only a scratch that had torn the scalp a little at her hairline above the right ear causing all the bleeding like scalp wounds do. Still, it was possible for trauma to occur to the brain from that kind of injury. For now, all she could do was clean up her face and wrap the head wound in sterile bandage, apply a pressure bandage to the upper arm wound to reduce the flow, cover her and place her on covered ground to keep her warm and prevent shock if she wasn't already there.

Eight minutes later the White Creek Rescue Squad arrived, and five minutes after that they were on their way to Southern Vermont Medical Center. While they were loading Jill, contact was made with Rogers at dispatch by cell phone and she was told that VSP headquarters was sending a team to take over the investigation. They wanted Gail to seal the area until troopers could arrive to take over. No one was to touch or move the other body. No one was to enter the house, barn or any other part of the property without authorization from headquarters and that included other law enforcement agencies. What the hell?

She questioned leaving a body on the ground with temperatures in the teens. There were, after all, problems with fixing time of death and always the possibility of changing weather conditions. Rogers replied that they didn't care about the body and she was to do as she was instructed. In other words, follow the yellow brick road and don't piss off the Wizard. He had a nasty temper.

Gail's hackles went up at the inference that some sort of cover up or power play was going on. Further questioning of Rogers merely got the standard – he was following orders and repeating what he was told. She asked who would be relieving her, but got no reply. She knew for certain someone would be there by 8:00 am but nothing more. It was now 4:40 am which meant the night was going to drag for another four hours. The New York deputies were asked to assist for an hour and agreed to leave one guy. The other had a court date.

He and Gail hung around the barn with the animals discussing what they had heard, done, and seen, trying to make sense of it all. She knew more details than he did and still couldn't figure it out. This was sheer insanity. Why would anyone break into Jill's house, and what were they looking for? If they thought she had what Gus had picked up on Wednesday, wouldn't they have expected Jill to turn it in? They must know she's an ex-cop. The intruder probably didn't know Jill had no knowledge of what Gus had found. Even so, why search her house for papers? It was obvious from the mess that he had been looking for something on paper or recorded. If he wanted what they had he should have been looking for a safe, or in the barn maybe. Apparently this guy didn't give Jill much credit. Only an idiot would go to their neighbor's house, discover illegal goods, and bring them back to her own house for safe keeping. Nah, that wasn't what was happening here.

Besides, how do you explain two shots out of nowhere that kill the bad guy before the cops get there?

* * *

Rick was talking on his cell from his quarters at Pittsford, "Yes sir, I understand. I can leave within the hour and be there by 0700. Do you have a team in mind or do I pick my own, sir?"

"Very well, sir. I will contact Trooper Filbert later today and keep you advised. If I may ask, sir, how much of this am I allowed to share with other personnel?"

"That will make things rather difficult."

"Yes, sir, but we can be equally culpable if it turns out that not every effort was made to be forthcoming with whatever information we did have either now or then and it proves the point. In my experience as a field officer, caution is best tempered with trust as long as both are used in moderation."

"Not at all, sir, I don't believe in sermons or lectures and meant no disrespect. Just speaking my opinion which you have told me many times you appreciated. If that is all, I need to take a shower and shove off before daylight. I understand we only have a Deputy Game Warden guarding the crime scene."

"Thank you, sir. Good night."

Rick closed the phone and put it on his desk. That didn't go well at all. Something was rotten in Denmark and he was being dropped right in the middle of it. Worse than that, Jill was almost dead, apparently her assailant was dead, and the Major didn't want a regular CSI team sent. The whole thing smelled like cover up and both he and Jill were getting caught up in it.

Right now his orders were to haul ass to the Hollow and take over the investigation. He was also to do a full background check on one William Robinson, private investigator from Burlington. A second background was to be run on Stephanie Kincaid, daughter of Professor Robert Kincaid. Results of these backgrounds were to be sent to the Major only. That also bothered Capt. Richard Dugan a lot, and for very good reason.

Major Benjamin Johnson of the Vermont State Police didn't often request special investigations from his senior officers. He kept pretty much to himself and stayed in headquarters or the State Capital most of the time doing whatever he was supposed to do. Lately, Captain Dugan had run into his name a few times in conversations with other LEO's in other agencies on seemingly innocent topics. Those topics always turned out to be related in a little way to something or someone Dugan was interested in. Now Major Johnson wanted him to do personal backgrounds for his eyes only. This was not a good thing.

* * *

Jill tried to brush the snow away from her eyes and realized she couldn't move her hands. Squinting at first, she could only see the back of his uniform which, of course, was creased to perfection and crisp beyond expectation. Then she focused her eyes on him. She couldn't figure out how Mike kept himself so sharp after patrolling for days on horseback with all the dust and rain and heat. But, that was Mike "Super Cop" Peterson, the most handsome and talented agent Jill had ever seen. Okay, so there was a little hero worship there, but the man was really good enough to take home to Mom. Never mind Mom, just take him home!

He looked at her and said with that wonderful grin of his, "Thinking like that will get you killed. I'm not sure it hasn't already."

"Thoughts like what?"

"Letting your mind go where you want it to go instead of concentrating on where it's supposed to be. Taking that bullet in the arm was a rookie mistake. Good thing he was a rotten shot."

"I thought I did a damn good job figuring out where he was going to go before he even got there. I can't help it if his route was shorter than mine."

"Come on Jill, you were scanning the woods trying to find him and started from the house. You wasted seconds on a useless exercise. What made you think he would be where he had already been? The smart thing would have been to start scanning from your right flank where you didn't know squat and scan left to his last known position. Then you might have picked up on movement by your shack."

"The operative word there is 'might'."

"Jill, the operative word is 'didn't' and you got yourself outflanked and shot. You wanted to beat him to the wall's end, and you wanted to see him approach so you could get the drop on him. You started looking from the left to make the sequence of events happen that you already had in your mind. It was a rookie mistake."

She hated to admit it, but he was right. It was a rookie mistake and it had cost her. "What about you, Mike, what kind of mistake did you make?"

His smile disappeared and his eyes, those beautiful bluish green eyes, took on a look of sadness so deep it was painful to look at him. He turned a little and looked down the valley from the trail where they were standing with the horses and said softly, "In a way you and I are tied together, but not as you would think.

"When I was a boy, my Dad told me about a friend in Vietnam who, with his squad, was separated from base. It happened frequently enough where they spent the night in the jungle and found their way back the next day. This time one of the men had stepped on a bamboo spike and he was in horrible pain from the crap that got into his system. He couldn't control his cries of pain and no one had any medication to give him to quiet him down. A decision had to be made as to whether the lives of the squad would remain at risk of detection or they would knock this one guy out. They decided to knock him out to save the group. Unfortunately, the hit was too hard and it killed him. It was an accidental death, although an intentional act.

"Dad said that although this was a very sad story, it was important to remember that sometimes to save your own, you kill your own." With that being said he turned and mounted his horse. The move allowed the sun to shine directly into Jill's eyes. She could still hear Mike say… "Sometimes to save your own, you kill your own"… over and over. The sun was so damn bright it was making her eye tear and she tried to lift her hand to brush it away, but it wouldn't move. "Why won't my hand move? And why is the damn sun in my left eye?"

And then the sun went away.

The more Bill thought about it the more he knew this damn case was going to kill every last one of them. He should have known it from the minute that woman walked into his office with that damn "I know you're the one who can solve this" look, he was biting off more than he could swallow. His instincts told him so. His gut told him so. Hell, his girlfriend told him so before she ditched him. Not that her leaving mattered; she was on her way out anyway. But even this was a bit much, why try to kill Jill Benoit? And why wasn't there any hot water on demand in this motel?

Here it was 2:15 in the afternoon and he still had to pick up the new rental car at the New Englander. He had slept late being exhausted from his travels and adventures of yesterday. TV news didn't carry much about the shooting, but conversation at the diner downtown had been full of rumor and speculation that ran from a massive shootout between several gunmen and five or six police officers to a break-in gone bad with one suspect killed and one retired officer critically wounded. He'd have to see Jill at the hospital to find out the truth. He could only hope it had nothing to do with his case.

While shaving, Bill thought about the other deaths and close calls since he had started investigating the initial hold up and events of the standoff in '71.

There was Janice Beemer who hated to talk about anything to anyone, but talked about the hold up with bitterness that matched Stephanie Kincaid's – almost. Her rendition was curt and to the point. The one called Zeke had grabbed her by the hair and dragged her to a storeroom in the bank's basement where he tied her hands and feet and gagged her. She saw him and him alone maybe four more times when he would untie her feet and take her to the washroom for five minutes only. She was allowed to drink water and once they gave her crackers from a vending machine they had broken into. She did not hear any shots until just before one officer opened the door and saw her. One shot was fired just as the officer approached, stopping his progress. He told her to sit quietly and wait for his return, as if she had a choice. Several minutes and shots later, the officer returned and escorted her out, but not before she saw Sam Donaldson face down on the floor with the back of his head blown off. After two days of captivity, that sort of tipped her over the edge and put her into hysterical mode. She was later identified as the teller Cpl. Metcalf rescued and was photographed with.

She had reason for her bitterness. According to her, there were several alternative exits that would have been safer, quicker, and easier on her psyche to get her out of there. She had begged him to take her out the closest one and get her outside quickly to safety as she was sure her emotional stability was questionable at best. Metcalf deliberately chose to go through the main part of the bank as if he wanted to have her see all the gore and exit the front doors for photographers to have a photo op. The blood and bodies was just too much for her and that, in her opinion, was what he was counting on. It made him a hero and her a helpless victim. After two days of being scared to death, tired, hungry, and tied up, Janice was on the verge of collapse. Even an idiot like Metcalf knew she couldn't take a bloody crime scene. She never forgave him for that. That was all she had to say about it.

It was apparently more than she should have said, because two days later she was found by her neighbor in the back yard sitting among her beloved flowers, quite dead. The autopsy report said she died from anaphylactic shock probably from an insect bite or bee sting. Without family to contest the issue or evidence to the contrary, Bill was at a loss to dispute it. But, he questioned whether someone as bitter about the event would calmly sit in a garden of flowers regardless of Florida's weather or reputation as the Sunshine State. Wouldn't someone with allergies to stings carry the injections to prevent shock? It wasn't a big stretch to confuse a sting site with a needle site. But, with her being the first survivor to die after the fact, no one was interested in his theories and told him to go home.

The John Doe at the airport who tried to kill him in the men's room was the most convincing of all that forces of evil were conspiring against him. He wondered if that was the same guy who tried to run him off the road in Killington last month. It would help him to rest easier if he knew there was only one man actively trying to slit his throat and one giving the orders. Cpl. Metcalf was now an Agent with the US Border Patrol and not willing to talk. Bill had called some time ago asking for a meeting and been turned down flat.

The Vermont State Police had a chain of command to go through to find anyone who had been on scene and were processing his request to interview officers still on active duty. They would also provide him with a list of names of those who had left or retired since then. That list would be made available sometime around the second Tuesday of next week as the saying goes. In other words, forget it. No one protects their own like cops do. The teller who hit the alarm was missing and had been for over twenty years. Finding her was a long shot but Bill had friends in high and special places who were working on it. His secretary had called this morning saying a letter had arrived from one of those friends and maybe that had the lead he needed.

Now that he was thinking of these convenient deaths, he hoped Jill's friend in LA was okay. He felt like shit having brought this to her doorstep. That invoice wasn't really that much to go on even though it might have tied in somehow at a later date. Right now it only brought up another question in a puzzle that had too many already.

Bill called a cab knowing that stewing about this wasn't going to solve anything at the motel, and shoved off for the hospital. He had been wondering when VSP would show up and, looking out the cab window, he wondered no more. Bill was looking at a very business-like and intent young trooper blocking the front entrance to the hospital. Trooper John

Filbert made some comment about being glad he could relieve Bill's mind of concern and then asked him to go to the Shaftsbury Barracks to answer some questions. He was being polite enough, but his body language and position indicated that choices were very limited. When asked about the type of questions, Trooper Filbert deferred saying Captain Dugan was the one requesting.

When Bill asked to see Jill first, it was suggested he wait. It seemed to be a touchy subject. He was asked if he was family or related in some way. Bill responded ... only by common cause. Trooper Filbert then suggested they leave as he had other things to do.

Had Charlie been looking out of the ICU window upstairs, she would have seen the two men, Bill and Trooper Filbert, having their discussion. Instead, she was sitting next to her best friend Jill, trying to listen in on the conversation going on next to the room's doorway. The group continued to talk softly for another few minutes before the doctor came in and introduced himself as the man in charge of ICU in general and Jill in particular.

Charlie wasn't impressed with his look, but then at her age younger doctors didn't impress. He looked to be old enough to be a high school drop-out in surgical scrubs. California was full of them, although on the west coast most were cosmetic specialists or some other useless specialty that cost a fortune and didn't do a damn thing to help a normal person survive normal health problems. Dr. Joaquin Cruz was maybe 35, married, if the ring on his left hand meant anything, and looked terribly concerned. If nothing else, she would give him high marks for reading her mood right. He didn't give her any crap about not being family or for being in ICU for two hours without leaving. Good thing, because she wasn't planning to leave anytime soon. As a matter of fact, she wasn't leaving at all until her best friend in the world came out of this. *Sorry, God, if you made other plans, you are going to have to put them on hold. We made a pact when we were kids and that takes precedent.*

The doctor was saying it was really a question of time and waiting for her brain to heal itself from the trauma. Every test they had run came out negative for internal injuries or damage inside the skull. There was no foreign object, or clot, or blood seepage. The laceration caused by the bullet wasn't deep enough to even scratch the skull bone. Her unconsciousness was most likely caused by a combination of blood loss from the arm wound and the concussive power of the bullet.

Jill had been under tremendous stress and in a weakened condition prior to the injury. She was lying in the cold for an extended length of time and her body systems had shut down to minimize effort and maximize survival. Comas were not always bad things in the short term. It's when people languish in them for extended periods that they become worrisome.

They had given her plasma and fluids to make up for her blood loss and antibiotics to fight infections. The small tear in the artery had been fixed along with the laceration on her scalp. There wasn't much more they could do except monitor her vitals and wait for her to come around.

Charlie asked if Jill could hear her if she talked. She wanted to know if there was any truth to the concept she had read about in journals. There was a lot of evidence that people do hear and even feel touch while in comas. It had also been shown to help in some cases. He was all for it.

"Does she have any family in the area and have they been informed of her condition?" the doctor asked.

Charlie had been waiting for this. "Jill comes from a big family but they're really spread out all over the place. Parents are gone, she has a daughter in Wyoming who's trying to get here, but it's going to take a while. Her closest relative is in Albany, and I've talked with him by phone. He's okay with my keeping him informed of Jill's status, and gave me his numbers for contact if you need them. I passed them on to the nurse at the desk. Did anyone check to see if Jill had a living will on record with the hospital? Her brother asked me and I didn't have the answer."

That was one of many details Charlie had not known about and for good reason. Jill and Charlie hadn't been in touch for almost five years when this Robinson character showed up on her doorstep. That had prompted Charlie to call the house, and when she didn't get an answer, she called a mutual friend, Jean Dugan. Charlie had met Jean in college and stayed friends. Jean had married a trooper from Vermont, and Charlie stayed in California with her honey Jake. Later on, Jill and Rick had become close friends on a different timeline and all of them wound up a fivesome on two coasts. For a while it was a sixsome until Jill's ex- husband bowed out. She never did understand what broke those two apart. They didn't talk about it.

"There is a paper here that says anything over thirty days on machine support, if brain dead, will be terminated. There is no power of attorney for health care decisions. That means we would need next of kin for surgery or other extraordinary measures if required."

The look he gave her clearly sent the message that under no circumstance was she going to interfere in Jill's treatment should extreme measures be required.

"Not to worry, doctor, I'll be the first to call when the shit hits the fan. I'm her best friend, not an idiot."

He smiled, turned, and left the room, leaving her to sit by Jill and wonder why anyone would want to hurt her pal.

They had grown up on the western side of Pittsfield knowing that nothing would ever change the bonds of friendship between them. It was instant and unquestioned, this loyalty they had. Charlie was a year older, descended from German/Hungarian parents, stronger (which pissed Jill off), and always thinking that the world was what you made of it. Jill was tough in a different way, Canadian through and through, pig-headed, and always fighting the battles of rowing upstream. She had to be smarter, climb bigger trees, and try scarier things. Yet she was a loner who stayed away from socials and parties, anything that had to do with groups. They got along great as long as it was just the two of them.

They'd spend hours hunting rabbits in the great woods behind the residential neighborhood where they lived. Their weapons were souvenir knives Jill's brother had brought back from Germany when he was overseas and the woods were a small group of saplings and brush next to undeveloped fields. Charlie was not sure they ever saw a rabbit, although she remembered Jill throwing a hatchet at something running through the field once. Hatchet? It was a roofing hammer maybe, with a bladed edge. Ah, they were fierce in those days.

"We were always off on adventures that put us in pickles with our parents. Do you remember riding our bicycles to Lee and back without permission and against the law? No bikes were allowed on the highway we used to get there. Let me tell you, I caught hell when I got back. Your mom was only four eleven and she was nice.

I was grounded for two weeks and had to do dishes for a month solid.

"Remember the time we talked Dad into taking us deer hunting when we were eleven or twelve or something stupid like that? He took us out into the forest and we thought we had walked for miles in the snow. It was what, a hundred yards? Then he stuck us on an overturned tree stump and told us not to move or make a sound. Said he was going to go over the ridge and be back in a bit. We froze our friggin' asses off. Both of us had to pee so bad we wet our snow pants which made us colder. But would we give in? Heck no. Finally he came back and took us back to the truck and drove us home. We didn't think we'd ever thaw out. Later he told Ma it was just a joke when he said he'd take us. He never thought you'd show up at five in the morning and never thought we'd last on the stump. He was only a few yards away from there watching us freeze and finally gave up when he started getting cold."

She kept watching Jill's face and holding her hand waiting for some sign of life, some movement, some blinking of an eyelid that would indicate she knew Charlie was there. Damn it, they had known each other for fifty years. They had been at each other's weddings, and kids' births, baptisms, birthday parties. They helped bury each other's mothers. She held Jill's head over the toilet bowl when she got her final divorce papers. "Wake up for Pete's sake!"

"Jill this is Charlie. You need to wake up. You're needed here and you're needed now. I can't stand to see you like this and I refuse to sit here and watch you die. I have a business to run and a husband who can't be in two places at once especially if one is in New York and the other is Los Angeles. I have appointments to keep, people to see and places to go. You may be retired but I'm not!"

A nurse walked in and asked if something was wrong. Charlie reassured her that other than her best friend being on another dimension and her being too loud, everything was just dandy.

She sat next to the bed with her head in her hand covering her eyes not thinking of anything in particular. Exhaustion was beginning to catch up with the jet lag. It was midnight California time so there was no sense in calling Jake. She hadn't checked into a hotel or eaten since the plane so both those life sustaining activities would be worth looking into pretty soon. She must have said something about leaving out loud because the next thing Charlie heard was a very faint "Leaving so soon?"

At first she wasn't sure she had heard Jill talking so, like an idiot, she said, "What?"

Jill turned her head a little and winced from what must have been pain from the laceration, and did a slow blink.

"Seems like you just showed up and already you're complaining." That was about the limit of her reserves and her eyes closed again to rest. That was Charlie's cue to run out into the hall and find someone, anyone. Jill was back and they'd better not lose her again.

Shake a leg folks, and get in here. Do your stuff. I've done mine.

Fifteen minutes later Jill was a little less covered with tubes and wires but still being monitored and still getting fluids intravenously. Meanwhile, she had been given a few sips of water and if she could hold that down they would continue to step her up through the food chain until she was back to normal. Once she was "tube free", she could hop onto the solid food wagon and head for home. It appeared that the worst was over.

"About time you returned to the land of the living," Charlie grumbled.

"Nice to see you too, Charlie. How the hell you been, and how the hell did you get here?" Jill's voice was not her usual low pitch tone, but rather a dry and grating monotone that hurt the ear listening as much as it hurt the throat that was speaking. The nurse brought in two containers with water and juice which Jill eagerly started to sip. That helped to ease the dryness in her throat and loosened the vocal cords somewhat.

Charlie helped move the water pitcher back and answered the questions. "I was just fine until some guy called Robinson came to see me yesterday, I think it was yesterday, and started asking me questions about an invoice and some shipment of stuff we picked up in Canada in 1988. I can't remember what I had for breakfast this morning. Anyway, I called you after he left and you didn't answer the phone. I called Jean and she told me about the shooting. I took the red eye to JFK and Rick had a friend in the New York Troopers Unit run me up the line where some VSP guy picked me up. I must say you rank pretty high around here."

Jill seemed to be taking a lot of time and working hard to talk. Obviously her recovery was going to take more than an hour or two. "My feeling is that this case ranks high, not me. Robinson is the connecting rod so far and he thinks I'm the connecting rod. Not sure either one of us know anything much. Do they know who was in the house and shot me?"

"I can answer that." The deep authoritative voice from the doorway spoke up from behind and the surprise caused Charlie to knock the monitor back an inch. Captain Dugan walked in with a smile on his face that showed genuine pleasure at seeing his friend awake and talking. He walked over to the other side of Jill's bed and took her hand into both of his causing hers to totally disappear.

"You look a hell of a lot better than the last time I saw you. Wasn't sure you'd be joining us again. Glad you decided to."

"Well my good captain, I can't let you have all the fun chasing after bad guys. Did you catch up with the guy in my house? I think I hit him with the .45."

He looked at me and smiled, "Charlie, could you give us a minute?"

She stepped outside and went to the ladies' room which had been calling for some time.

CHAPTER

11

As a child and young adult, faith was not something that I questioned or analyzed a great deal. My mother made sure we all went to church and observed the traditions and rules of Catholicism. More than that she exemplified to us what it meant to believe in something greater than yourself. To trust that an Almighty and Everlasting Being was going to provide answers to prayers or the strength to endure what she couldn't change was my mother's firm belief. There has always been a part of me that has wanted to believe in that type of faith, and for a good part of my life did.

I don't know where I heard it, but there was an expression that "there were no atheists in foxholes." As someone who has professionally served in uniform and put her life in harm's way, I can assure you that you may not choose to become a prophet when on death's doorstep, but it is highly unlikely you will not hope that God exists. It wasn't strange to me at all that the last thought I had when that blurry figure came into my gun sights and his flashlight hit my eyes was whether I had led a good life and done what God had intended for me to do.

The next thought I had wasn't really a thought at all, but more like a vision. I was walking up a hill towards a single tree sitting at the top with a couple of big boulders on the side. The tree had a huge canopy of branches and was filled with leaves. Once I reached the top, the view was expansive and showed the neighborhoods with their lower middle-class lawns and filled with flower gardens, trees, and shrubs. Off in the distance you could see the hills of Bousquet Ski Area. It was all quite picturesque.

Looking at the tree trunk there was a knothole where a branch had fallen off years ago and age had rotted the remains leaving a hollow the size of a softball. Inside the knothole there was a pack of cigarettes with book matches tucked inside the cellophane wrapper and two cigarettes gone from the pack. They were the latest in our efforts to be "adult", Charlie and me. She was a year older than I was and maybe a bit stronger, but I had more freedom from home and that more than made up for it. I took out a cigarette, lit it, and sat on the rock smoking, waiting for Charlie. Where the hell was she? I thought I had heard her. And what did we call this place, Tree Hill? The Rocks? Boulder Hill? Damn, I couldn't remember these days. Too much booze was killing...Murder Hill! That's what we called it, Murder Hill. I wonder why we called it that. Maybe someone was murdered in the old house on the other side of the Big Pines.

Then I heard her talking again, something about that bike ride to Lee and hunting with her dad, but that was years ago, as in forty almost fifty years. What the hell is she talking about and where the hell is she? I can't see her. Everywhere I look I see grass, shrubs, overgrowth, fields, but no people. Then everything started to fade into a whiteness that made all the shapes around me blend into a blank screen. It was the same as sitting on a sheet of white copy paper. No sight, no sound, no smell or taste to make any distinction between being and not being.

Then I heard Charlie again yelling off in the distance that I had to wake up. I was needed and she had other things to do or something to that effect. Leave it to Charlie to save the day and leave at the same time. What a pal. Wait a minute, what was she doing here? Was here still Bennington? Guess I'll have to open up the old eyeballs and find out.

I was just beginning to be happy about being awake and talking with Charlie when Rick walked in. He then proceeded to chase her out and take over my life. This was getting to be a pain in the ass this business of having people in my house, in my yard, shooting at me, calling me, talking to me, manipulating my life. When did I get to be retired and enjoy the fruits of my labors?

"Okay, you have my undivided attention. Who broke into my house and shot at me? And tell me you caught the bastard."

"First of all when Gail got to your place, the suspect was shot twice by person or persons unknown. She had two deputies from New York with her and all three think it was one shooter, but the result is the same. And yes, you did wing him with your last shot but he also got you on the side of your skull. You were lucky this guy had lousy aim." Rick seemed to be enjoying his role as story teller.

"Well, what's this guy's name?" I didn't try to hide the irritation in my voice.

"Zeke Faraday, do you know him?" Rick's face looked so innocent.

"I've heard of him. He was one of the suspects in the First National Bank job in '71."

"Why would you know about that case?" His demeanor changed quickly to one of an interrogator not a friend. This wasn't sitting too well with me, and I didn't really feel up to a game of wits. There was obviously more going on here than I could handle.

"Rick, I appreciate that you have an investigation to run, but I'm just a little under the weather right now. Do you mind if we continue this later?"

He didn't look a bit happy but wasn't in a position to argue, especially since Charlie had returned and was pacing in front of the doorway.

"I'll come back in the morning when you've had a chance to rest up. Sorry if I was pushing. There's a lot of pressure on me from upstate on this one, but keep that under your hat." With that quiet comment he kissed me on the head and left saying goodbye to Charlie as he left. Now what was all that about pressure and being quiet about it? I wasn't part of his troop and didn't need orders from him. I just wanted to be left alone.

Charlie came back in with a backward glance at Rick that said she wasn't at all pleased to have been dismissed by him. She tended to be protective of all things injured especially if they were family, and I was most definitely family. Her smile may have been trying to say welcome to the nurse who had walked in behind her, but her body language and position was most definitely saying she wasn't leaving anytime soon.

The nurse recorded some readings on the monitor, checked the IV, made certain I was comfortable and took a look at the dressing on my arm. She asked if I was hungry, saying I could have Jell-o if I felt I could keep it down. That sounded like a positive step and off she went to retrieve my hearty snack.

"Charlie, what can you tell me about the invoice Robinson had?"

Charlie looked a little annoyed and tired at the same time. "You just come back from the dead and all you can talk about is some old invoice?"

Now it was my turn to be annoyed, "Look, I wouldn't be here and neither would you if something hadn't interrupted both of our lives and not in a nice way. It seems to revolve around this guy Robinson and some case he's working on. His connection to you is that invoice. I'm just trying to figure out if it has any connection to me. Who knows, maybe you, or Jake, or both of you may be in danger also."

Charlie's facial expressions flowed through a series of changes from annoyance to anger, fear, and back to disbelief. It was easy to see that fatigue and probably hunger was taking its toll on her ability to make decisions.

Charlie confirmed my thoughts when she said, "Let me think a little. I'm really tired and not processing information or retrieving it very well."

While she was thinking about the past, I started to think about her present. There had to be some way of her getting some rest without being on her own. I didn't want her out and about in Bennington or at my place without someone to watch over her. My normal recourse would have been to call Jean, but with Rick on the case that was out of the question. Gail had more than proven herself reliable, but she too was involved. Robinson I didn't trust. That leaves who? I guess Tom is the only one I trusted who might even consider doing me a favor at this point. Speaking of which, where was he?

Tom Broman was a retired New Hampshire State trooper who lived by himself on Cross Road between Shaftsbury and White Creek. He had built himself a place in the woods off the beaten track and kept pretty much to himself. We had met first at the University of Vermont when UVM was affordable. Later, when I was stationed at Newport, we worked a few cases together. In Richford, we met again at a seminar held by Homeland on domestic terrorism and related topics. Both of us were divorced at this point and looking at retirement in the near future. Tom was looking to buy land and build; I offered to help with real estate information in Vermont.

The two of us hit it off and formed a close bond based on a mutual respect for each other's talents and recognition that personal space was essential. That was the main reason we never moved in together or married, it didn't work the first time for either of us and we had no illusions that it would work the second time. Apart, we let absence do its thing with the heart until fondness makes us choose otherwise. It works for us.

I'll bet Tom hasn't heard anything or else he would be here. He didn't have a scanner, seldom watched TV, and listened to NPR as I did. He would check the internet for national news, but I didn't think my being shot up was important enough for the BBC. Not many people knew about us so I imagine no one bothered to give him a jingle on the phone. Guess it was up to me.

"Charlie, I'm going to find a safe place for you to stay, and please don't argue." She just stared at me with a blank look that registered almost nothing.

"What are you talking about?" she stammered.

"Whatever is going on, your physical safety may be in question. I'm a little under the weather at the moment, and I don't know how complicated this threat is. I do know that Rick is involved in the investigation and staying with Jean is out of the question. Other people that I would trust with your safety are also involved in some manner so they are out. I have one person that I do trust with my life, therefore I would trust with yours. Would you mind if I gave him a call?"

"Do you really think someone would try to hurt me over a stupid invoice?" The question was tentative, but I could tell that Charlie wasn't sure about anything right now.

"At this point I'm inclined to believe it, that just being around me or at my house is enough. And yes, the invoice could be enough also."

"And who is this he?"

"Tom Broman, he's a very close personal friend of mine. I've known him since college. He's a retired New Hampshire trooper living around my area in Shaftsbury. You'll be well taken care of."

Charlie's eyebrows went up and a big smile crossed her face. "And just how close a 'personal friend' is he?"

"This is hardly the time or place to get into that." Sheesh, she could still make me squirm after all these years. You'd think she was my mother.

"Well, I suppose I should meet and check him out. Besides, I'm dead on my feet and it's too late to search around for hotels. It never occurred to me to stay with Jean. Rick just pisses me off with that VSP crap."

"Good. Let me use your cell phone. Tom probably hasn't heard anything yet and I'd like to tell him first. It'll save the environment a small explosion."

With that I called Tom, who was indeed sleeping, and told him the events immediately prior to my call. After explaining that I needed a safe place for Charlie, he said he'd be at the hospital in forty-five minutes to see me and pick her up. I also asked him to call Abigail Buskirk and find out what if anything was happening with the animals at my place.

True to his word, Tom came in forty minutes later looking every bit as competent and handsome as I knew he would. He quickly introduced himself to Charlie and thanked her for staying with me, which pleased her to no end. He also made it clear that putting her up at his place was the least he could do and not any imposition at all. We talked for a few minutes about what had happened in broad strokes to give an idea of what the threat level might be.

Apparently, Gail had made arrangements with the boys who delivered hay and feed for the horses from the local feed store to check on supplies and adjust as needed until notified by me. Tom was going to pick up Fundy from Gail later and bring him back to his place. Both Tom and Charlie would take over the feeding chores and check the house as soon as Charlie had some sleep.

"I really don't want Charlie being interrogated by anyone including Rick or Bill Robinson. Anything you can do to prevent contact with those two gentlemen would be appreciated. Charlie, that means I really don't want you to come back here."

"Now just a second, you aren't telling me what I can or can't do after I flew cross country just to wake your little ass up."

There was no mistaking that German temper when it got riled. Those eyes could drill holes through plate steel when she got that pissed.

"Simmer down before you bust something. Rick is already starting to question me about some old case. Robinson and I met late last night and some of the stuff we talked about includes an old case that Rick is connected with. He told me confidentially that he's under a lot of pressure from upstate on this investigation. Add this up and you can bet he's going to be questioning anyone he can as hard as he can. If you show up here again, he's going to want to question you too."

"So what, I don't know anything about any cold case. Why should I care if he questions me?"

The expression I read along with the words said this argument could go on forever. This was taking way too long. Charlie needed to leave. I gave Tom a pleading look and he stepped in.

"I think I'd better get going, Gail is expecting me to pick up Fundy and I have to swing by the house first. We can settle this by phone if necessary later on."

His voice was so smooth and matter of fact that no one took offense. I'll bet he was one hell of a cop. With ease he gathered Charlie's things and motioned her towards the door. Stopping by my side, he kissed me good night. "Don't worry, I've got your back. We'll be in touch as soon as the details are taken care of."

I think I was asleep before I saw his strong, straight, tall frame walk through the doorway.

CHAPTER

12

By Saturday morning every doctor and nurse who came within ten feet of me was more than ready to sign discharge papers. Tom and Charlie picked me up at 9:00, by 10:00 I was defending myself from a very ecstatic yellow lab that couldn't stop jumping and head-butting my still sore body. I was glad to see Fundy but my arm wasn't quite ready for defensive maneuvers and still needed a sling for support. Tom finally had to clip a lead on him until he calmed down into his licking phase.

The horses gathered around the fence to say hello and all gave me their respective muzzles to pat, although I think it was more in anticipation of feed than a welcome home. No one seemed the worse for wear given they had been in strange hands for a few days. Barn and hay storage seemed taken care of along with the water supply. The lack of organization made it obvious that strangers had been around, but at this point I wasn't complaining.

Crime scene tape was wrapped around the trees and briars in the area of the shooting and around the shack, although there were no guards posted. I walked out briefly to have a look. Most of the blood had seeped into the snow and been covered over by another layer of snow dust. It looked like Mother Nature's version of a powdered sugar coated strawberry pink cake. An outline of both the suspect's body and mine remained for future reference along with a line of tape that marked the path Faraday had taken from the shack to the corner. There was no need to see where or how he had reached the shack since it really made no difference to me at this point. I would need to reassure myself later that the person I tried to intercept was the person who shot me, but for now I wanted to go inside the house and see what carnage had been left for me to deal with.

Charlie was fixing coffee and a light lunch when I finally got around to walking into the kitchen. The smells were intoxicating after three days in the medicinal atmosphere of the ICU. Fundy was lying on the floor behind her patiently waiting for any small scrap to hit ground zero where it would immediately disappear into his mouth with one swipe of that enormous tongue. He had obviously gotten over his excitement of seeing me home.

Tom and I went downstairs to look at the results from the home invasion. As my foot touched the bottom step, my eyes caught the full brunt of what was the focus of the search. The room was totally trashed. There wasn't a book left on shelf, a drawer left in place, a piece of paper left where it had been originally. I had left my old file boxes from the attic down here and they were totally taken apart and scattered on the floor. It would take days, maybe weeks, to put all this stuff back together and in order. To make matters worse, some genius from VSP had been here dusting for prints and there was dust all over the place. Only someone who had the misfortune of cleaning up after a crime scene could understand the depth of my despair at the thought of cleaning up. Print dust was the worst. Rick would hear about this. The need for prints I understood. Leaving the mess for me to clean up I did not. And where was the list of things taken by VSP for the case file? I had no doubt they had taken stuff. Never knew them to go to a crime scene and not take something for their evidence file. It was not only common courtesy, but I thought, required to leave a list behind of the items taken or whatever they had in their possession. It was supposed to protect them from being accused of theft and help victims reclaim their property after a case was closed. Someone was slipping up big time.

Putting aside the mess downstairs, we sat around the table talking after lunch, discussing what to do next. I explained to Charlie about the attempts on Robinson's life and what I knew about the possible connection between his cold case, the invoice, the deaths we knew of, and maybe what had happened to me.

Charlie was not pleased that she was now somewhat of a target, and even less excited about my suggestion that Jake also consider removing himself from LA and perhaps joining us in Vermont for a spell as a precaution. She was far less of an alarmist than I.

"Are you intending to hold Jake and I hostage here? We do have businesses to run. I love you dearly, my friend, but Jake doesn't do well with poverty."

"Oh hell no, you'd talk me to death in less than a week if I had to hold you hostage." That didn't have the desired effect of lightening things up. "I just want both of you here where Tom and I can control the environment around you a little better. We can't do that if you are in LA or New York. Right now LAPD and NYPD are not involved in any related investigations and we can't count on their help. I don't want them to become involved by finding your bodies."

Both looked at me with very different expressions. Tom was thoughtful, processing everything in a logical and methodical way. I could see the cop analyzing risk, assessing information, making connections and trying not to assume facts not mentioned or reaching conclusions that couldn't be supported. He may have thought I was being paranoid trying to protect someone who didn't need protecting, but I could tell he was having a hard time getting around my logic.

Charlie, on the other hand, was looking at me with something between concern and incredible disbelief. As I talked and made my case, I could see her eyes change from disbelief to anger. At least I could deal with an angry friend as long as it was channeled in the right direction.

Tom was the first to answer, "I don't know what you have in mind for a plan, but I think you're probably right in that Charlie and Jake could be targets if someone is taking out people looking into that cold case." He turned and looking at Charlie said, "I think you should at least consider working something out if you can. I've been in law enforcement for a long time and I've seen crazier things happen. Jill could be wrong, but she might also be right. I'd rather see you safe, myself."

Charlie sat back and looked at the two of us with a smirk on her face. I couldn't quite read what it meant, too many years had gone by. "If the plan is reasonable and Jake can comply, I will agree. But let me go on record as saying I think both of you are nuts. I don't know anything that could get me hurt."

After a little pause, I asked Charlie, "Do you and Jake ever go together on trips for the shop or long vacations?"

She laughed, "Sure we do, it happens two or three times a year. We usually do a five or six country buying tour for shop items in the spring and fall. Depending on business, we'll take a week's vacation in early summer and one after the holidays."

"Your operations in LA and New York City operate alright with the personnel you have in place? You trust them?"

"Both shops run just fine without us as long as we have inventory. Our manager in LA has been working for us since '85, and our gal in New York came on board ten years ago. She's fantastic, a genius with antiques and a people person. Has a lot of contacts that she brought with her in the south and mid-Atlantic states which opened up a lot of areas to us."

I nodded, "So if Jake flew out here and the two of you stayed here as our guests for a while, your business would not suffer?"

"I don't think so. At least it wouldn't be a strain financially. Our inventory is fairly high right now and the staff is stable. This time of year isn't our busiest in either location. I'll have to run it by Jake and see what he has to say about this. He doesn't usually give me a hard time, but one never knows. What about you Tom, you think this is a good idea?"

Tom had been sitting very quietly watching the two of us go at it, not saying a word. He looked back and forth from me to Charlie and back again with a curious expression on his face. It wasn't a look of complete distrust, but close.

"You two are the ones who dragged that poor kid up that mosquito infested, muddy, over-grown mountain trail for four hours thinking he was climbing Mt. Greylock? Then when you crested the top, dragged him up another mountain saying you had climbed the wrong one? And you think I'm not worried about any plan you might come up with that involves me?"

What Tom was referring to happened a zillion years ago when Charlie and I were kids. Her cousin Billy came with us on a hike up Mt. Greylock via the Appalachian Trail. We walked up this huge mountain after about a week of rain. We were all complaining about the mud holes, the bugs, the branches, how tired we were, you name it - we were complaining about it. We get to the top of this mountain and I'll be damned if it isn't a different mountain than the one we thought we were climbing. There in front of us was Mt. Greylock just as big as life with the monument staring us right in the face.

We were beat, hungry and covered with mosquito bites. A decision had to be made. Did we cheat and walk up the road (not too far to our left) to the top, or continue the trail and risk missing our ride home? Didn't take us long to figure that one out. We banked left, walked the road to the top, sat for ten minutes and started to walk back down the road, blisters and all. I think someone gave us a lift half-way down and dropped us at the bottom. I don't think I ever admitted I didn't hike to the top. As far as I was concerned, we did. But I'll bet Billy talked.

Charlie and I were laughing so hard both of us were crying. Tom brought back the coffee pot from the counter and refilled everyone's cup, tossing the box of Kleenex on the table.

We dried our eyes, discussed a few more details concerning our bold plan and decided to split up for a while. Tom was going back to his place to do what he needed to do. Charlie and I would tackle the invoice, Robinson, and call Jake. I liked Tom's job better than mine, but it looked like I was stuck. As I walked Tom out to his car, we talked of other things a little more personal and a lot more fun. Tom had a way of taking my mind off whatever was aggravating me. Moments later he was gone and the aggravation was back.

Back inside Charlie and I settled in for the afternoon. The invoice was first up on the list of topics. I was really hoping Charlie had maintained her habit of remembering details. "Walk me through the conversation with Robinson about the invoice."

"Sure, he told me he was given an invoice that showed my shop received a box of materials from somewhere in British Columbia, Canada back in 1988 from someone named M. Johnson. The invoice indicated that US Customs had cleared it but wanted it held unopened by the recipient, our shop, until an agent picked it up. That notice of delay was typed in at the bottom and initialed but I couldn't decipher the initials.

"If you ask me, the invoice was phony and the shipment didn't exist. First of all, anything that screwy, I would have noticed and remembered. I probably wouldn't have complied or I would have called Customs and told them to pick up their shit. Second of all, I don't have people sending stuff to my shops. Either Jake or I buy everything that we sell. Even my managers don't ship stuff in. They may suggest people and places to contact for purchases, they may accompany us, they may bring people in to see us, but no one ships to us. There's too much danger for smuggling."

Charlie was absolutely right about the smuggling danger. "Did Robinson have any additional information about what was in this shipment?"

She shook her head, "Not that he mentioned to me. All he said was that it would have been a crate, fairly large, and would have arrived by truck. I told him that was a sure bet since all of our materials arrived by truck, UPS, FedEx, USPS or our private hand delivery. Some of our merchandise is quite valuable and if at all possible Jake and I prefer to freight it ourselves rather than risk damage by going commercial. But, naturally when it's a big or heavy item, we have to go commercial and insure the hell out of it. Most of the time we luck out, but once in a while we lose. In the end the winners outweigh the losers."

"Who was working for you back in '88?" I wondered if someone could be using her shop for illegal shipping.

"If memory serves me right, I had a college kid working part time in the front to meet and greet. He would cover for me while I cleared up the paperwork in the office and took care of inventory downstairs. Sweet kid too, had an older brother who worked Border Patrol up in Washington somewhere either before or after you were there, I think. Can't remember the kid's first name but I think his last name was Metcalf. On Tuesdays, Thursdays, and Saturdays I had this wonderful young woman, Gretchen Czerwinski, who was a whiz with cataloging and inventory control. She knew where everything was and could find any piece we had whether it was out front, in storage, being shipped by Jake, or just waiting someplace on a dock. I relied on her a lot for information. She's the one Robinson should be talking to about that invoice. Gretchen would know the answer." Charlie got up and left the room for a minute while I digested her last news flash.

At the sound of Metcalf and Gretchen Czerwinski, I had a mental heart attack. I shouted after her, "Did Robinson ask you about your employees back then?"

"Yes."

"Did you tell anyone about his visit or what you talked about?" Charlie thought for a minute or two after she sat down again, "Not directly, there were people in and out of the office when we were talking but I seriously doubt they could hear much of what was being said."

"Did you look anything up or open any files?"

"Of course I did. I had to make sure I didn't have any carbons of that shipping invoice, which I didn't. I also had to check old personnel records to see if I had any full time people. I wasn't able to locate records for 1988 back to 1985, which baffled me a bit."

"Is Jake at the shop right now?" I was beginning to have a peculiar feeling in my left eyebrow that people who knew me well called the Sherlock look. I have no idea why that particular nickname got attached to it. It was merely a twitch I had developed over the years. Whenever I was stressed out trying to solve a case my eyebrow would arch involuntarily when a detail made sense. I guess they figured it was my Sherlock Holmes look.

"He should be, we don't close for another two hours. Why?"

Okay, Jill, turn on the charm you don't have, and try not to panic your best friend while you play investigator with old, worn out skills. You really shouldn't be doing this even if they did take a shot at you. "I want you to call and ask him to check your office and any place where you have records to see if things have been disturbed."

"What are you thinking?" The expression on her face suggested I not sugar coat anything.

"I'm thinking that either one of your two helpers in '88 may have had that crate shipped to them and used your shop for cover. I'm thinking that whoever is trying to stop Robinson may try to cover the trail of information at your shop especially if the two are connected. And I'm thinking I'd like to know if they left a trail themselves."

I didn't add that I thought I knew who the "helper" might be as I wasn't sure I was ready for that piece of information either. For all I knew at this point, it could be both.

"One more thing, did Gretchen have anything physical about her that stood out and made her memorable to you?"

"Do you mean a birthmark or a limp, something like that?"

Jill nodded, "Anything that would make her stand out in a group of women if they all had the same eye and hair color."

Charlie thought for a long minute, "You know, there was this habit she had of talking with a southern drawl every time she got upset or frantic. We used to kid her about it a little and asked her to be careful especially on the phone when dealing with overseas accounts. Some clients took offense and thought she was making fun of their accent. I think she came from the south or southwest originally and tried to lose the accent on purpose but would forget when she got stressed."

Jill thought about her conversation with Gretchen earlier in the week about the Hummers and how her neighbor's twang had irritated her so early in the morning.

"Thanks, you'd better call Jake now."

Charlie called Jake and they talked for some time while I went in the bedroom and changed clothes. I took a look at my arm and decided to change the dressing as my quality time with Fundy had started a little seepage. I looked at the incision and decided nothing major was wrong. A little clean up, some fresh antibiotic cream, sterile padding and gauze wrap completed the task. It was a wound that would heal in time but would probably be more inconvenient than painful.

The gash on the side of my head wasn't covered and looked like one of those makeup jobs gone bad in Friday the 13th movies. They had shaved my head around the wound and did a very nice job of cleaning it up. There were several butterfly stitch tapes trying desperately to hold my scalp together. Personally I hoped they succeeded. Hair does not grow in scar tissue and the thought of a barren strip above my ear didn't strike me as a fashion statement I could pull off. However, there was no care involved in its recovery other than to watch out for it when I shampooed.

When I returned to the kitchen, Charlie handed me the phone, "Jake wants to talk with you."

"Hi Jake, how are things out west?" Did I really say that? No wonder they question my people skills.

"What the hell are you doing Jill, trying to get us all killed? I thought you had retired?" Angry would have been an understatement in describing Jake's tone. Perhaps it was warranted, but it certainly wasn't helpful.

"Hold on a second. I didn't start this. Why yell at me?"

I liked Jake LaFleche a lot. He was not only married to my best friend, he was genuinely a nice guy. But, like most Canadians, he could get really hot and overly protective where his wife was concerned. A bit like I was about my family and friends. Guess I could cut him some slack, one Canadian to another.

His tone changed a little when he said, "Sorry, by the way how are you? I heard you were shot. Is everything okay?"

"Yeah, I'm fine. A little sore and undernourished, but I'll live to fight another day. Did you see any signs that someone searched or screwed around with your records?"

"I should say so. The office wasn't bad. It was hard to say at first. Not much of a mess to see. But as I went through the file drawers I could see that the older files from the eighties had been pulled and replaced out of order. When I went through those files, there were what I think may be invoices missing. Of course there isn't any way to be sure. I'm just guessing based on fade marks. Our copies of invoices wouldn't be sequential on stuff coming in. They're all different."

I asked, "What about files in storage, basements, places like that?"

His voice changed considerably, "They were not as considerate there. Perhaps they thought no one would check. It's a mess. Boxes are tipped over, papers are pulled out of containers and dropped on the floor. I have no idea where they belong. They spilled coffee on an entire stack of payroll records. If the IRS ever decides to audit us, we'll have a bitch of a time trying to provide records. It will take months and hundreds of man-hours to straighten this out."

"Is that the worst of it or is there more?" The reason I asked was because I couldn't believe Jake would be that mad at me over tossed paperwork. Something else must have happened.

"I found a photograph tacked up to the inside of my house door. Not the office, but my home door, where Charlie and I live, on the inside. They were in my house!" Now he was shouting. I couldn't blame him. I knew exactly how he felt.

"What was in the photograph?" I tried to sound calm and reassuring, but to tell the truth I was anything but.

"There was a guy at the bottom of a cliff. I would say it was a cop maybe, but dead for sure. On the back of the picture it said, 'If you don't want the same, mind your own business' whatever that means."

"Did they do anything else in your home? "NO! Wasn't that enough?"

Somehow I had to get Jake calmed down and into some sort of comfort zone. We needed that picture and we needed to get Jake out of LA and with his wife.

"Can you hang on just a second, Jake? I need to ask Charlie something."

I turned to Charlie and asked if she thought she could get Jake here with the picture. She agreed that she could calm him down and had already explained the plan to him, but he was reluctant to leave the shop for fear the intruder would torch the place or the house. We settled on calming him down for now and faxing the picture. I'd have to come up with some other way to get him out of there.

As Charlie did her thing on one line with Jake, I got a hold of Tom on the other and explained the situation up to and including the picture. I didn't like Tom's advice, but had to agree it was pretty close to the only option…call Rick.

I had so many questions going on in my head; it felt like a bingo cage rotating with two loads of balls and no one pulling any out. Where was Bill Robinson? I hadn't seen him since Tuesday and Wednesday when we met at Rick's. I expected at least a call from him, if not a visit. Where was the Brinker family and was Gretchen Czerwinski aka Gretchen Brinker? Why did Zeke Faraday care enough to shoot me? Why not just search and run? Why search? What was the Metcalf connection? Was the younger brother as much of a scum bag as the older brother? Was this an old bank robbery or something else, like a smuggling ring using legit businesses, or both? How did VSP play into all of this other than the shooting and break in? Why was headquarters putting pressure on Rick?

And the big money question, what the hell did retired Agent Jill Benoit have to do with any of this?

Right on cue, two things happened simultaneously, Charlie got off the phone with the news that Jake was on the next red eye to JFK. Rick drove into the yard in his personal vehicle with Jean. Both events were unexpected and in my present state of mind had me a little off guard. Exactly what that meant for my immediate future remained to be seen.

CHAPTER

13

Bill never realized, as a rookie cop in Burlington, how tough it was for the public to give him respect. Not until he stood there in front of Trooper John Filbert at the hospital. It's tough to be in awe of a kid hardly old enough to drink legally, standing in the "at ease" position, with his Smokey the Bear hat two fingers from his nose, and Ray Bans. The look was absurd. Bill half expected to find a wind up key stuck in his back. He wondered if this boy had seen his first dead body yet. How would his polished look stand up to a three car fatal where all you could find on the highway were body parts? Would he still look so ram rod straight and proud after he was forced to shoot and kill an armed black suspect and the public called him a racist murderer? There was a lot more to gaining respect than a good looking uniform worn properly and a military stance. He wondered if Trooper Filbert knew that.

Sitting across the desk from Captain Richard Dugan, those questions never came to mind. This man commanded respect from everyone including Bill Robinson. His occupation as a private investigator was not taken lightly nor was it put down as so many cops did just because they could. Rick Dugan didn't seem to be from the school that believed PIs were people who didn't make it as good cops and used this as a fall back position. As long as he was going to treat him with respect, Bill was going to reciprocate. That was probably how Rick managed to make captain and continued to be an effective officer.

"Mr. Robinson, I want to thank you for coming in. I'll try not to take too much of your time." His voice was deep and polite, but authoritative.

"It's not like I had much of a choice." Bill liked the guy, but he needed to be clear about the level of cooperation. A blocking move followed by a cruiser ride wasn't exactly what he would call a voluntary office call.

"I understand your lack of appreciation for the invitation. It was important that I speak with you before you saw Jill Benoit again. You will understand after we talk. In case you haven't connected the dots, it was my home office the two of you met in the night shortly before Jill was shot." There was a long pause while he waited for a reaction. There was none.

"Bill, may I call you Bill?" Bill nodded. "I'd like you to fill in what you can about events leading to Jill's shooting incident. I'd like to know where she met up with you, when, exactly where you traveled, and what was discussed."

After squirming in his seat for a second, Bill answered, "You do know I'm a private investigator hired to find things out for other people. I'm not required to share that information with you. My clients wouldn't like it very much if I spilled all their secrets to the cops whenever I was picked up for questioning. I wouldn't stay in business very long.

"I've only met Jill recently and mostly in reference to one case. What I can contribute will be limited. It's not that I don't want to help, it's more that I can't help without a release from my client on certain pieces of information."

The expression in the Captain's eyes said this was not what he wanted to hear. No matter, Bill didn't want to say it either. They don't show in the movies how difficult it is to be a PI and have to wrestle with these damn moral dilemmas. He was an ex-cop. He was also a PI. He had crucial information that could solve a case and get the bad guys. That information was paid for and gathered at the behest of his client, therefore it was the property of his client.

As long as he wasn't obstructing an investigation, what could he do?

"Well, let's give it a try and see how close we can get before one of us wants to punch the other out."

The smile was there, but it wasn't full of warm fuzzies. The Captain started to talk about Bill's background with Burlington, some of the cases he handled and then dropped the bomb about the '71 cold case.

"Since you've started this case, one bank employee has died, one has disappeared, one person interviewed had their business ransacked, one person has been shot, and one of the original bank suspects has been killed. You've had a close call with death on several occasions, yes?"

"Yes. But I'd like to clarify that the bank employee that disappeared went missing after the bank job, not because I was involved. You make it sound like all this crap is my fault." What else was Bill going to say?

"Care to elaborate on anything?"

"About my near death experiences, I won't say anything unless you promise not to sic your dogs on me for suspicion of assault or some other felony. I don't need to be arrested in the middle of the night on bogus charges because VSP thinks I'm holding out on them."

The Captain put down the pen he was holding and sat back in his chair. "You know I can't promise, but if you can keep it vague without detail, I will keep it off the record."

That seemed fair enough, "I've been involved in a few demolition derby-type incidents on the highways that ended poorly for the other drivers. I was kept overnight once in the hospital with a concussion and walked away from the first. The other drivers both disappeared and I don't know what their injuries were if any. There was a sneak attack to stick me with an ice pick while my back was turned recently. That guy didn't make out too good, but it wasn't my fault really. I had him disarmed and landed a good right cross to the guy's jaw. He went down like a sack of potatoes and cracked his head on something else. Can't say as he made it but I didn't stick around to check."

Captain Dugan was very good at hiding his reactions even when they rang his bells as hard as they were right now. There was no proof, but he'd bet his paycheck that his new friend was the answer to a riddle over in Albany. Meanwhile, he had a question of his own to ask and see how well Bill did with hiding his reactions. "Did you know that Zeke Faraday was the shooter at Jill's place?"

That brought Bill up straight from his casual slouch. Holy shit! He wasn't even sure Faraday was still alive let alone in the area. What the hell was he doing using Jill for target practice? What does she have to do with this case?

The Captain raised an eyebrow, "That seems to have caught your attention. Any particular reason you can say why he should be taking pot shots at my friend?"

His emphasis on friend was not lost on Bill. He was obviously an intruder here under suspicion and couldn't blame him. He had brought all this crap here. Now the moral dilemma of how much to divulge to the captain was back.

Bill started to sweat a little, "Let me tell you the easy stuff first. I was hired by Stephanie Kincaid, the daughter of Professor Robert Kincaid, to find out who gave the green light order to shoot in '71. If you don't already know, Kincaid was killed in that robbery by mistake, so she says. Her story is she doesn't want revenge, just wants to know who gave the big okay. She gives me this case file, where she got it I don't know. I pick up the official Vermont State Police file from your archives and compared the two. First thing I see is a whole shit load of differences. She's got stuff you don't; you have a few things she doesn't. I made a list and chased those down. Then I started to track the people who were still alive and set up interviews.

"One unique piece of information kept showing up and the only person who could shed some light on it was Jill Benoit. But she kept showing up in the information as a Border Patrol Agent not as a private citizen. That's why it took me a while to track her down. As it turns out, another piece of information from Kincaid's file connects Jill with a person in LA who turns out to be her friend from long ago. I think they grew up together or something like that.

"Once I had a chance to talk with Jill, more questions came up than answers. We were really tired and getting nowhere at your barn office, at least I wasn't. I had just flown in from LA on the red eye and was starved for sleep. It was close to 3:00 am when we split. We set another meet for later that never happened.

"That's all I can say. The rest needs to clear my client first. I got to say that so far I'm thinking the bank job was some kind of cluster that may have been VSP's fault somehow. I don't see any connection with the garbage that's going on now, at least not yet, but if it is I'd stay away from it. Cover ups and such are always nasty and it's the guys downhill who end up taking the fall."

Captain Dugan stared at him for a long time. It was not a comfortable silence. It was impossible to guess if he felt threatened, angry, belligerent, ambivalent or merely taking a nap with his eyes open. Finally he leaned forward, placing both elbows on his desk, clasping a letter opener in the shape of a battalion sword that he twisted. His words came out slowly and with a measure of control that spoke to his strength as much as his authority.

"Mr. Robinson, you not only misjudge me, but insult me if you think I would waste one second of my time covering up any crime or breach of rules committed today or any day in the history of the Vermont State Police. No one is perfect. No agency is perfect. I have no reason to believe that VSP has or has not been guilty of screwing up at a crime scene. I can only account for my actions and those of the men and women under my direct supervision. However, I have not and will not directly contribute to any cover-up. I respect this agency and have given my word to protect it. If you think I would do anything less, you are mistaken."

The Captain carefully moved his chair back, stood, and started to walk towards his office door. "You are free to go."

With a red face Bill jumped up from his chair and walked quickly to intercept.

"Sir, I'm sorry, please, I apologize for being rude, or insulting, or insinuating you might be less than honorable. I didn't mean that at all. Look, I've been scared to death for weeks and people have been getting hurt or dead everywhere I go. I've been a cop too, and while I served Burlington, I did what I felt was the best damn job I could to protect the honor and integrity of the force. I was too dumb and didn't have the courage to figure out what to do with the information I had and stick with it. Instead I cut and ran. That doesn't mean I can't recognize an honest officer who does have integrity and can do the right thing.

"You're a good guy and officer, but I suspect there may have been a few rotten apples back in '71. I have no proof and I'm not certain I'll live long enough to get it, but from the little bits and pieces I've gathered, the picture seems to lean that way. I was only trying to warn you out of harm's way. Jill speaks very highly of you and I know you mean a lot to her. That's all I meant by it. I didn't mean to be insulting. Honest."

God, he didn't know how to grovel any lower than that. If this guy went over to the dark side, it would be impossible to break through any barriers on the State side of this case.

Dugan looked Bill straight in the eye. Bill didn't dare blink for fear the captain would take it as insincerity. Seconds later Rick offered his hand and said, "Apology accepted. I think we all get a little off plumb when one of our own gets hurt. I've heard from the hospital that Jill is out of danger and on the mend. She has friends staying with her for a while until she's up to par. I'd like to ask you to wait a day or so until you see her again. Can you find something else to do for a couple of days?"

Bill exhaled a long sigh of relief, "That's not a problem. I still have people to locate from the original list. The trace may be in by now." He started to walk out the door and turned around so fast his shoulder hit the side of the doorframe. Bill bounced backward towards the open door being held by Rick, and ended up lurching into Rick's chest with his other shoulder. Both men stumbled back into the office and quickly regained their footing.

Rick was the first to speak, "Are you this smooth on the dance floor?"

Bill blushed, laughed, and apologized for his lack of grace, then said,

"Oh! I almost forgot to tell you something. Coming over to Bennington from Albany Airport, I was followed by a black Jeep Cherokee. I lost him in the parking lot at Man from Kent, but not before I overheard a cell conversation. He told the person on the other end that he was tired of doing their dirty work and not to threaten him. He said the other person knew as well as he did that if he turned up dead, Dugan would put two and two together and come up with the person he was talking to. I'm assuming the Dugan he was talking about was you."

"Did you get a plate number?"

"I did." He started to fumble through his coat looking for the airline ticket stub he'd used to scratch it down on. It was in his shirt. "Ah, here it is, Vermont 125 CXJ."

"Are you certain there was only one person in the car?"

"That's all I could see. I checked as often as I could. It didn't look like there was a passenger."

Rick wrote down the information and asked Trooper Filbert to give Bill a ride home. The transition from office through hall and out to the cruiser went more smoothly, and without incident, the second time around.

There were three messages on Bill's phone when he returned to his room from the barracks in Shaftsbury, two were minor business calls about other cases that were pending upstate, and the third was from his friend in Washington D.C. who had a lead. It seems the missing bank teller, the last known witness to the '71 bank job, had turned up on his skip trace. Bill was off to Canada.

It was an easy flight to Spokane, a drive to the border at Oroville, Washington, and an overnight in Osoyoos, British Columbia. Driving was long with few passing lanes and multiple vans and trucks to contend with. There were no interstate highways in this part of Washington State although the roads were well kept with wide shoulders and smooth surfaces. He had to admit that the country was spectacular to look at. Miles of desert scrub and volcanic mountains followed by squares of orchards, vineyards, and fields just waiting for spring to cut them loose. This place must really rock once the water gets put to it.

Next morning, Bill headed north to Oliver, British Columbia where his missing teller was last known to be living with her sons. Paula Savant lived in a small two story farm house just north of Oliver but pretty far off the main road. He had tried to call in advance but no one answered. Around 11:30 am, Bill drove into the yard and saw a middle aged woman working in a large garden with two dogs lying nearby. There were assorted out buildings, fences, a paddock with two horses, a tractor with baler, two hay wagons, assorted pieces of machinery in various stages of decay, and one extraordinarily large wood carving of a black bear.

This was no ordinary wood carving. It had to be 15 feet tall from base to the top of its head. The spread of the extend paws was at least six feet on the inside. The diameter at the base of the trunk from which the beast had been carved must have been four to five feet. Two trees had to have been used and glued together to form this work of art. It couldn't have been carved from one tree. And the coup de grace was the finishing coat – it was lacquered in black. Black marble or a similar stone were used for the eyes.

It was the most ferocious and beautiful carving he had ever seen in his life.

Bill had no idea how long he was standing there with his mouth open before finally hearing the soft voice asking, "Can I help you?"

"I'm so sorry, I must look like an idiot. That is such an amazing carving. Where did you get that?" He must have sounded like a kid in a candy shop.

"It was carved by a very close friend of mine who is deceased. It comes from the Northeast." She wasn't going to volunteer much and certainly didn't sound like sharing with strangers. It was time to stop drooling and get back to work.

"Again, sorry about my manners. My name is Bill Robinson and I'm a private investigator from Burlington, Vermont." Her face turned white and he thought she was going to faint.

"Please, I'm not here to cause you any problems. I'm just looking for some information about a robbery that happened in '71 that I think you witnessed."

Paula Savant looked at him for one second and passed out cold.

It took the better part of an hour to revive Paula and convince her that Bill wasn't a threat, but they were now deep in conversation and amazing things were coming to light. She was on the phone talking to a customer when the robbery kicked into gear and she had been the one to trigger the alarm. She had been puzzled at how easy it was to reach the alarm and how sloppy the suspect had been to turn his head with her so close to it.

This had angered not only the other suspect but Dutch Donaldson as well. Paula and Dutch had never gotten along well and mutually disliked each other. Like the others, she was isolated for two days and only saw the one suspect who had tied her up in the back supply closet with one exception. She was almost positive she saw Donaldson talking to Kincaid in the hallway leading to her closet when the door was opened for her to use the facilities.

The look was cut off abruptly with the slammed door after Kincaid yelled "Johnson!"

"You saw Robert Kincaid and Sam Donaldson together?" This was news.

"It was fast, and I had been sitting in that closet for probably four or more hours. But I had been listening to the voices of two men arguing for about ten minutes before the door opened. Every now and then one voice got pretty loud and I remember thinking it sounded like Dutch's voice. The one who shouted Johnson was the other guy. It was a different voice, but when he turned to move out of the hallway, the silhouette had the short beard and glasses like Kincaid and the loud voice could have been his."

"I don't remember anything in the files about your tagging either of these guys."

"I told one trooper, some jerk, think his name was Metlap or Medcap. I really don't remember his name. He said it didn't matter because they were both dead."

On a hunch he asked her, "What do you know about Sam Donaldson that the rest of us probably don't?"

"If I told you, you wouldn't believe me."

"Try me."

"For one thing, he was a fanatic. He would rant and rave about everything from gun rights to freedom from government. He was convinced the government was going to invade our homes, take our property, and spy on us forever. A paranoid right wing nut case is a good description of Dutch Donaldson. He was a big militia honcho. The local cell was run with him and Kincaid mostly, but there was another guy involved who was connected somehow to an outside organization. At least that's what he bragged about to me. The guy gave me the willies.

"Kincaid used the college for communications and networking, Dutch was the training guy. He lived in the mountains somewhere and had this big spread where he hoarded arms and had a training course. He was never around the bank for overtime or special audits. Never covered for anyone or filled in. How he got to be Head Teller is beyond me. I don't know what the third guy did."

"Why did Dutch tell you this stuff? Wasn't it a dangerous thing to let you know he was a leader of a militia?"

"Truthfully I wish he hadn't. I didn't like him before and liked him less after. I was twenty years old, fresh from junior college, looking to succeed at my first job. At first I thought he had knowledge I could benefit from. I don't know what he thought I would or could do for him. He was just the kind of guy who had an ego the size of Brooklyn and no brain to match. Maybe he thought he could intimidate me enough to keep me quiet. If he did, he was right. I never told anyone until now."

"What about Kincaid? Did you ever think that someone should know about his militia ties?"

"You're kidding, right? Robert Kincaid was almost a god in that neck of the woods. Everyone loved him. I'd be willing to bet the college has a building or wing named after him."

"It's a library."

"Right, a library, and you want me to ride into the middle of town saying their hero is an anti-government, militia leading, gun- toting, subversive?"

She had a point. This was definitely not going to be easy to explain to Stephanie. Did she already know? If she did, why was he here? Was he tracking Paula down so someone could …son of a bitch! Now he was getting pissed. It was never about finding the person responsible; it was about eliminating the players. Somewhere there was a piece of information, a link between then and now that had surfaced and threatened someone who was still around and could pay the price.

"When did you leave Vermont?"

"The day after I finished testifying, I went back to my apartment, packed one suitcase after saying goodbye to my Mom, and took a plane to Atlanta. It took a month to end up in New Mexico where I met and married the love of my life. He died in '88 and I moved here two years later. Immigration to Canada was a lot easier then. I'm really surprised you found me. That's not easy to do and frankly worries me a bit."

"It worries me too. Now that you've told me what you know, I think I might have been hired to find you and others connected with this case. Several people I've talked to have had accidents and other misadventures following our meetings. I'm not comfortable with bringing this to your doorstep. Do you live here alone?"

"I actually don't live here, I'm just visiting my son. My permanent home is some distance from here. We set this up when the technology changed and skip tracing became so invasive. My husband's death was not accidental and my children felt the need to protect me. I'm sure I'll be fine once you leave. Both my sons already know you are here and will be arriving within the hour."

"I'm impressed. May I ask what your married name was and how he died?"

"What does that have to do with your robbery?"

"Perhaps nothing, but my gut says something's come up that connects the present with the past and points an accusing finger at someone. That person or persons is trying to get rid of anyone connected to their crimes. Maybe your husband was one of the spiders in the web. I don't know, just guessing."

"I was married to Field Operation Supervisor Mike Peterson of the US Border Patrol. He was killed in Sumas, WA in 1988 while on horse patrol in the mountains searching for a group of smugglers. There was an ambush, some logs were rolled down the mountainside at his horse. Cochise backed up some but not enough and went down throwing Mike off and over a cliff. He died on impact. The other officer, Agent Benoit, was unable to pursue the only suspect she saw on the mountain ridge due to the location and the fact that an officer was down. No one has ever been arrested for his murder."

There were tears streaming down her face. He noticed the wedding band on her left hand and knew that it was Mike's. It seemed cruel to continue with questions, but he didn't want to bother this lovely woman again after today. She had given too much of her life to tragedy already and didn't need him to remind her.

"Do you know any details of why he was there on that particular mountain when he was killed?"

"Mike didn't talk about work very much. He knew about the bank thing with me and said that kind of trauma was enough for one person for one lifetime. He didn't need to share details to cope with his job. Once in a while other officers would come over for cook outs and talk about stuff, but I never had a sense of what it was about.

"Once there was a hold up that ended up in some sort of stand off in Oregon. I've forgotten a lot of the details, but the end result was a big shoot out with locals and ATF agents that had a high body count. A lot of civilians got killed including children. When ATF got into the building they found huge amounts of smuggled arms and ammunition plus some C4 concealed under the flooring. They traced the arms somehow to the border frontier that Mike was working at and that had him really upset. Come to think of it, that was eight months before his accident.

"You know who might be able to give you better answers is Jill Benoit. She worked with Mike on the smuggling case for the last two months before he was killed. She took his death pretty hard. I think she felt personally responsible."

"Anyone who wears a uniform does. You should know that I've met and talked with Jill Benoit. I've just come from her place in Vermont, and since she can fill in the gaps, I think maybe it's time for me to go. I would like to wait until your sons get here to be sure you're okay."

She had no objection and they finished off the afternoon with a tour and idle chatter. Her sons, Mike and Joel, politely thanked and escorted him to the road where he turned left and started the long journey back to …what?

CHAPTER

14

The greetings between Jean and Charlie were far friendlier and longer than anything that happened with Rick. Hell, it was more than happened between Rick and me. You'd think someone would be happy I was alive and well besides Tom. Jean gave me a hug and showed genuine concern at my close encounter, but it was definitely Rick's cool attitude that had me wondering what the hell this courtesy call was all about.

Charlie and Jean were very close friends in college, and I knew from my own history with Charlie that absence didn't make a difference with her when it came to reconnecting. You just picked up wherever it was you left off two days ago, two years ago, twenty years ago, whenever. Charlie didn't miss a beat. Jean was the same way. That's what I liked about her. Now both of them had settled in on the couch, coffee in hand, catching up on the past however many years it had been since the last time they had talked.

Rick said, "I don't think Jean has said that much to me in three weeks."

"Have you been home long enough in three weeks to hear that much?"

"Ouch, that was harsh. What have I done to you?"

"For starters you come waltzing in here unannounced, in street clothes, and sit here with attitude. What gives?"

He just looked at me with that expression men get when they question your ability to handle information. I hate that. It was such a friggin put down. I'm not even sure men know they do it.

I must have sounded angry. His reply was defensive. "If you want us to leave, we will. I thought we were friends. We came to see how you were doing and Jean wanted to see Charlie."

"Thanks for the concern, and yes we are friends. Friends don't keep things from each other, and you are hiding something from me. I can see it in your eyes. If you have questions get at it. You know me. Something really stinks around here and I'm going to find out what it is with or without you."

He sat there few a few moments and then got up from the table, "Take a walk with me."

We went out to the car where he removed a file from his briefcase and we walked down to the barn. Inside he spread the contents out on the bench. We reviewed the photographs and reports of not only the shooting but also the Fish and Game inventory of the Brinkers' game bags and garage search. This was mind twisting. There were bricks of C4 and detonators coated with blood and hair from the deer meat lying next to them in the photos. The amount wasn't impressive, but just being there confused me. Why was Brinker hiding illegal government explosives in illegally poached game?

"Jill, you have to give me your word that none of this information will leave here. No one can know I showed you this file."

"For crying out loud, Rick, get a grip. I worked Border Patrol for twenty-five years and saw more than one case go south because cops couldn't get over themselves with this information sharing bullshit. What is it about territory that you guys get all pissy about? Doesn't it make any difference at all that sharing might make a case close faster?"

"In this case it isn't about territory, and don't take that preachy feminist tone with me." Rick continued, "The reason I don't want this information shared is a hunch there may be an agency internal link or leak in one or more of them. Your pal Robinson knows stuff that he's not giving up, claims client privilege. He did mention a conversation that linked me to a threat some guy made to someone else. In it they implied I could make a connection if this person turned up dead. When I ran the plate number Robinson gave me, it came back to a Michael V Johns of Plainfield, VT. I had that name run through the FBI computers by a friend of mine. I asked him to do whatever he could and to track any leads that came off of it as far back as possible. The trace took forever for a couple of reasons: they had to run a facial recognition scan to come up with an ID and get fingerprints, and this guy is a long time escapee from prison. For some reason escapees get lost in the system if they've been off the grid for a long time.

"Our mutual friend is Maxwell Vincent Johnson of the original National Bank heist in '71. He is presently under FBI/ ATF surveillance as the leader of one of three active militia cells operating an arms/ explosives smuggling ring. His brother is a major with VSP and my boss in Montpelier."

I jumped in, "Is that why he hasn't been picked up and put back in prison? In my day if you break out of jail and someone like the FBI knew where you were, they put you back in with a longer sentence. Especially if you were serving time for robbery with two homicides involved in the process."

Rick didn't even bother to cover the look of exasperation he felt. "Look, I don't know what the FBI or the ATF is or is not thinking about Maxwell Johnson. All I have here is that he runs this militia group, is a sharpshooter and survival expert, and has been described as tall, muscular with full beard and ponytail. His cell mate was killed during his escape in '73 and Zeke Faraday is suspected of being his lover....maybe. That's all I have. You now know as much as I do about Max."

I thought about the Major being Rick's boss and asked, "Do you think Max has been in touch with his brother?"

"I have no reason to believe that he has called or is in any way connected with his brother in militia activity or any activity at all. But, I do have to be very careful about where I step, what I say, and what information gets kicked around. That's one reason for the gag request."

He looked to see if I had any questions then went on. "What is particularly interesting and brings you into sharp focus here is something I learned from Albany Airport Police today. The unidentified body they found in the men's room a few days ago has been identified as Joseph

Brinker Sr. Who also happens to be one of the three militia cell leaders the ATF is watching.

"Cause of death appears to be subdural hemorrhaging caused by blunt force trauma when he fell and whacked his head. The floor had caution signs placed in a couple spots, so it had recently been washed and was slick. Brinker could have slipped and hit his head. The curious thing is, why no ID in his clothing or on his person? Gives the Airport Investigators enough reason to theorize he was there for illegal purpose or that someone else stripped him clean after a crime. I also have some recent information indicating he might have been sent there on a mission that went wrong."

I asked, "What kind of mission?"

Rick shook his head, "I really don't want to say too much since I can't prove anything yet, and may not even want to. Brinker may have been militia, but I doubt he was trained to be more than that. If he was told to do something like assassinate someone, he could very easily have botched the job and gotten himself killed in the process." Rick continued, "My theory still leaves questions unanswered. Where is his family? For everyone to have gone missing at the same time indicates several possibilities: one or more were involved in Mr. Brinker's death, the entire family went missing for the same reason but in different directions, or they all planned to disappear but Mr. Brinker had an accident and the rest of the family isn't aware of it yet. This could be tied to the game and explosives find or something in the house as yet undisclosed."

The frustration Rick felt clearly showed in his scrunched up eyebrows, raised voice, and the pieces of broken, dried, hay stems that were beginning to form a pile on the bench next to his file. His hands were absently picking them up from the surrounding area and slowly breaking them into one inch pieces that dropped into a neat pile while he continued his rhetorical questioning. "Why did Brinker have bruising on his right wrist and a dislocated right thumb? Forensics thinks someone twisted his right hand and forcefully removed something from his grip. That would fit my theory of a hit gone bad, but is that really what happened?" He stopped for a second, and then asked Jill, "Can you fill in any answers?"

My heart went out to the poor guy. So many questions and so few answers, and me without a clue to help. "Hell, Rick, you already know more about Joe Sr. than I do. I've only talked to the guy once or twice from the back of a horse riding by the house. He's a lawyer and I don't talk with them unless I absolutely have to. Gretchen never discussed him much when she talked with me. She'd call if he was out of town and she needed something. Always claimed she felt safer knowing I was around when he was gone. I saw him leave real early the day he went to the airport, but didn't think much of it. That was the same day Robinson called and the four prowlers came calling. Maybe there's a connection. Don't know what it has to do with me, but maybe the four guys are militia. As to whether there's a connection between Robinson, Johnson, and Brinker I'd say probably. How? That's speculation on my part and I'd rather not do that."

Rick thought about that for a minute and then offered another large piece of information that surprised me more than the thought of my neighbors being closet radicals.

"There's another matter that's come up with your findings. The serial numbers matched a partial shipment that was taken from an armory several months ago in upper New York State, and the ATF has been tracking it trying to find its final destination. They've been working with VSP and Border Patrol in an effort to break up a fringe group of extremists who have been smuggling small arms and explosives across the Canadian border and state lines. They use local militia groups and poaching rings to move materials a little at a time all over the place. The organization is so loose no one can cut off the head and break it up. The funding comes from bank robberies and armored car hold ups, usually small in the amounts taken and no casualties. The last time anyone was killed happened in '71 at the National Bank. Everyone pretty much agrees on that.

"If someone gets caught with contraband it does nothing to the overall situation because the rest of the stuff dribbles through in a dozen other places. Gus found enough C4 to blow up a bunch of stuff, but it was only one quarter of the amount stolen from the armory. The rest of it could be scattered from New Jersey to Texas for all we know. Most of the intel gathered has stayed with the departments that have gathered it, and it hasn't been until recently that we've noticed a lot of it overlaps. Mostly because you, Robinson, and a few other civilians have been stirring the pot and agencies have been bumping into each other in the field."

As I was sitting there on a bale of hay, my mind was trying to fit all these people and places together into some sort of puzzle or framework that made logical sense. The images of events and faces were like news clips you see on TV that flash for two second intervals one on top of the other. My eyes wandered into the corner above the bench where Rick was sitting and I saw a moderate size spider web left over from last year with a few dead bodies still trapped on its surface. Following the line of the beam, I found several other webs of various sizes in the same condition. It reminded me of how difficult if not impossible it is to rid a house or barn of spiders or webs. I don't care how many spiders you kill, webs you suck up in the vacuum, or rooms you set off insect bombs in, sooner or later they will show up somewhere else. Maybe they will be little spiders in big webs or big spiders in little webs, but you always have spiders and webs.

This business with Brinker, Kincaid, and Faraday, banks, militias, poaching, shootings and all the other crap was like an ugly weave with a bunch of ugly spiders. The awful thing is that it began to set off bells in my memory.

This was all starting to sound so familiar in ways that were clear in technique but eluding me in where I had run into it before. The brain cells were not as sharp as they used to be and memories fade when you don't pull them back very often. Of course it could also be just my pet peeve about agencies not sharing. Gets harder to tell the longer you let things stew.

"Rick, I've been trying to remember a case way back when that reminds me of this kind of diffuse system but I don't have all the specifics. Seems to me Mike Peterson had something going like this that drove him crazy. He was stationed in Susma, WA when I was there and had been trying to break this smuggling ring, at least I think it was a ring, for a while when I came in. He never did find out how they were getting stuff across the border."

"Are you two still in touch? I'd like to talk with him about it."

I had never told Rick about Mike. No one except Charlie knew about Mike. This was going to be hard. Maybe I could think about it as police business, a professional discussion about a case that became a tragic event. And maybe my arm would stop hurting and heal in the next five minutes. One had as much of a chance of happening as the other.

"Mike Peterson died in the line of duty pursuing a lead trying to find those very smugglers. The ATF, or some other federal agency, confiscated a crate of small arms and C4 that had been smuggled across the border by shipment to some antique shop in California. They claimed they could prove that the customs clearance and special instructions for holding and pick up could be traced to a station section that came under Mike's supervision. Mike knew nothing about it, but he knew that what was crossing over had to have an inside person to make it work, either a Customs officer or an Agent. He told me once he thought it was one of us and had an idea who, but couldn't prove it. Around the same time there was the big shoot out in Oregon with the high casualty count and arms cache found under the flooring. Again ATF said it came across in Mike's area but that time he had a lead.

"The day we went out on patrol up into the foothills, he told me that if anything ever happened to him, he had a personal file called 'FTB' with all the information on it. It was all circumstantial stuff and nothing he could make a case with. It had names and dates of surveillance he was doing and who he thought was involved. In the event of his death, I should make certain to get his horse Cochise and his tack. Our conversation was interrupted before he finished explaining. We never got back to it although I did manage to ask what FTB stood for. He said it meant Find the Bastard."

My mind was filled with clear pictures of Mike and I gearing up for patrol. Remembering that day was knotting up my stomach like a bad case of stage fright. My emotional control was tenuous at best. "On the way up a narrow one sided trail, a log trap released and Mike's horse lost his footing. Mike was thrown over the side and fell landing on the rocks below. My horse almost went over the side. The two pack horses panicked, turned and ran half way down the mountain before they stopped. I looked up the side of the rock ledge, but only saw the back of one figure clearing the ridge and disappearing behind the rocks. Cochise, Mike's horse, was up on his feet again but bleeding and holding one hind leg up off the ground. It didn't look like he was going to make it."

Now I was there. I could see him. I could feel the fear, the pain, the total certainty that I had failed my partner and gotten him killed. "I couldn't get down to Mike to see if he was alive. There was so much blood around his head, it was doubtful he survived the fall. His arms and legs were all twisted and at weird angles.

Funny what you remember when faced with your partner's death. I didn't want to go down there because I didn't want to live the rest of my life remembering him any more grotesque than he was from the top of that cliff."

Suddenly I realized that my face was wet, my vision was blurry, my heart was breaking, and I couldn't stop the pain from pouring out. It all came in a flow of shaking sobs that Rick's shoulder absorbed with the silence of understanding that only a kindred spirit can share. All those years of holding in the feeling of loss and guilt at having watched your partner go down without so much as lifting a finger to help, broke open. You're trained to take fire. You're trained to fight back, to attack, to be brave, to conquer fear, to serve and protect. They don't train you to stand and watch your best friend die. They don't teach you how to handle guilt, how to answer the endless questions of what you could have done better, quicker, different. You spend endless hours alone in the darkness searching for the answer to the question that has no answer: what should I have done to save my partner's life? No instructor teaches a rookie that survivor's guilt happens to cops. I never forgave myself for losing Mike, for not seeing the trap and warning him, for not going down to see if he was still alive, for having survived his death.

Rick was more than willing to call it a day. I wasn't quite ready to face the girls until I had a bit more composure. There wasn't that much more to tell anyhow.

"There wasn't much that could be done from where it all happened, and I had to ride out about two miles before I could reach base by phone. They sent in rescue and removed Mike and Cochise by chopper. I was surprised they took Cochise out but they did. Took about a year but Cochise recovered and I was able to get him as my mount when I posted at Coleville. I never remembered about the file until years after. I did get Mike's tack with Cochise but after going through it several times, I didn't discover anything that indicated storage of information. Whatever was there must have been taken or destroyed when Cochise was going through rehab.

"Paula disappeared after the funeral. I mean vanished. It was as if she went into hiding. I tried to find her and ask if she had any of his tack or equipment but could never locate her."

Rick had moved back to the bench and made a few notes on a piece of paper. "Don't take this the wrong way, but did you have a personal relationship with Mike?'

"Are you asking if I slept with him?" I wasn't quite sure if he was trying shock therapy or just being nosey, either way, it was irritating.

"Yes."

"Hard not to take that the wrong way. I don't see where that makes any difference to this investigation or is any of your business."

"There are a lot of things that connect or tie in that have been happening in the past few days around your house including the people, but none of them connect to you, at least not directly. I'm trying to find out why we always end up here."

He had a point. "As a policy, Border Patrol Agents don't fraternize and as a personal policy, I don't play where I work. I have always found that to be a bad combination. I never liked going to office parties where spouses were invited, especially cop parties."

"Jill, you're not answering the question. Did you have an intimate relationship with Mike Peterson?"

"Mike and I were closer than most partners were and probably too close for Jim, my hubby at the time. Nothing was ever said but there was friction between Mike and Jim."

"So you weren't in love with him."

"I don't know, maybe. Mike was married too and both of us had kids. There was a lot to consider besides body chemistry. We were working a lot of hours and that was pretty rugged country to be patrolling on horseback and snowmobile. Half the time we were working sixteen hour shifts with eight hours to recoup and then we'd be out again. Even if we wanted to screw around we'd be too tired or couldn't find a private corner to do it in.

"In any case, the answer to your question is no, I never slept with Mike. We never acted on any feelings we may have had. He loved Paula a great deal and I kept things to myself. You know as well as I do that Jim and I divorced in '89 and Mike died in '88."

By now the clock above the horse grain bins was edging towards 4:30 pm and feed time. I suggested Rick give me a hand with chores while we continue the conversation and then head for the house. Tom would be expecting Charlie and me soon, plus we had to make arrangements for Jake's arrival from LA. Rick seemed surprised to hear about his impending appearance and off we went again on the information loop about Robinson, the invoice, the crate, the picture…

Then it hit me, "The photograph! It has to be a picture of Mike at the base of the cliff. Why would they do that? Who took that picture? Why would they post Mike on Charlie's door?"

I must have been yelling in Rick's face because he slapped me and I fell back against the rail where the saddles were stacked. Rick had to grab my arm to keep me from falling over the tack box underneath.

"Get a grip, Jill. What are you talking about?"

I had to admit being slapped by Rick in my own barn had a sobering effect. Perhaps it was needed to give me a reality check, but grabbing me by the arms and squeezing a gunshot wound didn't qualify under my acceptable behavior column. My loud 'ouch' was both angry and warning that further action wasn't needed to get me back on track. He quickly let go, and with an apology backed up to allow me passage to the feeding bins. As I fed grain the story of Jake discovering the photo on his home entry and the ransacking of his business was explained along with his eminent arrival in New York. During the discussion the names of Gretchen Czerwinski and Metcalf came up. That brought Rick's head up fast enough to hit Tracker on the muzzle causing a bit of commotion in the paddock.

Once we had the horses quieted Rick came back to the subject. "Gretchen is not a very common first name. Do you think it's a possibility she could be Brinker's wife?"

"The thought certainly crossed my mind, but I would have no way of checking. I talked with Charlie about her trying to get a clue. It seems her clerk had a southern drawl when she panicked. My neighbor did the same thing. Charlie said Jake looked for the personnel records from that time period and they were totally unreadable or missing so we have no way of determining age or Social Security number. There are no prints to trace unless you can get a warrant to search Brinker's house and maybe find something to trace back."

Rick thought for a minute, "Well, with Joe dead in New York and next of kin missing, I think a judge might give me a warrant. What about this Metcalf kid, know anything about him?"

Obviously this was going to be my night for illuminating Rick with my historical gems. "I don't know anything about the kid, but I did know his older brother. He was, and probably still is, Border Patrol. I met him for the first time way back in the late 60's. He was one of you, a trooper with VSP in Shaftsbury. He was an asshole then, stayed an asshole with us, and is still an asshole."

"You seem pretty convinced he's an asshole. My guess is you have reasons?" His smirk did nothing to cool my rising temperature as I was forced to reminisce about Metcalf.

"You bet I do. Refusing to back up another officer on call for one, unprofessional behavior leading to the near dismissal of this officer for another, and just being a plain coward and all around scum bag for a third."

Rick sat back on his stool and propped his foot on the tool box below. "This sounds like some story."

"One night around 2030 hours when it was still light, I get a call that someone is shooting in the US National Forest campgrounds where I was working. They tell me to go and tell them to knock it off. I drive into this site where there are four tents in a semi-circle and no way out but the way I came in. Four very large, very drunk, fully armed men with two pit bulls are standing on the edge of a bank shooting at beer cans in the stream.

"I exit my security vehicle with my tiny little 9mm and portable radio that probably wouldn't reach base, and step ankle deep into a puddle of water. They very generously hold back their attack dogs. After a brief exchange of words, I thought we agreed that yes I have a badge, and the authority to tell them to knock it off. I smile, thank them and leave.

"I receive the exact same call at 2330 hours the following night. The men in that camp knew I would be responding. They were counting on it. I knew they would be drunk and looking to have a little fun at my expense. Before you ask, yes, I was scared. I didn't have the training to handle this kind of thing."

Rick shook his head no, but agreed, "Booze and guns in remote areas are not handled alone by anyone if they have half a brain and can get back up."

I was going to say something cute, but decided my smart mouth would quash Rick's approval. "I asked for back up. Trooper Jerome Metcalf was on call, on duty and available. He decided that he could not assist. He suggested on the air for all of scanner land to hear that I should use my own discretion. I did just that and continued my patrol in the other direction. I figured any injuries or fatalities that night were more his fault than mine."

Rick didn't look as if it was a big deal. "Granted that wasn't a professional way to handle an assist call, but he might have had reasons you didn't know about."

"Oh, he had reasons and he stated his case later to my boss at the NFS Office when I was filing my report. The Vermont State Police did not do private security work and if the security guards they hired were incapable of doing their jobs adequately perhaps they should get in touch with VSP headquarters and see if they could work out some sort of arrangement for proper policing of their campgrounds. He was using the incident to pitch a contract with the National Forest Service for patrol work. He damn near got me fired and that makes him a double asshole."

Rick smiled which made me bristle, but he raised his hand to stop me from saying anything as I started to open my mouth.

"You know how competitive departments are for cash contracts with any municipality or agency willing to pay for patrol work. VSP has made no bones about going after extra cash when our budget comes up short with cuts from Montpelier. But, I will give you points on his bad taste for walking over you to push it. That's a call his Post Commander should have made directly not him."

He made a few notes on a pad and went on, "Where did you run into him next? I'm assuming there was a next time judging by the smoke coming out of your ears."

There was smoke alright, but it wasn't because I was thinking about Metcalf. Why was I talking about this again? Oh, yes, my friend needed help solving a case and I had useful information. Gee, I'll have to ask Rick later how an asshole like Metcalf rates status as a person of interest and having his actions defended at the same time.

I went on, but with much less enthusiasm, "Newport, I was assigned there with the Border Patrol and he was a Senior Agent. We were out on snowmobile patrol looking for guys crossing the line. He and another agent had gone ahead while I answered a nature call. I took a different trail to catch up and ran across four snowmobiles hauling sleds loaded with cases heading for a frozen lake. I knew Metcalf would be cutting in soon from the other end, but at the speed these guys were going they'd be across the lake and down the road before he could stop them. I made a quick decision and headed for the lead guy. Didn't pay attention to where the last guy in line was and had my sled track blown out from under me. Metcalf was so pissed he made my life a living hell. I finally requested a transfer to Port Huron in Michigan when an opening came up."

"So what was the problem with him on that deal?"

Wow, Rick was really going to defend this jerk. "What? I thought it was pretty obvious Metcalf had problems with how I did my job. If I hadn't stopped and taken the other route, we never would have seen the four. He was taking a well used groomed trail that vacationing tourists use. No self-respecting smuggler would take that run to cross over. And second, if he had continued at the rate he left me, he would have come out on the other side of that lake at the same time I did. Instead, he was a quarter mile north of me. Close enough to see but too far to catch them. And third, he blamed not only me, but the other agent too for the lost collar. Forgot the guy's name, but he ended up on the southern border somewhere. Heard he got killed not too long after that. Why did he blame him? Why is it shit never sticks to this guy?"

This piece of information brought a look of worry to Rick's face. His concern and questioning about Metcalf was beginning to concern me too. Metcalf had always been a scum bag in my book, and I had worked with him only because my assignments with USBP had put me next to him. Twice I had asked for transfers and both times they had rearranged my schedule and duties to avoid contact with him. In other words, the men told me to suck it up or get the hell out of their playing field. You're with the big boys now, and if you don't like your teammates, get lost. Most of the time it was okay, I didn't have to physically be with him on duty. Luckily the work was spread out over such large areas geographically that agents didn't spend a lot of time breathing down each other's necks. A hostile environment was rare, and if it did exist the brass did everything they could to keep things down to a dull roar, including granting transfers.

Rick was asking, "Metcalf seems to have had it in for you or at least had the power to make life miserable. Does the USBP place agents by request or do they have a protocol for assignments?"

That was a strange question. Rick would know that, why ask me? "When I came out of UVM my grades were high enough that when I showed interest in Federal agencies they all came looking. I picked BP because I felt they were the least political and would give me the best balance of fairness and field work. My job offer required two years on the southern border. Then I could apply for postings to stations as they became available if I had the qualifications for those postings. I was always lucky with getting posted to the places I wanted when I wanted to go there. I spent four years in New Mexico and then went to Newport. From there I went to Michigan, then Washington, and eventually came back to Vermont."

Again Rick picked at the transfer questions. "Could officers request transfers?"

"Sure they can, but it has to go through command and the reasons have to be approved. The place you are applying for has to have an opening for an officer of your rank too. An agent can't arbitrarily request posting to Newport because they're bored with life on the southern border."

"Did you ever request or get a transfer?"

"I just told you I asked for Michigan after the Newport mess." Rick didn't need to know more details about transfers. "Besides, I only made Senior Agent by retirement, and that was such a big deal I figured I'd better keep my mouth shut before they noticed I had accomplished something."

He chuckled, "I doubt the USBP didn't know Jill Benoit was around."

Again his hand began to scribble little notes in the margins of the files and a small notebook Rick carried in his shirt pocket. After a long silence, his questioning continued. "Metcalf is still with the Border Patrol, so I imagine you had further dealings with him or heard more about him?"

I was beginning to feel like a witness in the hot seat at a trial. "Funny you should ask. It wasn't by choice, believe me. Metcalf and I were on a stake out, watching for some truckers who were supposed to be running false bottom flatbeds with small arms across the line and unloading at this warehouse out in the back country in Washington. It was pretty boring work. The kind of stuff I didn't think senior agents did, but he was there sharing the load. Actually I should say he was getting loaded. I was watching a trucker in the distance who at first seemed to have engine trouble, but then started to look suspicious. When I mentioned it to Metcalf, he came up behind me and put his arms around me to take the binoculars. When I ducked down to step out from under, we started a dance that ended badly for him. At first I thought he had lost his mind, and then I smelled the bourbon. He had me pinned to the wall briefly and I did a little creative restructuring of his private anatomy.

"He doubled over all apologetic, said he was sorry, didn't know what came over him, and staggered off outside. Said he wasn't used to doing stake outs with women, especially good looking ones. I told him to keep his distance and I checked the field again for the trucker. He was gone with the rig. We stayed for another couple of hours, but Metcalf stayed outside with his cell phone and ice pack. "I filed a sexual harassment suit although I didn't expect it would do much good. There was a disciplinary hearing with the brass, but I don't know what went on with him. I took a posting to Coleville. I don't know where he ended up. He wrote me a formal letter of apology which I used for a dart board."

"Did you ever see him after that?"

"Only in passing, we haven't spoken two words to each other and I don't intend to. I don't like him, don't trust him, and don't think he should be in uniform. I would have a very difficult time backing him up and I probably wouldn't. I never thought I would say that about someone in uniform, but that's how I feel."

Rick had returned to his totally professional attitude again. "Did you know he was involved in the National Bank affair?"

"Not until Bill Robinson brought it up. I saw the newspaper photo. Figures he'd be the first one in and the hero of the day. I'm surprised he didn't shoot himself in the foot or shoot a hostage."

"Why would you say that?"

"Why, because he's an asshole and in my opinion a coward. You would be hard put to convince me that Jerome Metcalf had the balls to enter an area of conflict without knowing full well he would come out untouched."

"Do you think Metcalf was involved in the robbery?"

"Do you? You know you've been peppering me with questions for five hours and I think it's time you start answering a few. Let's start with what you know about Metcalf and why you are so interested?"

Rick wasn't about to sit still for this turn in role playing. After all, he was still on active duty and I was retired. On the other hand, I was not going to break the silence and I was not going to move out of the way to let him pass from the bench to the doorway out of the barn. I was perfectly comfortable sitting on the hay bales next to the door frame with my feet propped on an overturned feed bucket. He could sit there on the work stool 'til the cows came home or start answering *my* questions for a change.

After a very long few minutes, Rick said, "The northern border states have always had a certain amount of smuggling going on. Different agencies do their thing the way they see fit and for the most part each manages to keep the lid on. After 9/11, Homeland Security, and global cooperation it became easier in some ways and harder in others to keep track of everything. One of the things that started to show up was how easy it is to move small amounts of anything back and forth across the line if you have contacts within a state or border agency.

"The other disturbing thing that showed up in the research was how far back people had been using this kind of system to smuggle. Some of the patterns could be tracked back to the 50's. The way it worked was pretty simple. You have small groups like militia, gangs, or patriots who are scattered across the states. You have one or two border crossings in strategic places that have a sympathetic official. You also have a few supportive state officers, local cops, or state game wardens. Your funding is totally done by small cash donations from sympathizers or small bank holdups with no casualties. You have to stay away from the high profile stuff that captures big headlines like hold-ups that have hostages or killings.

The other cash comes from arms and explosives sales. Arms come from armory thefts and construction sites for explosives, although all the C4 comes from government sites.

"Nothing is moved in large quantities so that any loss is minimal. The stuff we found at Brinker's is a good case-in-point. They move it in poached game, fruit boxes, empty tires, false truck bottoms, crates of coffee, and all kinds of ways."

This was a good story, but it didn't tie in with my pal. "That still doesn't explain your interest in Metcalf, although it's beginning to explain my innate distrust of him."

Rick held his hand up as if to say wait a minute, I'm not done yet. "Two years ago I was approached by someone outside of VSP about a joint investigation involving officers and smuggling. I was also told it would be a long and confidential investigation. I was to trust no one in any department including my own, and to question everyone's loyalty and integrity.

"When you were shot, I was given your case along with a caution to find out what was going on with Robinson's investigation and to make certain that VSP didn't get caught with their fly open. This was said because they already knew Zeke Faraday was the shooter and was dead. There is absolutely no way that any evidence could have shown or witness could have known the name of the shooter, and that information was available before you even made it to surgery. All I can tell you right now is that I have several officers in VSP who know more than they should if you look at the time frame. They have a close relationship with Metcalf who is still with the Border Patrol. You seem to have a lot of background material on several persons of interest regarding my overall investigation that I would really like to pursue."

My arm was screaming pain and the head wound was throbbing and needed care. After a lifetime of yelling about the lack of interagency cooperation I finally had my chance. Here I was smack dab in the middle of multiple agencies sharing information and cooperating on a case. Can you hear me now?

What Rick was really saying, or in fact asking, was if I would join forces and share my information with them. My hesitation didn't center on sharing, it centered on trust and with whom I was sharing it with. So far, Rick hadn't told me anything about his partners or who he was working for. He could be working for the enemy without knowing it. For that matter, who *was* the enemy?

I told Rick it was time to head for the house. Once inside, Charlie and Jean were nowhere to be found until a blast of laughter came from downstairs in the backroom where I had a treadmill and a Bowflex machine. Apparently the fitness bug had bitten them while they were waiting for us, along with one of my better bottles of merlot. There was a note on the counter that Tom had called and volunteered to go pick up Jake. Charlie and he had made the arrangements and all was set. Good, that left dinner and first aid the remaining tasks for the night, that and what to do with Rick's request for information.

"Rick, I'm going to go fix my wounds and take some meds. Would you go downstairs and see what those two clowns have planned for dinner?"

The bandage on my arm was soaked with fluids from Rick's rough handling, but the stitches appeared to be holding. Some medicated ointment, a few gauze pads, and a clean wrap with tape and that was done.

Again I looked at the head wound and marveled how the bullet had just barely touched me, and by doing that had probably saved my life. How very strange. Had it missed, I would have killed Faraday, disarmed him, tried to get back to the house, and either been shot by Faraday's killer or pumped out the rest of my blood through the cut in my artery. Instead I went into a coma and the cold slowed everything including my heartbeat, thus saving me. Who would have known such a thing could happen?

As I stared at the face in the mirror, my mind flashed back to the wall and the snow-covered ground. The light flashed in my eyes and the pain burned through my arm and on the side of my head as the sound of shots fired kept going off in my ears over and over. The sight of Mike's dead twisted body at the bottom of the cliff swam through the snow and disappeared leaving large pools of blood in the snow with my face staring back at me from the bottom.

I shook my head hard enough to cause an instant headache and decided daydreaming might not be the right thing to do at this particular moment.

After some Ibuprofen for pain and a quick wash up, I rejoined the rest of the group in the kitchen. Both Charlie and Jean were reliving their college days and filling in Rick on what they had been doing while we were in the barn. I inquired about dinner and was pleasantly surprised to hear that it was cooking in the oven and would be ready within the hour. Rick and I poured ourselves a drink and joined the conversation.

Soon it was way past my bed time and the stress of all the questioning caught up with me. Charlie didn't think Tom and Jake would make it back until early morning. Rick wanted to get Jean home and do some work on his own before catching up with me again. We made a tentative plan to touch base by phone around 10:00 am to see where everyone was and maybe meet up either here or at Rick's home office.

Around 8:00 am the phone rang while I was feeding the horses and I grabbed it in the barn. It was none other than my friend Bill Robinson.

"Where the hell have you been? I expected you to at least bring me flowers or chocolates after I went through all that trouble getting you a car and all."

"Yeah, thanks for the car I never had the chance to pick up. Your friends at VSP made sure I got the first ride out of town. They wouldn't let me in the front door of the hospital. Had a guard posted out front waiting when I drove up in a cab."

"You're kidding me. Rick wouldn't let you into the hospital?
Can he do that?"

"I don't know if he can legally, but he had some trooper there named Walnut or Hickory or some kind of nut politely ask me to the barracks for a one-on-one with Dugan. He made it clear I wasn't going in."

I laughed, "You mean John Filbert, and he's assigned to the shooting case with Rick. He's young but seems to be a decent guy. Did you and Rick have a nice chat?"

"It wasn't all that great since what he wanted to know was privileged information from my point of view. He got a little bent out of shape and we parted without drawing blood but we're not buddies for sure."

I was starting to get impatient with my obnoxious PI again. He had the most annoying habit of calling at bad times. "I don't suppose this is why you are calling at such an unholy hour. You know better. I haven't had coffee, fed the dog or put on my smiley face. Where the hell are you?"

"I'm on my cell and driving on some godforsaken back road called LaClair. I'm lost to say the least. There's a four way stop here and four different road signs but only two intersecting roads. Whose brainchild was that? How do I get to your place?"

"Who the hell invited you?"

"Aw, c'mon? I'll make it worth your while. I found Paula Savant, your old partner's widow and she said you were the one to talk to about a case Mike Peterson was working on. She thought it might have something to do with his death and you might have more clues than you think you do. Said it had to do with smuggling. I thought it might tie in with the heist since she's the last teller from the original National bank job."

I could feel the blood drain from my face. Paula was a teller at the First National? She must have been all of eighteen or nineteen years old, maybe early twenties. Holy shit, she had married Mike in New Mexico right after that. I'll bet she was running from the whole mess. I wonder what she told Bill. Only way to find out is to give him directions and feed him breakfast I suppose.

"Are you facing downhill?"

"Yes."

Quickly I ran through the lay of the land which would lead him to my front door in ten minutes, assuming he could follow directions. I hung up the phone and finished chores. Fundy was off chasing a rabbit but came readily when I whistled. Food always won out in the morning.

Back inside Fundy got his reward and I explained to a slightly hung over Charlie about our unexpected guest. She wasn't too pleased at the prospect of entertaining this early so she grabbed a mug of coffee and shuffled back to the bedroom with her laptop in tow and Fundy at her heels. I felt a little betrayed. Within ten minutes, a nice looking 4X4 drove in and parked out front. One grungy looking PI exited the driver's side and half slid half walked his way to the porch.

"I must say you are the sorriest excuse for a PI I've ever seen. When was the last time you slept?"

Bill just sort of sat there looking at me with eyes that didn't seem to register what I was saying. He finally blinked and answered, "I slept on the plane, couldn't get a flight from Chicago to Albany until tomorrow so I took a flight to JFK and drove from there."

After a couple mugs of coffee and some breakfast, he seemed to catch his second wind. "Okay Bill, you've been wined and dined, it's time to pay the piper. What did Paula have to say and where did you ever find her?"

CHAPTER

16

And so it began, Bill's odyssey from Bennington to Oliver and back seemed easy enough, but I knew from experience that tracking of that kind required sophisticated means or big bucks behind it to work. I didn't think he had either. His description of Paula was true enough and the details he supplied regarding Mike and his sons also rang true. I had no reason to doubt that he had actually met and talked to Mike's wife.

What had me sitting on the edge of my seat was the story of the '71 heist and her subsequent disappearance. She obviously had been frightened past the point of feeling safe in her own home. It takes a lot of courage or fear for a single young woman to take herself away from everything she knows to start another life thousands of miles away in another culture, another state, another lifestyle. It impressed me even more when I thought of the year and the times back in 1971.

That also clarified how it was that Paula had disappeared after Mike's death. She was no stranger to the techniques and requirements of leaving material things behind and starting over somewhere else with nothing to connect you to a life in the past. It did bring up a lot of questions, like why she felt the need, and why she felt threatened. Was there someone around to help her relocate? Was her relocation connected to Mike's case or death? It could have been connected to both or neither.

I didn't know Paula well. We had met several times and Mike had spoken about her a lot, but not in depth. I did know this: her maiden name was not Savant. She was listed on the record as a teller named Priscilla Sonja who lived with her mother and had recently acquired the position at the bank. Previously she had interned there as part of a school/work program with the community college, but details were sparse on who had arranged it or how she made the transfer to full-time employment. This I knew only because Rick had showed me the file last night.

Bill was sorting through his notes and looking for something in particular. I wasn't all that sure I cared what he needed. Finding Paula, and how he was finding people like Charlie and me, was beginning to rub the wrong way. If Rick had reason to believe there was some sort of conspiracy going on involving high level officers, or at least uniformed officers, why not use ex-officers turned investigators as well? Who better to track down loose ends without suspicion?

"You seem to have an inside track on finding some people who are hard to find. How did you ever come up with Paula?"

"I ran a skip trace on Priscilla Sonja, and came up empty. But, a friend of mine who works for the FBI developed this software program that ran possible name combinations using the first letters P and S against other lists in the same time frame, like plane tickets bought or trains, stuff like that. We did that for the days after the robbery. We found 54 hits but not all of them fit the physical description. All but four didn't match to her age. One had died since then, two were accounted for in other ways."

I was impressed. "That gave you a name, but it didn't tell you where she was."

"No, that took a lot more digging and some help from another friend who knew a friend of a friend in the State Department. I don't really know how it all came about, only my source knows for sure. He's not talking and neither am I. The lady wants to stay lost and I'm not going to be the one that spills the beans. If you saw the size of her two kids, you would agree with my call. Man, they grow them big up there in the woods."

Bill was being protective and gallant, but I took personal offense at that last remark. He may have pulled off the search of the century, but implying that I was somehow a threat to Paula was pushing his welcome way out on the edge of oblivion with this host. "And what is it that you think I can do for you?"

Charlie picked this moment to walk into the kitchen and eyeball Robinson as she poured herself another cup of coffee.

"Well, well, look what the cat dragged in, if it isn't Mr. Invoice. Still searching for the Holy Grail?"

Bill looked up, saw Charlie and stopped moving. He was speechless. It was clear he had no idea why Charlie was here and never expected her to walk into his life again. This was beyond his ability to react to.

The lack of words became uncomfortable. "Come on, Bill, you remember Charlie from LA don't you? You were out there a week ago looking into an invoice that was posted to her shop. You were asking questions about a case or crate that was held for delivery. Does it ring a bell?"

He shook his head and smiled. "Sorry, you took me by surprise. I thought Jill was alone and didn't expect to see anyone." He stood and extended his hand, "Nice to see you again. Sorry I wigged out there, I'm a little tired this morning."

She accepted the handshake without warmth. "I'm in someone else's home so I'll extend the courtesy, but don't consider it a pledge of cooperation. You have managed to not only close my business in LA but also brought threats to my home and pissed off my husband. And I'm sure you played no small part in getting my best friend shot up. You're a busy man, how do you manage to maintain a clientele with all that chaos around you?"

This was fun to watch. For once I wasn't the one in the middle taking flack or giving it. Let's see how fast Robinson can think on his feet. He'd best be good. He's up against the best.

"What happened to your business that's my fault?" Bill sounded tired and more than a little defensive.

Charlie glared, "Whatever your interest was in the invoice or anything else, your appearance brought others to our door. They ransacked our files, destroyed some, and left a threatening note at our residence making my husband's continued presence there a bad idea until this business is resolved. Whatever you are doing is contaminating everything it touches and the people you talk to."

Sighing, Bill said, "And you think I'm responsible for someone shooting Jill? Why?" I could tell he wasn't processing information very well. His notes consisted of a few concentric circles drawn like the Olympic logo, with the names of different people inside. I couldn't read the names from where I was standing. My best guess would have been the main characters in his case.

Charlie was still trying to reach him on a conscious level. "She was saving your butt and out until 3:00 am the night she was shot. Had she been home where she was supposed to be, the break in would not have taken place or she would have been in a better position to defend herself."

I had to admit this was entertaining but getting us nowhere. "Both of you need to understand that hindsight isn't 20/20 in my world, and listening to the two of you bicker about things that can't be changed is wasting time. Rick is going to be calling at ten to set up a meet with me, and Charlie, you need to call Tom and find out where Jake is."

I turned my attention to Bill at the table and went on as if the truce was a done deal. "Bill, if you want to know what I know about Mike's case, I can tell you it concerned smuggling arms over the line that ended up in Oregon. At least that's the case directly connected to his death. There was an incident there with multiple casualties. Federal authorities traced the arms somehow to Mike's jurisdiction and he thought he knew how or who had passed them through. We were following a lead when he was killed in an ambush. That about sums it up, anything else I can clear up for you?"

I could tell he didn't want to let go of the challenge from Charlie, but manners got the best of him and he deferred to my explanation with a question of his own.

"Did anyone ever pick up his case after he died?"

"I don't know. I shipped out soon after that."

"Did you know who the crooked cop was?"

"I never said it was a cop, and no, he never told me who he suspected."

It was my turn. "Did Paula tell you anything about his death?"

"Only that he had an accident while on patrol and you were with him. She said you were pretty shaken up about it. Said she thought you blamed yourself."

So she remembered our conversation at the house. I had stopped by before the wake to explain why I wouldn't be there. She understood and told me not to be so hard on myself, that Mike loved his work and knew the risks. He also had told her how much he respected me and respected my talent for the work. She knew that if I could have stopped this from happening I would have. How I had tried to believe her.

Everyone was silent, lost in their own memories and thoughts. When the phone rang, it was almost an insult. Charlie was the closest and answered with the practiced politeness of a seasoned business owner, "Benoit residence."

"Jake! I didn't expect you to be up this early. When did you get in?"

The chatter went on from there and Bill went back to his notes to see if more questions needed my input. I picked up dishes and cleaned counters. Fundy went out to chase the local creatures while the sun did its thing to the snow cover and turned white dust to glaring ice mirrors. It got to the point where you almost had to wear sunglasses inside the house the reflection was so bright.

Charlie hung up with news that she was heading over to Tom's as soon as she showered and dressed. The phone rang again and it was Rick with his view on how the day was going to progress. I informed him of the morning's events up to Jake's call, and he went so far as to say "shit". Apparently this was not part of his plan. With a quick mumble about calling me back in an hour, we hung up.

I threw on some boots and sunglasses and went down to the barn to check supplies for the trio and decided all was okay until next week. The hay barn was stacked until spring and refills were preordered. Out of nowhere Fundy came bounding in and damn near knocked me down. A voice from the house let me know that Charlie was ready to leave so up we went to play taxi. As I rounded the corner of the house, I caught a flash from the other side of the road halfway up the hill. It was something you'd see if sunlight hit binoculars briefly. Curious, it wasn't hunting season. Maybe the wardens were out scouting for poachers or keeping an eye out for sign of the Brinkers.

That was something I kept meaning to ask Rick about. What, if anything, had he heard about Gretchen and her son? They must be somewhere around here. No one had mentioned a word about them since the shooting and no one seemed interested in locating the family. It was curious that Rick always seemed to be asking questions about things in her life. Bill was asking questions about some cold case thirty years ago, and no one was asking questions about her next door neighbor who had a dead husband and was missing with her son.

Charlie was ready to roll and I told Bill I'd take him back to town as far as the main road leading to North Bennington. He could make his way from there. Just before we were about to leave I asked Bill, "Did you know that the girl who worked in Charlie's shop back in the 80's was my next door neighbor?"

Bill looked at me with a mixture of bewilderment and shock. "Are you talking about Gretchen?"

"Yeah, she's married to a lawyer and has two kids. They've been living in the house up the road for eight or so years. Rick and I are pretty sure she was working for Charlie when that case on your invoice went through the shop."

Bill was excited now. "Can we go talk to her? I've got a ton of questions about that case and the invoice."

"I'm afraid not, seems Gretchen has disappeared with her son. Her husband Joseph left for the airport last week and had an accident. Come to think of it, he died the same day you called me from the airport. He fell in the restroom and cracked his head on the floor. You wouldn't know anything about that would you?"

The look on his face made an answer unnecessary. I didn't know the details, but I'd bet my pension that Bill knew all about how Joseph Brinker Sr. fell and managed to meet his Maker. At the same time it shot down the theory that Gretchen was his killer, or that the entire family was somehow whisked away on a secret mission. It didn't leave any good theories around as to exactly where Gretchen could be, and that was worrisome.

Bill went out first and we followed in a few minutes. His car was running and I just assumed he would back around and follow when I pulled forward from the side of the house. I turned down the drive and glanced in the rear view but Bill's car wasn't moving. I stopped and waited a few seconds. There was no movement.

I put my car in reverse, hit the gas, and backed up quickly past my drive until I was across from his car where I could see him staring straight ahead. What the hell was he doing? I hit the horn but no reaction except from Charlie who wasn't pleased at the delay.

"Is that jerk coming or not?"

"Something doesn't look right," I said, "Wait here and I'll walk over to see what the problem is."

I left my door open in case a hasty retreat was in order and high-stepped across the snow to the car listening for sounds and watching for movements. My sixth cop sense was sending all kinds of signals up and down my spine. Bill's eyes were open but I hadn't seen him blink yet. Of course it was a bit difficult to see him clearly through the glass of the side window. Still, he had rolled it down some for air while his car warmed up… then I saw it. The small round hole near his temple with the stream of blood trickling down, and on the other side of his car there was plenty of blood splattered on the seat, window and interior to prove he had been shot and was quite dead. With both windows on the opposite side still intact, that meant the bullet had lodged inside. That also meant the shot had been fired from across the road at a pretty restricted angle to fit through the open driver's window and not exit the other side. Turning around I scanned the woods for possible vantage points or shooters but knew I would see nothing. Quickly my senses to protect returned and I told Charlie to slide down towards the floor of the car even though I doubted she was a mark at this point. I reached into his car and turned off the ignition, removing the keys afterward. While I was next to Bill, I did a quick check of his inside coat pocket and found his notebook which fit into my inside pocket without much effort or notice. I figured Bill wouldn't mind if we kept certain information about Canada between the two of us. Now I was more involved in this case than I wanted to be and the bullet hole in my arm gave me permission to stick my nose into this as far as I wanted to. These bastards were killing people in my front yard in addition to harassing my friends and I was damn well going to finish the job.

It was time to get Rick again. Why is it he's never here when the shit hits the fan? Funny how he was going to be here and then got upset when I told him Bill was here. He changes his mind, says he'll call me back but doesn't, and now we have another mess. It makes me wonder if this is coincidence or convenience.

I returned to the car and grabbed my cell phone as I drove down the drive. Charlie wasn't exactly pleased at my protocol and started in on me.

"What the hell are you doing?"

"I'm taking you to Tom's."

"Are you crazy? Bill is dead, right? You have a dead body in a car, in your front yard and the police are not here, correct? You can't leave dead bodies lying around without reporting them to the police and waiting for them to show up, can you? Well, can you just do that?"

I closed the phone and accelerated, "Would you rather stay with a dead body that was shot by someone you cannot see with a gun you cannot hear that may still be in the area and want to shoot you too?"

She just stared at me without saying a word as the car sped through the back roads at unholy speeds. That was an argument she couldn't win and we continued in silence a few more minutes. Then I reopened my cell and speed dialed Rick with the information on the shooting. He wasn't happy with my protocol either but I was at Tom's by then and promised to return to the house ASAP. Tom and I had a few minutes of private conversation and I filled him in on the few details I had. Tom had some information about a guy in town who was asking questions about me, but it was vague. I would have to research this later. Meanwhile, I gave Tom the notebook and asked him to hide it from all persons including Rick or cops of any sort. It contained sensitive material that I would need later and could be confiscated as evidence. I didn't want to lose it, but didn't want him in jail either. He just smiled and said he'd be glad to "hold it in trust" for me. Tom just loved to do things like that.

Back at the shooting gallery, Rick and John Filbert were going over the car while the medical examiner was doing his thing with the body. Two teams with dogs were off in the woods looking for tracks or scent but I doubted they'd find anything. Whoever fired that shot through a narrow slit of a window in a few minutes time with a silenced rifle was a pro. Too much of a pro to leave trace, tracks, casings, or other identifiable marks behind. Someone wanted Bill Robinson dead and they made it so. Rick wanted to know who, but I was much more interested in why.

I parked out of the way on the side of the house and kept Fundy in the car. Rick was taking pictures and Filbert was drawing diagrams, taking measurements, and trying to remember everything he had learned in Crime Scene Investigation classes over the past two years. It really isn't as easy as it looks on TV.

Rick shook his head and asked without really asking, "I don't get it. Why was Robinson here and why would anyone want to shoot him in your front yard? What is it about you that all this shit ends up at your front door?"

This was my friend?

"Thanks for the support Rick. I don't think this is about me at all. I think you have your head up your ass and don't know which case to investigate. By doing the old file shuffle game, you can't keep your eye on the ball. You don't know if you're investigating arms smuggling or a missing Brinker family. Are you investigating Joe Brinker's death or his involvement in illegal activities? Are you trying to break up subversive militant cells or find corrupt police officers? Now you have a sniper running loose who killed Robinson and may have killed the man who attempted to kill me." I was on a roll now.

"I'd be willing to bet my retirement that whoever conned you into this task force you're on has you jumping through hoops blind. Bill probably had more information than you do and now he's dead. The reason he's dead in my front yard isn't because of me, my friend, it's because of you. It's because you aren't equipped with enough information or resources to do the job you have been asked to do. Whatever Bill was working on may connect with me somehow, but you should be able to make those same connections if your people were giving you any kind of back up. So don't go pinning this on me."

Rick was pissed, "Are you saying you won't cooperate in this investigation?"

My temper had gone over the edge hours ago. "And which investigation would that be?"

Normally Rick didn't lose his cool, but today was an exception. "Oh for Christ's sake, Jill, the dead body in your front yard. What the hell do you think? You're not the only one who's tired of all this crap. I'm still required to investigate as long as I'm in uniform just as you would if you were in my position. So stop being an ass and answer my question. The sooner you do the faster we can get on to the next step.

"Getting shot doesn't give you the right to sit in judgment on the work that is or isn't being done. Just because you were a cop doesn't mean you know any more than anyone else. I may have chosen the wrong words, but even you have to admit that this house and *you* appear to be the center of activity for at least two deaths, one shooting, one arms smuggling discovery, one missing persons report, one break in with vandalism, and one cold case with more crimes connected with that. It isn't a figment of my imagination, it's for real and most of those calls, if not all, came from you. So stop bitching about VSP and start acting like an ex- cop who understands the job and its limitations."

Rick's cell phone rang which he answered so quickly and loudly, I wondered if the person on the other end suffered hearing loss. He apologized to the caller and walked away from me for the rest of the conversation. I went inside to cool off.

For the next hour I answered his questions and gave him my theory about how and by whom Joe Brinker was killed. It didn't really have much bearing on what had happened to Bill, but I knew it would help Rick close one end of his case and make up for some of my smart mouthing. I was more than surprised at Rick's lack of reaction to my theory. He acted as though he already knew. This only continued to reinforce my gut feeling that Rick was holding out on me. Who was he working for and why all the secrecy? Why couldn't he trust me? Slowly the yard cleared of personnel, cruisers, the ambulance and finally Bill's rental. Rick's parting words were standard and cool letting me know that for now, space between us was a good thing.

Fundy and I fed the horses and went back inside to a quiet house. Tom called and wanted to know if he should bring the notebook when he came over. I thought not tonight. All I wanted was Tom and a bottle of wine, not necessarily in that order. Investigation and detecting were not on my calendar for the night. I was tired and sad and more than a little worried about the future. Tonight was downtime.

CHAPTER
17

The snow was almost over the top of my boots and heavy with moisture making it hard to walk across the porch and down the steps. It must have snowed all night to get this deep. At least 13 inches lay on the ground and large clumps clung to the tree branches bending everything over. If the temperature dropped below freezing, this stuff would break power lines all over the place. I had to get to the horses and plow out the paddock so they could get to water and feed.

My legs felt like lead and the snow kept pulling my boots loose. I had to reach down with both hands and pull them up with each foot to take the next step. When I came around the corner of the house and started down the drive towards the gate, I saw that it was open and the horses were gone. There was no snow at the barn or beyond. It was all grass and the fencing was down. Agent Metcalf was standing next to the barn swinging a rope in one hand and holding Cochise's halter in the other.

I yelled at him asking where the horses were. What had he done with Cochise? He smiled, "Don't you worry, honey, Cochise is gone now and can't hurt you anymore." The panic in my chest was painful and the effort of trying to run towards the barn was physically exhausting. My clothing was wet with sweat.

I kept trying to explain that Cochise wouldn't hurt me. He was Mike's horse and Mike made me promise to take care of his horse. Metcalf just kept smiling and repeating that Cochise was gone and couldn't hurt me.

When I finally reached the barn, I tried to grab him. All I wanted to do was shake Metcalf so hard that he would understand that Cochise was my horse. He had to bring all of them back but especially Cochise. He had no right to take them away from me. The struggle inside me to yell loud enough to force him to understand was so painful and frustrating it brought hot tears to my eyes that somehow flowed into my ears. Metcalf had both my wrists grasped tight and I could feel his warm face next to mine whispering, "It's okay, Jill, you're safe. Calm down, relax, you're okay, I'm here."

Slowly Tom relaxed his grip on my hands as reality returned and we both held on waiting for the images in my head to fade and give me some peace. It took more than their fading to erase the tension and feelings of frustration left behind. The addiction my brain seemed to have developed for reliving the past had taken over both my waking and sleeping mind. Nothing I did helped stop the constant flashing of memories that were constantly erupting and interrupting the normalcy of my life.

Last night with Tom had been perfect for both of us, or at least it had felt that way. After a quiet dinner and half a bottle of wine, we had spent an intense and passionate few hours saying physically what we felt emotionally. It had been a while and neither of us held back. Falling asleep was not a problem for either of us, and I certainly was not worried about dreaming. On the contrary, dreams were an escape for me and had always been since I was a child. I've always dreamt in storybook form with a beginning, middle and an end. Sometimes in color and sometimes I dreamt of super powers like being able to fly or jump across canyons. I was always the hero, always survived death, once went to my own funeral, and also played multiple musical instruments. I've also solved many problems in my dreams both practical and personal. Dreams were my escape and my friends. Now, dreams were my own private hell hole. They were waking me up...and not in a good way.

"How do you want your eggs?" Tom was going to cook while I tended to animals.

"Whatever takes fifteen minutes to prepare? I'll be back by then."

Gratefully there was no fresh snow on the ground and no one waiting at the barn. Horses were all accounted for and happy to be fed. The thought of Metcalf was still in mind although I don't put much stock into dream analysis or their predictive value. My mom once thought she had some premonitions about things like my brother's car accident and the like, but even if it were true, I doubt those things are inherited.

After breakfast Tom reminded me of the informant who had called and his creepy guy asking questions, so we made a plan to part ways. He headed for home and his babysitting job while I went to find Chip. Later, we would meet to go over the notebook and decide what to do about Paula. I didn't want her found either, but my gut said I needed to find Mike's information to connect all the dots and she had the pencil to do it. Rick had plenty to keep him busy without having to include me. Besides, his little speech last night still smarted. It didn't matter that I probably had it coming. I didn't need a slap in the face when a tap on the hand would have worked just as well.

On my way into town I stopped at the clinic to see my doctor for a quick check of arm and head. Both were healing nicely, said the good man, but of course I was supposed to be home taking it easy and resting until sutures were out, risk of infection was gone, my strength was back to normal, immunity rebuilt, yada, yada. I did manage to get a concession from him about losing the sling which I had already done. He knew from experience I was a bad girl when it came to following medical advice.

Back in the parking lot I noticed a tan Toyota pick-up with rental plates sitting at idle way over on the side that is rarely used for patients of the clinic. I wouldn't have thought much of it except that it pulled out after I did and turned south to follow me.

In town I ditched the truck and back-tracked to a place where I usually buy my ammunition. I was carrying all the time now and noticed with my last check of the cabinet this morning that .40 caliber ammo was down to one clip. It never occurred to me I might have to stock up to maintain my status as a happy retiree.

Inside I spent a few minutes talking with the guys about fun stuff and picked up my favorite candy bar for later on. No day is complete without a Payday, right Dad? Just as I sat behind the wheel to leave, there was Mr. Toyota sitting across the street inside Dunkin Donuts. Who is this guy? So far I couldn't get a good visual because there was always a window between him and me. Best I could do was tall, what looked like a beard or heavy facial growth, pretty good build, and dressed from the waist up in a dark three- quarter coat with dark toke. The coat was a guess on my part, but it looked like a pea coat they wear in the Navy. My brother had one once.

I called Chip and told him about my shadow asking if this might be the guy he was talking about. Chip wouldn't talk on the phone. Great, this was going to be very difficult. I called Wilson Stedfelt at the Bennington Police Department and asked him if he could help me out with a quick ID project. He owed me a favor from days gone by. We set up Mr. Toyota in the Kmart parking lot where I pointed him out to Stedfelt. While he was questioning my anonymous stalker on some made up pretense, I went back to the armory and met up with Chip in person.

An hour and 15 minutes worth of conversation didn't improve my knowledge base enough to justify the trip. Yes, there was a 6'2", muscular, dark eyed guy with facial hair and military haircut asking questions about me. He wanted to know where I lived, my connection with Robinson, Rick, Brinker, and Faraday. He wanted to know if I had boyfriends, friends, relatives, or places around that I frequented often enough to maybe stay for a while. That last one had me confused as I had no idea why anyone would care or even think that I was in hiding. The best I could come up with was they thought I was hiding someone or something else. Maybe they thought I was hiding Charlie or had found Mike's information? Nah, that was a stretch even for me.

Chip was wired and ready to bust his mainspring. I had never seen him so jumpy.

"What the hell is wrong with you? This isn't the first time you've given me information and this certainly isn't earth shattering. You're acting like you've just given me Pentagon papers. What's going on?"

"You don't know what you're up against here. This guy is a real nut case. He's got information about people he shouldn't have, and carries some serious weapons. He must be some kind of Green Beret reject or something to be outfitted like he is. He had two pearl handled .45s in shoulder rigs that looked like something out of a Patton movie set. There was a throwing knife in his boot, and he was wearing one of those belts with something weird for a belt buckle that carries a garrote line or blows up things. I mean no one walks around like that unless they're nuts or a mercenary."

This guy sounded like a hundred others I'd run into in the mountains of Washington and Idaho. Most were ex-military who had retired to the forests and mountains to be left alone and escape their memories of war or other domestic problems. Not many LEOs bothered you out there. The rest were mercenaries of sorts, connected to drugs or other related businesses and quite capable of using those weapons and many others too.

"Maybe he watches too many Rambo movies. Did he threaten you or hurt you?"

"No, just the opposite, he was so calm it was creepy. His voice was soft and polite, almost pleasant. But I didn't buy into any of it. There's no way he could have known where my friend lived or what he did with cars unless he had an 'in' with some serious information sources."

"What are you talking about?"

"He found me through my friend who helped us with your friend that needed the wheels that night in Kmart. You know the one who just got himself killed."

"Robinson?"

"I guess so. This creepy guy shows up at my friend's place of business and threatens to turn him in and revoke his ..." Chip stopped himself before saying too much. I figured his pal was in Witness Protection but never brought it up. "He threatened him with life altering stuff unless he gave him information about you. When he couldn't come up with any, my friend volunteered me as a source of info. It would take serious money and skills to break into the files or bribe the people who know about my friend."

Chip might be right, but it also could be that someone on government payroll could come up with the same information. Whoever this guy was, clearly efficiency was not a flaw. In addition to being a weapons aficionado, he might also be a computer hacker of sorts. Witness Protection files were pretty hard to break into, but not impossible.

"Chip, did you happen to see what he was driving?"

"Yeah, I wasn't impressed. I offered to get him something better, but he said classy didn't suit him. It was the only time he smiled. He's driving an older model Toyota pick-up."

"How much did you end up telling about me and my habits?"

Chip started to cry. That's what his being wired was about. I should have picked up on it before now. I must be slipping. He felt he had betrayed me and couldn't handle it. I spent the next 20 minutes convincing him it was all good. I never expected him to defend me, but needed to know exactly how much Mr. Toyota knew. As it turned out, he knew damn little. Most of it could have turned up on an internet search. If he was a hired gun, he already knew more than that.

Stedfelt returned to the armory and let me know that Mr. Toyota was one Christian Haughey on leave from the Army and just passing through town. He apologized if he upset anyone by seeming to follow them, but assured the officer he was not. Presently he was staying at the Apple Inn, and would be leaving in the morning. He wasn't armed in the truck that Stedfelt could see and denied having any weapons.

With thanks for his help and a promise to explain everything later, I sent Chip home with Stedfelt. Now what? Think, that's what I needed to do, and get a plan. I needed to get back to Tom's and look over Bill's notebook. Once I had his information it was sit down with a large mug of coffee, paper, pen, and undisturbed quiet time until the light bulbs went on. There were too many people, places and events running through my head.

After dinner that's exactly what I did. Bill's notebook had several pieces of information I hadn't registered before. Between that and the files Rick had produced a few nights ago in the barn, my diagram on the newsprint was beginning to take shape. It still resembled a spider web made by an arachnid on crack, but the connections between people were taking shape. A few key relationships were missing or had no evidence to support them, but they were making sense.

Stephanie Kincaid starts it all with the hiring of Bill to investigate the '71 shootout. She's tied to one victim, the professor. Bill finds Beemer, and Savant aka Sonja for statements. At some point after her interview, Beemer is found dead. Along the way, Brinker tries to kill Bill for unknown reasons and Bill accidentally kills him in self defense. Zeke Faraday is shot and killed following a break- in at my house by person unknown. Dutch Donaldson is second victim at bank heist. Maxwell Johnson is still at large and believed to have been following Bill. With the exception of Brinker who wasn't there, that accounts for all the people within the bank.

What Bill had written underneath at the end of Beemer's interview was a list of questions concerning the dress of the professor and Donaldson.

According to the VSP report he had seen, the VSP guys were focused on two men dressed similarly with tokes and face masks. Both were visible through the windows and one had a phone to his ear when the order was given. But, when the bodies of Kincaid and Donaldson were brought out, they were in street clothes. What happened to the other clothing, hats, etc.? What happened to the phone forensic evidence which never shows up in any reports? It must have had blood or tissue on it. Why was no mention made of any fabric or foreign material being found in either head wound? Certainly a bullet passing through glass and a toke then hair would have left something in the entrance wound to be reported in the autopsy.

The next strange thing in Bill's notes was the invoice contained in Stephanie's case file that sent him to Charlie's shop. That connected Bill's investigation to Mike's investigation, but why did he have it and not the VSP file? For that matter, why did he have it at all? The invoice really had no bearing on the bank or the event he was investigating. It also brought up Metcalf's brother and Gretchen Brinker who were connected to me, sort of. Was their involvement contrived to bring Bill back around to the Hollow and me for some reason?

We certainly found evidence at Brinker's house. Mike thought both the unclaimed case at Charlie's and the arms found at the Oregon crime scene were related. He also had some tentative evidence that I had yet to secure. Unfortunately, I didn't see where that necessarily connected to the east coast and what was happening here. The only similarity seemed to be that the Oregon incident and the National Bank both involved militant militia group members.

The notes after Paula's interview were the most sobering. Not because she was Mike's wife, but because they were the last ones he made before being shot. Something about his finding her made Bill very dangerous. It had to be in these notes. I must have read those pages forty times before it finally dawned on me that because I wanted it to be there didn't mean it was. This wasn't a TV cop show where everything is resolved in an hour and we go to bed happy as a lark pleased that the bad guy lost and the good guy won.

It was interesting that Bill's theory connected the past with the future. It made sense that something had surfaced which threatened a bad guy or guys today who had been involved with the capper way back then. But how did that tie in with Mike? It must be through me since I'm the only common denominator. Now the question is, do I have this "thing" or do I need to find it? Let's assume I come up with the mystery evidence and connect the heist with the smuggling and Mike's murder. I still haven't solved anything. I don't know who killed Bill although my money is on Maxwell since he's the only original member who's still out there and unaccounted for. I don't know where the Brinkers are. I don't know who gave the order to shoot so I can't finish Bill's case.

Oh, and let's not forget Rick and the Task Force. There's no telling what the questions and answers are for that band of brothers.

I must have said something out loud announcing my frustration for soon the door opened slightly and a hand cautiously slid past the doorframe with a tumbler of JD on the rocks. Now there's a man who understands my limitations. It didn't take much of a smile and no argument at all to coax me out of the back room. It was obvious I had been neglecting my duties as a part-time host. This I quickly rectified. The four of us, Jake, Tom, Charlie, and me, spent the rest of the night playing cards, talking and generally ignoring the realities of the day. Jake and Tom went back to my place to tend to the horses while Charlie and I cleaned up and geared down.

Charlie asked, "What are you going to do now?"

"I've located most of Bill's key points from his notebook and mapped it out. It appears that somehow I'm instrumental in connecting two investigations, the one Bill was researching and one that Mike Peterson and I worked back in '88. This may be a long shot, but Mike once told me some hidden evidence existed and I'm going to try and find it."

Charlie's eyebrow arched a bit, "Isn't a twenty plus year old search a little optimistic?"

"No, it's insane. I don't have any choice. There are no other leads that I'm privy to and people keep getting shot at or killed in my yard. Besides, it's ruining the neighborhood and cutting into my love life."

After she stopped laughing she asked, "Do you think Paula will talk to you and help out?"

"Why wouldn't she?" I was starting to get a little edge in my voice.

"She didn't know about you and Mike did she?"

"Know about what? Mike and I were partners working cases together. We weren't having an affair if that's your implication."

Charlie looked at me for a long time and I glared right back. "I know you better than you know yourself. I've known you loved him since the first time you talked to me about him years ago. When he was killed, it damn near destroyed you and you know it. Don't even think of sitting there and telling me he was just an ordinary work partner."

Sometimes best friends just don't know when to stop. Charlie meant well, I'm sure, but this was not the time or the place for soul searching or wound cleansing. And it certainly wasn't the time for baring the soul. What went on or didn't go on between Mike and I was private and would stay that way...even from my best friend.

"Charlie, I never said I didn't love him. I said we did not have an affair and Paula has no reason to doubt my friendship. I never violated her trust. As for my relationship with Mike, this is hardly the time or place to be discussing that. I really need to keep my mind on other things."

We both apologized for being a little curt with each other and poured the rest of our drinks down the drain. This was not a good time to have our judgment impaired with alcohol. By then the boys were back and with brief goodnights we wandered off to bed. Tom and I discussed plans for the next few days, and he quickly drifted off to sleep. As I lay there looking at the ceiling, I thought of Cochise and his equipment. Over and over I went through all the possible places Mike might have secreted a piece of evidence. It would have helped if I knew what I was looking for. I didn't know if it was a piece of paper, or picture, recording tape, film, negative, maybe a weapon or other stolen item. Shit, it could be as small as a pin or as big as a saddle and I wouldn't be the wiser.

Saddle... I hadn't thought of that. When I had taken Cochise from his rehab unit, his tack box had been set to go. I checked everything to be sure it was there including Mike's saddle that he used with Cochise when not on duty. He liked it because it was padded with gel and the underside was sheepskin and soft on the horse's back. When I went looking for the evidence, I had pried apart or tried to pry every piece of tack and horse product that was in the case including the case itself. It had yielded nothing. No hidden compartments or secret papers under the coverings. I didn't take an in-depth look at his saddle thinking a horseman would never damage something that precious, or would he? Was it there? I had to know.

CHAPTER

18

The barn was always so peaceful at night. You'd hardly believe that people were dropping like flies. The moon was casting just enough light to make objects visible and the horses frisky. Tom will be pissed that I snuck out to come over alone but he needs his beauty sleep and I have no patience left.

The saddle was where I had left it and I didn't need lights to see what I was doing as the moonlight was coming through the open door and striking the cantle dead on. I had a flashlight just in case, but for now I was using my hands for eyes. I slowly felt over the flat surfaces of leather looking for bumps or ridges that would indicate something under the surface. Then I started a check of the stitching to see if new had been added or replaced old. I checked the gel seat pushing in with my fingers trying to find objects that might have been inserted. Underneath I combed through the matted sheepskin and checked the edges looking for slits or patches. Finally, I looked closely at the oversized stirrups. I came up with a big zero.

I could feel the anger boil up inside as the frustration once again took control. This was the last rock unturned. There was no other place to go for clues, no other place to look for hidden treasure. I had been so sure that something was going to turn up on the saddle, and again I came up empty handed. Without the slightest intention of stopping, I grabbed the saddle by the horn and cantle, hoisted it several feet off the rack, and with unexpected strength threw it against the opposite wall. The sound frightened Tracker who was in the stall next to the barn and he took off like a rocket to find Cochise and Nevada. The outburst did nothing to ease my frustration. As a matter of fact, it added to this damnable feeling of impotence that kept following me lately.

Frustration led to despair and I decided to head back to Tom's before my disposition got any worse. Picking up the saddle I felt rather than saw a piece of rock or pebble stuck in the seam of the horn where the thread for the stitching started around the top. It might even be the head of a small nail. With the saddle back on the rack, I tried to pry it out, but it wouldn't budge. Okay, if it wasn't coming out, maybe I could drive it in. I hit it dead on with a punch and hammer and the entire front of the horn popped open a quarter inch. When I pried it the rest of the way with my fingers, a piece of paper was visible. I poked inside and found that the interior portion of the saddle where the horn rested had been hollowed out. It contained a cassette tape along with several other papers and documents bearing Mike's writing and signature. My hands were shaking.

With care I removed the contents and found a corner of the barn up in the second story where my light couldn't be seen from the outside. After taking a deep breath, I began to go through the contents.

The first paper was a brief description of how Mike had listened to the tape, and identified one of the voices as that of Jerome Metcalf. It also stated that an independent informant had sworn to him that the other voice was that of Maxwell Johnson, a convicted felon. It gave a case # 3467 FBI Task Force as reference along with several other references that were beyond me. I was still shocked at the names and was now beginning to understand a lot more about the past and present connection.

A second piece of paper was simply a statement from Mike that he had been helping a Federal Task Force trying to stop a national smuggling operation with uniformed officers of various agencies involved in and supporting the actions of that ring. To date he didn't have any large accumulation of information, but he had been watching Metcalf and Johnson long enough to know they were part of whatever was going on.

A third piece of paper, which was really an index card folded in half, had lists of dates and times with notations. One said 'Metcalf/Johnson warehouse post NatGrd break-in'. Another said "Metcalf/Johnson storage lockers East St post WelsFrg Bnk hold up". There must have been a dozen dates listing meetings between Metcalf and Johnson at various locations, apparently following break-ins and hold-ups. Thinking back to the incident with Metcalf that led to the sexual harassment charge, I guess that was also part of his cover-up and a better choice for him than losing a load of whatever was in that truck. That son of a bitch used me.

On the back of the index card, Mike had written his name, and corresponding case numbers of the crimes for which he was watching these two birds. I wondered if we went back into BP files if we would see any mention of Metcalf or Johnson as possible suspects in any of those cases. I couldn't do any of that research, but I knew I could at least find out what was on the cassette. I played the tape on a small recorder I carried in my car and heard Metcalf's voice give an order to the first VSP officer to take the shot at the National Bank Heist in '71. There was a lot of confusion in the background but you could clearly hear his voice as if the mic were very close to him. Then you could hear a second voice saying they would meet him inside the bank and he'd better be alone or the deal was off. He was also told not to be late. Then there was more commotion but soon it got quiet and then the off button was pushed. I wonder what kind of deal Trooper Metcalf made with the devil. Whatever the deal, Mike had paid with his life to find out, and so had Bill. Was Metcalf calling the shots and Maxwell pulling the trigger?

There were still a lot of important questions that needed answering and Rick was the one I needed to ask. I'd be gracious enough to let him get up at a reasonable hour, but not by much.

It was getting on to three in the morning and I was tired. This evidence had been safe here for 20 some odd years. I guess a few more days will be fine until I could figure out what to do with it. I made sure there was no sign on the saddle or horn that it had been tampered with, and then cleaned up the area where I had thrown the saddle. When I left the barn it was as if no one had been there.

Just for fun, I drove into Bennington from the house. I wanted to see, first of all, if anyone was watching the house, and secondly, if I was being followed. I didn't get a good answer to the first, but the answer to the second was yes. My near and dear friend, Mr. Toyota, picked me up but not until

I had reached North Bennington. Guess he wasn't the rural type. I pulled around to a Dunkin Donuts and waved him by. He must have been insulted as he sped up and continued past heading south towards his supposed motel. I grabbed a quick coffee and donut and went back to the car.

As I started north through North Bennington on 67A, I noticed a car stopped on the railroad tracks with the hood up and some guy leaning on the fender. This was not good. Trains don't usually go through here at night, but still it wouldn't do to see this and not report it at least. Slowing down with cell phone in hand, I punched in the Shaftsbury barracks number... mistake number one.

I had just noticed the driver's ponytail when the dispatcher answered.

"State Police Dispatcher Bevins. How can I help you?"

"10-32." That was all I could say, and that was risky. I brought the phone down from my ear slowly and carefully placed it on the floor between the door and the seat hoping the movement couldn't be seen in the dark by my surprise visitor. He motioned for the window to be rolled down. I was looking at the barrel of a semi-auto being held by the man I was going to help and decided compliance was a damn fine idea. This would have been a good time for someone else to come along and help me. Given the circumstances, "man with a gun" is not a bad call sign to give a police dispatcher. Of course it would take a series of miracles to be sure I didn't disconnect the line when I dropped it the last few inches, and hope Bevins kept the line open long enough to identify and trace, then take the ten codes literally and send in the cavalry. Was that asking too much?

"Both hands on the wheel and move very slowly."

The voice was pleasant enough but the intent wasn't. He opened the passenger door, got in and placed the barrel of the gun gently against my temple.

"Let's not have any accidents. Back up and park your car behind the post office. Please drive carefully."

I did what I was told. He turned off the ignition and removed my keys placing them in the glove box. Then he reached behind my back without moving his gun and removed my gun from my waist band.

"I'm going to ask you once if you carry two guns. Lying will cost you."

"I only have the one tonight." This guy was very professional. Not too tall, older, military background from the looks of the haircut and tattoo on the back of his hand. Full beard and mustache with plenty of grey, but the eyes were not those of an old man. I couldn't see his frame under the bulky winter clothing, but my guess was it didn't carry much flab.

"Now I want you to listen to me very carefully. We are going to get out of your car, walk over to the car on the tracks, and you are going to get into the driver's seat. I will be behind you and tell you where to go. If for any reason you are stopped or fail to do what I ask, you will die."

As he spoke he attached a silencer to what I now recognized as a Beretta. "Let's go."

I couldn't grab my cell without disconnecting or making it obvious that it had been on. On the plus side, my vehicle was being left in a spot that would irritate the USPS and get an early response from VSP. He was driving a Crown Victoria which at least gave him credit for good taste in cars. We got moving fast. As I turned the corner to head north on 7A, I was certain I saw Mr. Toyota sitting in his truck behind Paulin's Short Stop. *What the hell? How many bad guys were out there anyhow?*

Vermont is a beautiful state filled with small towns and winding roads that take you through valleys and mountains filled with rustic dairy farms, saw mills, and all sorts of tourist industries like skiing, etc. It's also a place where big time crime doesn't tend to happen because this is where big time criminals have their second homes. At least that's the theory I have. You don't shit where you sleep. Vermont is one of the major drug corridors but comparatively little stays here. It's just passing through on a journey south or north depending on the cargo.

What makes Vermont most useful to guys like my friend in the back seat, is its hundreds of miles of isolated roads with few residences that no one notices or even cares about. It's ideal for storing people of questionable reputation or questioning people of any reputation. You can scream to your heart's content and not be heard. Police can search forever and not find a missing person. My guess was I would soon be a resident of such a place.

"Do you have a name or should I call you honey?"

I couldn't see his face in the rear view, but something told me he didn't have a sense of humor. I also had a damn good idea who he was.

"Max."

"Ah! You wouldn't be the infamous Maxwell Johnson would you?"

That brought a sharp pain to the back of my head from the barrel of the Berretta. It was hard enough to bring stars and bright lights to my eyes. The car swerved some before my vision cleared.

"Just keep your mouth shut, lady, and drive."

"Look Max, in case you haven't noticed, I'm driving. Knock me out and we both crash. If you don't want us stopped, try being a little more civil. I'm sure your boss would prefer seeing both of us alive."

"Just shut up and drive."

So much for being friendly, and now I have a headache.

Perhaps Max thought I didn't know much about Vermont back roads or didn't care if I could find my way out. No attempt was being made to make our destination a secret other than his not telling me where it was. Even in the dark, I knew I was somewhere on the backside of Stratton Mountain probably in the town of Winhall where skiing was the major industry and rich people kept second homes and condos all over the place. The police force was pretty good but small, and had to be diplomats first if they wanted to have a happy day.

It was no surprise that our destination was at the end of a mile long dead end road. The only other residence was on the corner and appeared unoccupied. Their driveway was piled high with snow that had not been cleared for most of the winter. Whatever the owner was paying for maintenance, he wasn't getting his money's worth. We headed for the end of the road and a private drive that had to be 1000 yards long. It curved left to the front of a single story hunting lodge-style house that cost maybe two million to build. Max had me pull over to the side where an overhead door opened for us to drive in. There was nothing inside the parking garage or house to disappoint my expectations of grand and expensive tastes. I didn't know who owned this place, but they had beaucoup bucks.

"Walk over to that fireplace and stand there with your back to me. Don't turn around and don't move."

I did as I was told. So far my hands were free and I thought if I behaved they might stay that way. On the table next to the fireplace there was a photograph of three guys in hunting clothes with rifles and big smiles standing next to a Range Rover. I couldn't tell where the picture was taken, but two of the men were Maxwell Johnson and Jerome Metcalf. The third looked enough like Max to be his brother but I wasn't really sure.

Without moving my head, I tried to see more of the room and managed to catch a glimpse of some bookshelves on the right. Most of the books I could see didn't reveal titles. I did notice on the bottom shelf there were several magazines, the top one being Gall's. Gall's was a cop's one stop shopping source for all things he or she needed to serve and protect short of guns and ammo. *Oh shit! Please don't tell me this is Metcalf's place.*

I could hear Max on the phone behind me. There was a bit about my being there. No, there wasn't any trouble. Yes, he'd looked for a tail. No, I hadn't been questioned yet, was he supposed to wait for "him". With that the call ended, I was handcuffed with the plastic type and told to sit down.

I asked, "What happens now?"

"We wait for Metcalf."

"He lives pretty well. I like his house."

He laughed and almost looked happy. "Are you insane? This isn't his place. My brother owns this and him too. Metcalf can't hang onto three cents without scotch tape. He's a disaster with money. If my brother didn't watch out for him he'd be in jail by now."

"Wow, and all this time I thought Metcalf was the brains of the outfit. Looks like everyone's barking up the wrong tree thinking Metcalf pulled off the National Bank thing."

What did I have to lose? If he was going to have me questioned I might as well see what I could get out of him first. Besides, this brotherly love thing might help me out. Who the hell was his brother anyway? I should know this. Somebody told me and I seem to have forgotten.

Max took the bait big time. "That National Bank job was a cluster from the beginning with Donaldson and Kincaid running their mouths off all the time. Metcalf was such a freaking wimp, we practically had to hold his hand through the whole set up. He actually thought we were there only for the money. My brother had to threaten to kick him out of VSP before he finally got with the program. What a candy ass."

"I don't get it, if you weren't there for the money, what was the program?" This was news to me.

"Oh we were there for the money, alright, but Metcalf was supposed to show up alone and take out Dutch and the professor. I told Ben he'd screw it up and he did. But I fixed it like I always do."

"Why is he coming here if he's such a jerk?"

Now I knew where I had heard about Max Johnson's brother. Rick had told me his boss, Major Johnson, was his brother when we talked in the barn. Crap, if Metcalf was coming here and was not at all respected or a leader, chances were good they would kill both of us and make it look like he did me in. Metcalf gets the blame for all the shootings, probably gets blamed for all the smuggling, the evidence dies with me and the Johnson boys get away with everything. They don't need to find Paula or bother with Charlie anymore because the link is gone with the two of us dead. Wow, this is a pretty good move. Let's hear it for the bad guys.

"He thinks you have something that belongs to him. Something that incriminates him that your boyfriend gave you before I knocked him off his horse…"

I didn't hear much after that. The rage must have been evident in my face because his lips stopped moving for a few seconds and then broke into a wide smile. He knew his words had struck home. There was a very clear communication in those dark eyes that he thoroughly enjoyed telling me he was responsible for the murder of Mike Peterson, and I couldn't do a thing about it. He would get away with that crime too.

What Mr. Johnson did not realize was that his enjoyment and confession had created a very dangerous person. The second I knew for certain he was the one, his arrest or death became my only job. He killed my partner and, by God, I would bring him to justice or die trying.

"You seem to have two facts wrong in that last statement. I don't have any evidence on Metcalf or anyone else. If I did I would have given it to Captain Dugan. And, if you are referring to Agent Mike Peterson, he was my partner in an investigation, not my boyfriend. I'm not sure I would go around confessing to murdering Border Patrol Agents if I were you. Your brother might see that as goading the enemy and not take it too kindly. He is, after all, a brother in arms."

The noise that came out of his mouth was supposed to be a laugh but it sounded more like a choked off yell.

"My brother wouldn't waste a bullet on your filthy carcass. He's a patriot and a good man. The only reason he's with your kind is to keep track of all your subversive activities and watch where you people store the weapons and bombs you plan to use to take away the freedoms of law abiding citizens. We know what the Feds are up to, and we know they've infiltrated the State Police and the universities. That's why we have to be careful and keep ourselves small and distanced from each other so we don't get caught. My brother knows how to handle all that stuff and he relies on me as his right hand man.

"I'm the one who keeps him safe. I'm the one who gets the jobs done. Metcalf is just a puppet like my brother says because we need someone in the Border Patrol who has seniority and can move back and forth across the northern border. If we had a replacement, he'd be gone in a heartbeat. He's outlived his usefulness anyhow."

Max was over the top about the cause and his brother. I had hit a verbal nerve and for now it suited my purpose as he was pacing back and forth around the living room while spewing propaganda and the party line. My hands were cuffed with plastic ties and in front which made movement a bit risky. I did carry a pocket knife which was still in my jeans, but removal from a front pocket took time and finesse.

Having accomplished that, it also took considerable time to figure out how to cut and then to accomplish the cutting of one tie without separating my hands. Without a gun, I needed surprise to affect any escape. Max was a well-built guy for his age and in much better shape than I was. Add to that the fact that women are on average 60% as strong as men, and I needed a lot of surprise. Looking around for a weapon I spotted my .40 caliber on the fireplace mantel. There was no way of telling if he had left the magazine in place or if there was a round in the chamber. His Berretta was holstered in a shoulder rig, left side. That meant he probably had removed the silencer. I didn't see any gun cabinets or rooms where there might be another source. I did have my pocket knife with its 2 inch blade. Given the opportunity I could sever the artery in his throat. Like that's going to happen.

Well you'd better come up with something because I have a feeling time is running out.

"How long before Metcalf gets here?"

Max stopped talking and just looked dumbfounded. "Huh?"

"When is Metcalf expected to arrive?"

He looked at the clock then checked his watch. "He'll be here pretty soon. Don't worry about it. He'll be here. He wouldn't dare cross my brother."

"Do you mind if I get some sleep? I've been up all night."

"If you can sleep sitting up that's fine with me."

"Can't stretch out on the couch?"

"Nope."

"You're all heart, Max. Remind me to tell your brother how well he raised you."

All that got me was a glare of hate, but that was good enough for now. A little nap would be good for me. I needed to recharge the brain cells and come up with a plan. After 15 years Mike's killer was within reach. He wasn't getting over the top of that ridge again.

CHAPTER

19

It was hard to distinguish the shapes against the background of trees and bushes covered in snow outside the oversized living room windows. It was still dark and the clouds pretty much eliminated any moonlight that might be available at this late hour. I couldn't see or hear anyone close to me in the room and didn't want to move or open my eyes too wide to be noticed as having returned to the land of hostages. As best I could figure, there were two maybe three figures having a pretty heated discussion on the other side of the living room, although I couldn't decide if they were inside or outside.

My position in the chair had me facing in their direction and I was slouched down with one leg over the arm and the other on the floor. My back was killing me and my neck was stiff, but sleep had been a good idea. There was some light coming from the kitchen area and another seemed to be on in the hallway leading to the garage. What I thought to be the back bedrooms or office areas were dark. I wondered if there might be a back door in that direction or a sliding glass door in the master bedroom. If I were rich, I'd have a deck and hot tub off my master bedroom.

The trick would be getting from here to there without being noticed by the Three Stooges. I looked at my ties to see if they were still cut, and yes they were. I checked the mantel but couldn't see in the shadows if Max was dumb enough to leave my gun up there. Okay now what are you going to do? Another look at the window showed what I thought were two figures facing a third at a slight angle to the window. The single figure could see me out of the corner of his eye, but the other two had their backs almost totally turned in my direction. If I moved slow enough and waited for the conversation to get really revved, I might be able to slide out and behind the chair unseen. Then it would be a short crawl straight back to the edge of the fireplace, a slow stand, grab the gun and pray it was still loaded. After that I could exit out back through a window or door and find my way to a phone or car and get Rick.

Speaking of which, he should be getting a call about now from a very testy postmaster concerning my leaving a car in his sacred parking area where their truck can't unload mail. That's a federal offense and he'd better arrest me or some such thing. I wondered if Bevins had made any sense at all of my using the 10-32 call sign for "man with a gun" and traced it to my cell phone. I'm not sure she could have done anything with it but it was all I could think of doing. Must not have worked too well if I was still here and no one was beating down the door.

I started to get my body ready for movement with little isometrics and mini exercises to get the blood pumping through my leg and arm muscles. As my mind became more alert and the adrenaline started to flow, my hearing keyed in to the sounds of the house and tried to pick up what was going on next to the window. When the volume seemed to go up and everyone appeared intently engaged in the argument, I moved my leg down off the arm rest and readjusted my position. Then I watched with eyes slightly open to see if it was noticed.

Several minutes later I got an unexpected break when the third man threw his hands up in disgust and turned his back on me. Without hesitation I left the chair and went straight to the side of the fireplace where I grabbed the gun and flattened myself against the wall. A quick check told me it was loaded. Dropping to one knee, I chanced a look at the window and saw no one. Shit! No time to waste here. There were three of them, one of me, and 16 shots in my possession. One of them was a marksman, one was Metcalf, but who was the third? It could be the Major I suppose, and if it was, what kind of killer was he?

One was sure to be running around to the back figuring I'd head that way. It was a good bet all three knew this house better than I did. I think my better choice is to find a good hiding spot close to an exit and take a couple out before making tracks. Behind the fireplace there was an alcove that led to a storage area for skis and other outdoor sports equipment. This in turn led to a door that must have opened to a small porch or landing. To the left across the hall was a partially open door and I could see a desk and bookcases. Good, something solid to catch bullets. Inside the room it was a dream come true, not a window in the place and only the one door. A check of the desk drawers produced a Model 1911 .45 with two boxes of ammo which I promptly stuck in my belt and pockets. Not wanting to be lax in my search, I checked the closet and, son of bitch, if the good major didn't have an AR-15 semi- auto rifle with a full clip tucked in the corner. How thoughtful of him.

Pulling out the rifle dislodged a piece of clothing that fell to the floor of the closet with a dull thud. It turned out to be a very nice Kevlar vest! I broke out in the biggest smile I've had on my face in a month, almost yelling for sheer joy. Now they had no idea who they were messing with. This enhanced my plans considerably and gave me a bona fide kick in the ass boost of confidence. Escape was no longer my goal. I wanted these guys and as far as I was concerned, they were as good as got.

Listening at the room's doorway I could hear the latch sounds of a door closing coming from the garage side and then the hall light went out. You can't really hear someone walking on rugs as much as you can feel their presence. When waiting in the dark, it helps to think like the people who are coming after you and imagining where you would be in their shoes. When the sounds do come, you are already keyed in to the direction they may come from and better prepared to guess at how close they are. It was no surprise to hear the squeak of a rubber sole as it crossed the hard surface of the kitchen area and circled towards the living room where I had first entered. A second man must be coming straight down the hall towards the room area where I was. Man number three would be outside or coming in from the opposite side of the hallway to cut off escape in that direction. That's fine with me.

It was starting to get a little lighter outside but unless someone was in front of a window I couldn't see well enough to take a shot. I'd have to go for the fire light of burning powder as it exits the barrel of a gun or muzzle flash. One guy moved a chair that seemed several feet away from the fireplace where I had been sleeping. I thought he was heading in my direction; I would see his silhouette as he rounded the corner with the big windows behind him. Number two guy coming down the hall had me worried. His movements were extremely quiet and hard to detect. I had no idea how close he was to me or how much cover he had to shoot from. For me to fire at him meant that I had to lean out of the doorway and expose my position. That would be a risky shot to take without a clear target. I was good, but maybe not that good. Those diving tuck-and-roll shots Clint Eastwood makes look great on film but are they humanly possible?

Suddenly a voice from my right spoke to the guy at the fireplace to stop. At the same time a shot hit the doorframe next to my thigh on the left, but not before I spotted the muzzle flash and fired twice into the same spot. I dropped to my knees and leaned right before the second man fired two shots where my muzzle blast had been. From my crouching position I touched off two more to the left and six inches lower than the muzzle flash from the living room. I figured if he were half as smart as I was, he would have dove to his right for cover. One of his caught the fabric of my vest, the other went past into the room. I didn't miss him entirely as I heard a yelp of sorts and something metal hit the fireplace brick.

No more shots were fired from the hallway. There was little movement from the living room but I could hear noise. I waited for the third man to come down the hall. There was no sound. Then I heard an engine turn over and a vehicle drove out. It was probably a safe guess that the third man was gone. I was going to have to chance moving in on the living room man to check his condition. It would be nice if I could find a flashlight. Looking out the office door slowly I could see the big windows across the house and daylight starting to lighten up the room a bit. Unloading the AR-15 I set it aside and grabbed the .45 which was far more convenient for sneaking around the house. I also left the two boxes of ammo on the floor deciding they were overkill at this point and more than a little heavy. What was I thinking?

Instead of going directly to the living room, I went down the hall to check the first man who was happily Mr. Johnson and quite dead with a neat hole in his forehead. From there I circled through the kitchen and located a very miserable Agent Metcalf bleeding profusely all over the major's rug. He wanted to shoot me with his gun but couldn't quite reach it with his shattered arm that had a rather large hole in it, as did his right shoulder. Besides that, he passed out on me.

I called Rick on his personal line and told him what had happened. I also told him about the third man that I suspected might be Major Johnson. As I expected, Rick yelled a lot and then told me he was almost at the house anyway with the cavalry. Apparently they had figured things out between Bevins and someone else who saw Max going through town. He'd explain it all later. Suspecting that someone might have called Winhall PD, I asked him what course of action he preferred to take with them. Rick had that covered. Metcalf muttered something about medical care at that time and I mentioned to Rick he might want to bring a band aid for one of the suspects and signed off.

I looked down at that miserable piece of crap with all the disgust my weary body could muster.

"You don't really think I give a shit if you live or die do you?"

Metcalf turned his face to look at me and realized that any movement caused great pain since it caused the shoulder wound to reopen and bleed again. I couldn't stand watching him wince like a baby. Moving the furniture out of the way and checking his person for weapons first, I pulled him flat on his back out on the rug and threw some pillows under his head. I found some plastic cuff ties on Johnson and cuffed Metcalf's good arm to the solid oak table in the middle of the room which didn't look like an easy item to cart around. Then I went searching for towels to stem the bleeding.

Johnson was the next item to care for. Dead or not everyone gets cuffed at a crime scene. Weapons were picked up for safety's sake after I marked where they had landed with some duct tape I found in a drawer and a black marker pen. I looked for a camera but didn't find one. A walk down the hallway did lead to several bedrooms and a master suite which indeed had a deck, hot tub, and back exit. Looking through the double glass doors, I could see tracks where someone had approached and tried to open the doors, but a lock bar inside would have required them to break the glass. That certainly would have made enough noise to warn me of their presence and ruined any chance of surprise. Good reason to give up and leave after a series of shots followed by silence and your buddies don't come out to get you.

Back I went to my wounded suspect to see if pain and reflection might make him a little talkative. I wasn't very hopeful, but it was worth a try.

"So tell me, Jerome, what made you decide to become a career asshole?"

"You think you're so smart, you tell me. I don't see you living the great life. Just because you put in 25 and got out with a pension doesn't amount to shit. Do you think anyone cares about what we do out there or cares about what we deal with day in and day out? Think of all the times you sat on a dumb horse in the pouring rain or freezing snow for days at a time just to check a fence line that some smuggler cut across days ago and was already long gone. They just want cops when they're in trouble and then get out. They don't want to pay us for it either. We're supposed to work 24/7 for peanuts for what, for God and Country? Bullshit. At least I got paid and paid well, and crime would have happened any how. I just made it easier so no one got hurt."

"Oh really, and what about the women and children in Oregon who were killed? What about Mike Peterson? What about Robert Kincaid? What do you think we should tell his daughter?"

"His daughter, what do you mean what should you tell his daughter? He didn't have a daughter!"

"Professor Kincaid, Robert Kincaid, the man who was killed at the National Bank in '71 by sniper fire did not have a daughter named Stephanie? You are positive of that?"

"I am absolutely positive of that. Who told you he had a daughter? Bob and I were friends for years and grew up together. I was his neighbor for a while. He wasn't even legally married. He just said he was so the college wouldn't make a big deal out of it and he could run the recruiting thing for militia on campus. The woman he lived with didn't want kids of her own. I think they had kids living with them but they weren't theirs. They were foster kids or something like that and only stayed for a few years."

Well I'll be damned. The weirdness continued in spite of me. Interesting, there's no real daughter named Stephanie Kincaid, so who hired Bill Robinson? Better question to ask would be who is this person that hired Bill and why did she claim to be Stephanie Kincaid?

Blue lights were flashing through the window and it was time to let the big boys in to do their thing. Rick and John Filbert were first in with the crime lab boys next in line. Rick and I stepped into the office area and chatted for a few minutes.

"Rick, you have to let me in on this task force stuff in an official capacity."

"Why?"

"Why? I should think that would be obvious. Whether I like it or not the connections between past and present cases are through me. I can't get my life back if people keep shooting at me, shooting people in my yard, or picking me up and threatening to shoot me. It's just not healthy. If I'm going to be able to help, I need some inside information and some authority to affect arrests or use the strength of the law.

"By the way Maxwell Johnson confessed to me while I was cuffed waiting to be executed early this morning, that he was responsible for the murder of Agent Michael Peterson. I'm now the only one alive who can close that file because Johnson is dead unless we can get that information out of Metcalf or Major Johnson. That is assuming they had any connection to it. As you can see I can assist if I'm part of the Task Force."

Rick thought about that for a while then said he had to talk with his contact before giving me an answer. My answer was not to wait too long because there was more and time was getting short. I didn't explain what that meant.

Three hours later we were finishing breakfast at a local diner and Rick was handing over a faxed copy of temporary authority to assist in the investigation. It didn't look like much to me but I'd stretch it as much as I needed.

I started to ask questions about the Brinkers and what he knew about Gretchen and Joey. To date they were not dead or being held for ransom. Joe senior had been sent to eliminate Bill before his trip to LA, hoping to stop further inquiries into the bank job.

Joey was a recent recruit of the southern branch of a new militia cell of which Joe senior was the legal advisor for in addition to being a member. It was unknown if Gretchen really bought into the whole patriot deal but she obviously wasn't going to turn in hubby or son, be it because of love or fear. The night of the four wanderers through my place was some sort of training thing for Joey, and the game and smuggling stuff I found was the result of a similar thing. Gus and Gail were told to keep their mouths shut and stay out of it once Rick was called in. That was why I never saw either one after I was shot.

The mystery of their whereabouts starts with the day of Joe senior's death. Joe lost his tail going over to the airport and it took a long time before VSP knew he was dead so no one was particularly noticing the movements of Gretchen or Joey. She was being watched also as a matter of interest but not very closely. She was seen heading into town with her son but the officer assigned was called to another duty and had no reason to think it was more important to keep track of her. She was last seen in her SUV with Joey heading towards SVC where her daughter attended classes. Tracey is still there attending classes but has no clue where her mother and brother are and doesn't care. She had a major falling out with the parents over some boyfriend several years back and left the home never to return or reconcile some 18 months ago.

An APB, or All Points Bulletin, was put out for Gretchen's vehicle with no results until it was found parked in the garage at home. Somehow she got help either through a friend or the group for transportation. That explained why her trail was never picked up. She continues to be on a national list with all police agencies as a missing person of interest wanted for questioning in the death of her husband Joseph Brinker, even though Bill has been proven the most likely person responsible for the accident. No arrest warrants are issued for Gretchen, but she is to be detained for her own protection along with her son.

We talked a little about her working at Charlie's with Metcalf's brother and how that all played out. Rick didn't think that was anything we could work on yet because there was no tie between Jerome Metcalf the BP Agent and the smuggling.

"I beg to differ, my good friend, I have written evidence that one Agent Michael Peterson observed on several dates, meetings between Metcalf and Maxwell Johnson at various warehouses and storage facilities following the break-ins and hold-ups of banks and other establishments in the same area. There are case numbers, dates, times and all manner of recorded information. I found the information Mike wanted me to find if something happened to him. It's still in safe keeping. I can also tie Metcalf to the National Bank as the one who actually gave the shoot command to the first VSP sharpshooter. It wasn't an accident, it was an execution set up by persons unknown to get rid of Donaldson and Kincaid. Metcalf was supposed to do it on his own originally but screwed it up. What happened was Maxwell's way of fixing it and probably his way of blackmailing Metcalf."

Rick looked at me for a very long minute trying to decide if he wanted to kiss me or kill me.

"One of these days, you are going to push me over the edge and I'm either going to die of a coronary or serve out my retirement in solitary. Why didn't you tell me this before?"

"I didn't find it until this morning just before Johnson took me for a ride. It took a while for me to be able to put all these puzzle pieces together and get enough of a picture to make some kind of sense. You try working a case that's 20 plus years old with something unrelated clear across the country and a bunch of people with no apparent ties to each other."

Rick was exasperated. "Fine, I have to go find the major before he disappears too. Go back to his house and see if you can find something, anything, that helps locate Gretchen or Metcalf's brother."

"Wait a minute, Metcalf's brother is missing too?"

"Yeah, didn't I tell you that? We were keeping an eye on him when he moved to Burlington and then they lost him."

"Who the hell is on this Task Force?"

"Doesn't matter right now. You need to get back to that house and I need to get other stuff done. Move, unless you can't get your sorry ass in gear."

There wasn't much activity left at the major's house. Bodies were gone to morgue and hospital. The crime scene boys had finished with pictures, dusting, measuring, collecting, and packing up. One trooper was left to tape off the door with crime scene tape and to secure the house. I asked him to leave one door unlocked and enough tape for me to finish the job when I left.

Inside I started with the least likely places for files to be hidden in order to narrow the search quickly. All flooring was checked for hidden safes or drop down stairs. All ceilings were checked for hidden access points, hide-a-ways, vents, false tiles and the like. The bathroom and kitchen were checked for false cabinet backs, phony appliances, false bottom drawers, shallow shelves, hollow walls behind medicine cabinets, and the ever handy plastic bag in the toilet tank. Next were the closets and storage areas with boxes and cases that were either inside them or anywhere in the house. So far I was coming up empty.

The master bedroom closet had nothing but clothes, shoes and a duffle bag with hunting gear. There were a few empty suitcases in the corner but no secret doors or hollow walls. The night table didn't have anything either which struck me as strange. Everybody keeps something in their night table. It was time to check his office, which is probably where I should have started. Walking past the king size bed next to the glass doors, I slipped a little on a puddle of water where the snow from outside had melted on the brick inlay next to the shag rug. The locking bar had been removed, probably by the VSP boys, to take photos of the tracks and prints from the door. Someone was a little sloppy and didn't replace the bar.

I had the crime scene tape in my jacket so I stepped outside the doors and taped across in the traditional X formation. Ducking underneath the tape without tearing it, I closed the doors from the inside and placed the locking bar in the track. I listened for a minute to the sounds of the house thinking I had heard a thud down the hall. Lack of sleep and the ringing in my ears from firing guns indoors was making reality a hard ride these days.

Down the hall and inside the major's office, I went to the desk and sat in the chair. Slowly I looked at the entire room trying to imagine where I would store vital information I needed to remain absolutely secret but available to me. I'm rich, I'm a cop and I've been getting away with this for a long time by being smarter than everyone else. It's also information I use for blackmail purposes so I need to get at it now and then. Where do I keep that information? The room itself was simple but very elegant in a manly way.

The desk was gorgeous dark red oak and massive with only a few tasteful carvings on the drawer pulls. I had already checked the drawers and come up empty.

The bookcases that lined one full wall were of the same wood and partially filled with books. The remaining spaces were filled with awards and pictures of his service in the State Police and different events or trips with buddies. It was all well balanced and tasteful. Now I would hide papers in books or behind them. I started checking for false books or openings behind shelves.

About halfway down and behind a couple of "do it yourself" books, I caught a reflection off a knot in the paneling that didn't quite look like authentic wood product. I pulled out a few more books and ran my fingers lightly along the woodwork until I found the seams of what appeared to be an inlaid piece of paneling. Depressing the unusual knot triggered a spring opening the door.

Inside were a series of files and pictures, some tapes, a couple stacks of money, a leather pouch and some other objects I couldn't quite see in the back. I'd say the interior of this hiding box was about two feet long, one foot high and eighteen inches deep. It was so well concealed, it didn't need a lock. The find was a mixed blessing of sorts. Great for Rick's case but more work for me. All this stuff had to be put into evidence bags which I didn't have. Maybe there were plastic bags in the kitchen.

After I had pulled everything out of the enclosure and placed it on the desk, I got a couple of bags from the kitchen and went back to bag it up. Just past the door I felt a sharp pain in the back of my head that felt oh, so familiar.

"Would someone please come up with an original way to get my attention? This gun to the head thing is pissing me off. Who the hell is it this time and what the hell do you want?" I felt like saying go ahead and shoot.

"I'm sorry you got dragged into this Agent Benoit, but it's too late now. I have my own problems. Please put your hands on your head and lace your fingers."

The voice sounded old and tired. It was also very polite for someone with a gun stuck in my ribs. And the orders were definitely those of a cop. My money was on this being the major.

"Welcome back, Major Johnson. Did you come in through the front door or the master bedroom?"

"Master bedroom, I'm afraid Captain Dugan has some more training to do with some of the officers on how to secure a crime scene." While he was talking, he had removed my weapon. "Now if you would please sit down on the floor over there behind the desk with your back against the wall."

Moving over to the front of the desk, he placed the contents from the secret wall enclosure into a briefcase and pulled some papers off the shelf in his closet which he also added to the case.

"Major, if you don't mind my asking, do you know where Gretchen Brinker, or Joey, or Metcalf's brother happen to be at this moment?"

"Where they are now is not where they will be soon. Just as where you are now is not where you will be in ten minutes."

"And just what do you mean by that?"

"I have to leave and you cannot be left to possibly follow or tell someone I was here. I'm so sorry. I really thought it could all be controlled and damage could be kept to a minimum. Sometimes to stay safe you have to kill your own."

Suddenly a flash of memory brought back the dream I had of Mike and his Dad's story of his buddy. I could still here Mike repeating, "Sometimes to save your own you kill your own." Great, just great, the major was all bummed out about how bad things were, but heck he could fix his problem by taking me out. "Does that mean you intend to kill them too?"

"They know nothing of me and as long as they continue to do what they are told they will be fine."

He had positioned himself between me and the door making escape impossible even if I were standing. He was close enough for me to take him but it would have to be fast and soon since the end was near in more ways than one.

To my surprise he said, "Turn around."

"What?"

"Turn around."

"What for?"

"Would you rather see it coming?"

Well, if that didn't beat all. That little coward was really pissing me off. "It's a little different when you have to look an officer in the eye and pull the trigger, isn't it major? Murder isn't all that much fun anymore when it's you doing the killing and not your brother."

His face stiffened, and between tightened lips he rasped, "Fine, have it your way."

With that he pulled back the hammer of his Berretta and a door slammed in the garage. It was enough of a distraction for me to gather my feet under my body and push forward towards his belt line with my right shoulder and every ounce of energy I could muster. Using both hands I grabbed for the gun. With one hand I jammed my thumb between the hammer and firing pin while the other locked the slide and pushed up. Both of us slammed into the desk and rolled off the edge onto the floor where I ended up on the bottom.

I could feel the skin tearing off my thumb and warm blood running down my wrist but I knew taking it out of that position was a big mistake. At least he couldn't fire a round if the hammer couldn't strike. Then his left fist collided with my jaw and daylight went black.

When I came back to reality, the major was on the floor unconscious with his hands cuffed, and I was staring up at Mr. Toyota with a .45 and some woman in black with very expensive taste in leather boots and equally well armed. My hand was wrapped in a towel and a bag of ice was next to my jaw. I decided this was too crazy even for me and passed out again.

CHAPTER

20

Every bone in my body ached and the headache I had was beyond medical help. I was vaguely aware that the floor had changed to something softer, but it would take much, much more than that to make me happy after the past 24 hours. The thumb on my right hand was burning and throbbing as well as my left arm where it had hit the edge of the desk on the way down to the floor during the struggle. Of course it had to hit within inches of the previous wound which was not quite healed yet. I knew physically I was beat up and just about finished. What I was going to do about Mr. Toyota and how it would be done would require nothing less than a miracle given my present condition. And who was the new player?

A body sat down next to me causing my right arm to slide off the pillow it had been resting on. A hand removed the towel from my hand and started to wrap it in gauze while a female voice spoke to someone on a phone. I opened one eye and recognized the lady in black sans weapon or jacket who now had a nifty chain around her neck with a pretty leather piece dangling from it. In the middle of the leather was a shiny metal badge with Department Of Justice stamped around the edges. How nice to meet a new friend under such circumstances. Mr. Toyota walked up behind her with a bag of ice for my jaw, and clipped to his belt was a similar metal badge. I also noticed his matching .45s and unusual belt buckle. This must be Chip's visitor as well as my shadow. I now had both eyes open and just couldn't wait to hear who these two were. It's not that I wasn't grateful that I wouldn't be shot or beaten up beyond recognition. It wasn't even the realization that I wouldn't have to pray for another miracle to save my sorry butt that had me just a wee bit angry. It was all the damn cloak and dagger shit and me thinking I was being followed by a hit man that got me.

Without making any effort to disguise my anger, I growled, "I don't believe we've been introduced although the big guy here has been scaring half of Bennington and pissing me off for weeks."

He smiled but she answered, "My name is Stephanie Kincaid and I work for the Department of Justice as a special investigator. I'm assigned to the Task Force on smuggling, terrorism, and militias in the northern sector. This is Christian Haughey who also works for DOJ in the same capacity but mainly as a field operative and investigative support person. He was assigned to keep tabs on you and Mr. Robinson until other personnel could be brought in to pick up the slack. Obviously we failed with Mr. Robinson. Luckily, we were able to maintain a tracking device on the major's car and arrived in time to save you."

How sweet of her to state the obvious. "Are you the wonderful Task Force Captain Dugan has been talking about?"

"He is part of this Task Force and actually reports to me. I was the one who sent the authorization to add you to the team."

Couldn't tell if she was being arrogant, annoying or both. "Do you know where Gretchen Brinker, her son, or Metcalf's brother are?"

No point in wasting time to ask questions if she felt she knew everything. There were some folks who just couldn't resist answering. She hesitated and looked away at Christian then back to me. What, she needed his permission to answer? She wanted him to leave? I had bad breath? Maybe it was the pain in my head, or the throbbing ache from my thumb to my wrist that was giving me attitude, but Kincaid was really rubbing on my nerves.

She answered coolly, "Joey has disappeared into the militia underground and so far we have no word as to his whereabouts. Gretchen is at her sister's in Wyoming and under surveillance. We suspect that some day she'll return to Vermont or turn herself in and talk to us about what she knows. For now she's refusing to cooperate. She does know that her husband is dead.

"Paul Metcalf has been arrested for conspiracy in a recent smuggling case involving arms and explosives which has no connection to any cases here. As far as we know, he was not involved in anything his brother was involved in and has no militia ties."

Well that answered a bunch of stuff. So Gretchen was okay and with her sister. I didn't even know she had family.

"Did Paul or Gretchen have anything to do with the crate or box that went to the antique shop in LA?"

"I don't know which case you are referring to."

The hell she didn't, that invoice came from the file she gave Bill.

"You don't? I'm referring to the invoice you gave Bill Robinson to investigate. You included it in the National Bank file when you hired him to do your work."

This did not make me a new friend. She took offense at the possibility that I thought she had used Bill beyond ethical boundaries and failed to provide him with the back up or information he needed to stay alive. Well think away, Honey, because you are right on.

Defensively, she shot back, "The last contact I had with Bill didn't seem to support that theory. He thought it was an effort on Johnson's part to put Paul in jeopardy because he, Johnson that is, hated Metcalf so much. He never trusted Metcalf and tried to screw him every chance he got. Part of my early investigations into this ring turned up a rumor that Maxwell Johnson actually had a voice tape of Jerome Metcalf ordering the State Police sharpshooters to fire in the '71 National Bank hold up and in fact executed two militia members. That tape has not been found."

It was my turn to be smug and smile, "You should learn to have patience and a lot more faith in people. The tape does in fact exist and I have it along with other evidence connecting Metcalf and Johnson in multiple crimes."

This stunned her and immediately she wanted it turned over. Not so fast. I had to ask, "Are you or are you not Professor Kincaid's daughter?"

"Metcalf told you I wasn't, right?"

"Yes he did."

"I am his adopted daughter. He never admitted to it mostly because I turned him in to the local police for wife abuse. The cops never did anything to him even though his wife was hospitalized for two days. There are papers of adoption on file and it is a fact." Now this was giving me a bona fide migraine. I couldn't quite figure why the daughter of an executed radical, caught in the middle of committing a crime, would go to such extremes 20 or so years after the fact. So far it didn't make sense. I couldn't let go and kept asking questions. "Was this so called case you gave Bill a legitimate DOJ thing or some sort of revenge trip?"

The reaction from her was mystifying to say the least. Anger, indignation, even righteous rage would have fit, but not laughter. It actually left me speechless which takes some doing.

"May I call you Jill?" I nodded my assent. "Jill, you don't honestly believe that I reached this level of my career by seeking vendettas do you? I'd be writing parking tickets at Capitol Hill shopping mall if I did that. The decision to hire Bill Robinson as a private investigator was made by several members of the force much higher up on the totem pole than me. They used me only because it made sense given my relationship. We all agreed it would be easier for a PI to develop information than anyone officially connected with the government or uniformed LEOs. We just weren't getting enough leads from the people we have undercover inside the militias concerning who was on the outside."

Stephanie had finished with my medical needs and moved over to another chair. I sat up on the couch but kept the ice on my jaw while she continued her story. "I was young when the '71 hit happened but I remembered a little about seeing a trooper around our garage late one night. I thought they were finally going to arrest my father. Then years later when I was up around Derby Line on a different case, I heard about this crazy BP agent who tried to stop a string of smugglers by herself and almost ended up at the bottom of a lake. Something smelled about that incident and our agents ended up catching a couple of those guys in Connecticut."

As I sat there listening, I could still feel the fear in my stomach of flying uncontrollably through the air after that track busted. The sudden stop and landing in the lake were just blurs. "Did anyone have suspicions about Metcalf at that time?"

"I was DOJ liaison working with ATF on an advisory basis then and I knew some of those guys investigating the smuggling issues thought a BP agent was or had to be involved. No one mentioned his name specifically. We met several times for briefings and I recognized him from photos of the bank job. I was pretty sure he was the trooper at the house. Over the years his name or face has appeared at various locations all across the northern border on dozens of cases, but we've never had any evidence to connect him directly to any crime, at least not enough to go to trial and convict."

"What about Mike Peterson? Where does he fit in to all of this?"

"Mike was working for us as much as he could without compromising his duties as an agent, pretty much like Rick does here for VSP. If there are corrupt officers within the ranks of enforcement agencies, only uniformed officers stand a chance of finding out who they are. It's even tougher to weed out top brass because your access to information and informants is extremely limited. Mike was unable to get information to us very often because Metcalf was the Supervisor in Charge and controlled his schedule. Mike did tell us that he had a partner that he trusted and should something happen, she would know where to find anything he had. So we knew you were told about his information, but we also knew you couldn't find it. Without that, we couldn't do a thing about Metcalf."

"What about Mike's wife, Paula, is she ever going to be able to live a normal life out in the open? Seems to me all her bad guys are dead now. Shouldn't she be able to come out of hiding?"

"As far as we are concerned, she can. It might be wise for DOJ to do a little research first to be sure that is fact rather than wishful thinking. I understand from Rick that Maxwell Johnson confessed to you he was responsible for Peterson's murder, and everyone in the bank heist is dead. By the way, we will need statements from you concerning his confession for files."

Her cell phone rang causing a brief pause in the conversation. Not much was said on her end and then it was back to my answers as if it had never happened. Stephanie Kincaid was definitely a horse of a different color, as mother used to say. "Paula should be fine. We can contact her or you can if you'd like. My experience with militias and patriotic groups is they want attention to their cause in a positive way. They want people to join up. Killing Paula would be revenge and very bad publicity for them."

Kincaid had a good point. "I'd like to be the one to pass on the news about Johnson, if it's all the same to you. I owe Mike at least that much. One last thing, before Gretchen left that morning she dropped off a package at my place that held a very peculiar item and had been mailed in a very odd manner. Do you know anything about that?"

Stephanie nodded her head, "Your badge and ID that disappeared after the accident was mailed to you through a series of post offices at a series of duty stations where you served."

Well, well, the lady in black gets the gold star. "Very good, now could you please explain to me why?"

"There was another officer with you on that patrol, Roman Mantillas, who was the first to reach you in the lake. When he pulled you out, he removed your suit which was soaked with cold water to avoid hypothermia. He also called the local rescue on his cell and was answering questions, one of which concerned allergies and medications. He went looking for your wallet and ID and pulled it out leaving it on the ground afterwards. It got kicked into the water during your extrication and was found a few years later by accident. One of our guys was up there fishing on vacation with his two boys. They were digging around in the mud for buried treasure and found it. They gave it to dad. He gave it to me."

She had this great way of talking all around an answer. Did they teach this at their academy or was it an elective? "Great, that's how you got it. Why send it to me?"

Stephanie looked annoyed at the interruption of her monologue. "When we hired Bill Robinson to start the investigation, we knew he might not be able to get your cooperation voluntarily. We didn't want to get Rick involved tipping his hand as being on the Task Force. I decided to stir your interest, or at least try, by mailing the ID back through a series of old duty stations that might make some connections for you. I don't know if it worked or not. Did it?"

I had to think a little. After all the events and traumas of the past weeks, it was hard to go all the way back to the beginning. So many memories had been revived, new friendships had been made, old one's reinforced, and so many rotten people had popped up all over the landscape. There were enough dead bodies to keep an undertaker happy for weeks. But had the return of the badge helped to get me involved? I guess I'd have to say no, not by itself. "Not by itself it didn't. The badge brought back memories and later on helped connect some things. With Bill around it made a few things more concrete, but I'd have to say that on its own it never would have recruited me to the cause. Nice touch though."

Rick walked in with Tom and an armload of coffee and fresh pastries. Finally, someone who knows how to treat a survivor. Tom came over and sat with me on the couch checking the bandages and other bruises that were now making themselves abundantly visible.

"Are you through playing Zena for a while?"

"Yeah, I think so. We'll have to check with Uncle Rick, but I think all the bad guys are gone and the good guys have prevailed once again."

Rick walked over with coffee for both of us. "You'll have to come to the table if you want food."

I asked for heavy duty aspirins and got a selection of four different types from Stephanie and Christian, or Chris as he preferred to be called. Then Tom and I sat down for the first of what was to be many debriefings and retellings of life gone bizarre.

EPILOGUE

It seemed like a lifetime had passed since the time Joe Brinker drove down the drive past my house. The coffee smelled the same, the window view was almost the same minus a few inches of snow, and even Fundy chasing furry things was the same. So why didn't it feel the same? It was more than the scars of flesh or the painful reliving of old failures and loves lost. There was a deep sadness inside my soul that wondered if any of the past weeks' events meant anything in the long run.

The conflicts between people, who believe that the rights of individuals supersede the rights of the collective, or the reverse, or that government should control us all, or that the law is meant to be broken will continue until there are no more people. We will either kill each other off one by one or in one gigantic explosion. Or maybe we'll learn that it's all about getting along and maybe we don't need to take more than enough and sharing isn't all that bad.

Whatever lesson was meant to be learned from the Heavenly Powers during the past month was wasted on Zeke Faraday, Maxwell Johnson, Bill Robinson, Joseph Brinker, and Janice Beemer. They were all dead. Major Benjamin Johnson and Agent Jerome Metcalf were scheduled for trial on several federal charges and according to the latest conversation I had with Stephanie Kincaid, it was very likely they would serve considerable time in prison. All of that time would be protected, of course, due to their being law enforcement and all. How was that justice I wondered.

They did manage to get some information from Metcalf on operations but very little. Johnson gave hardly any and the bulk of discovery on Vermont militias came from the papers and documents found in the major's wall hideaway. It looked like the system of small loosely organized cells would continue to rejuvenate. It was and would continue to be a system of little spiders in a big web that no matter how many you stepped on, enough always got away to continue the growth and spread of mayhem.

We had found one killer, stopped two corrupt cops, and broken up one militia cell. We had also solved and closed at least four investigations covering more than 20 years. That was pretty good work on anyone's watch. You couldn't look at all the evil in the world if you wanted to survive as a cop. You took it one success at a time and today had been a good day.

Still, I had to wonder, was all the killing and shooting worth it?

Charlie and Jake stayed with us for a few more days and we actually relaxed. No one shot at us, the animals loved the attention and exercise they got, and we had great food with long nights and lots of cheating at cards. Both Charlie and I cried at the airport when they left and we promised to get together every year for a week somewhere for a vacation.

Rick turned down a promotion to fill the major's job. He was more interested in retirement and didn't think a couple years in that spot fair to the service he loved so much and had devoted his life to. A younger man to lead VSP was a better choice in his opinion. He and Jean took a two week vacation in Jamaica and started to think of places they might retire to.

Tom and I tried to return to normal, but I was restless. I knew there was one more thing I had to do before I could put all of this behind me. Tom and I were casually talking about things that had to be done when he asked **the** question. "When are you heading to Canada?"

With a start, I replied "What makes you think I'm going?"

"Jill, you and I have been together, sort of, for five years now. Give me some credit for knowing you a little bit. We do share more than a bed and a few laughs now and then. Both of us are cops and I know how I'd feel if you had been my partner. I'd want to be the one to tell your spouse the bastard who killed his wife was dead. Especially if you meant to me what Mike meant to you."

Well I'll be damned. This guy was getting to be downright irreplaceable.

"I'll tell you what, if you come with me, I'll go. We could take the horses and make a vacation out of it. We've talked about doing it before and spring is a good time to start something new. This isn't a trip I want to make alone. I can't tell you why because I don't know myself."

It took some convincing but eventually I won. We drove the three horses and Fundy cross country on a great trip that did more to heal my soul than anything I could have done in the Hollow. It was wonderful to see the Rocky Mountains again even if the truck hated the elevations and the brakes burned with the weight of the trailer and three horses. Cochise was more alive than I've seen him in years. Tracker and Nevada couldn't wait to get out and hit the grass when we would pull in to rest areas specified for horse travelers where grazing was available. They had died and gone to heaven.

After ten days, we planted ourselves at a campsite in Washington not far from Oliver, B.C. We secured the horses for a few days and I left with the truck to find Paula. It wasn't as hard as I thought it would be. One of her sons, Joel, ran a lumber yard in Oliver. I explained who I was and why I was there. He immediately called Paula who met us at Joel's house half an hour later. Bill was right in his notebook that was the biggest carved bear I'd ever seen in my life.

Paula and I hugged as soon as we saw each other with tears following. Time had been kind to both our memories and only the good stuff remained. I explained all of the events gone by especially the confession and death of one Maxwell Johnson. I also told of the evidence found and the crucial role her husband played in gathering the evidence that would convict a corrupt Border Patrol officer. That alone was something that Paula needed to understand was a big deal for Mike. I didn't know anyone else in the service who loved Border Patrol more than he did. She asked about Bill and was deeply saddened to hear of his murder.

"He was such a gentle man when he was here and so considerate of my situation. Did he tell you I fainted on him when he introduced himself?"

I shook my head no; she then proceeded to tell me all about his visit in such a soft voice. Anyone could see Bill had impressed her.

"I didn't have much of a chance to talk with Bill after he came back from Canada. I do remember his saying how nice a person you were and no one was to find out where you were. I think you impressed him too."

To this she smiled and we went on talking about Mike. After an hour or so we were both pretty drained emotionally. I decided to ask, "I have driven to a place in Washington with a close friend, and three horses. Tomorrow Tom and I are going to ride the trail up to where Mike was ambushed and place a memorial wreath at the site. I need closure to get on with my life. This has been eating at me for years, and now with the case closed, I think I can do that. I would be honored and pleased if you would join us. Your sons are also welcome although I don't have mounts for them."

Paula sat there holding my hands with tears running down her cheeks saying nothing for the longest time. I wasn't sure if I had insulted her or simply shocked her.

"Do you know that tomorrow is his birthday?"

"As a matter of fact I do. He used to get razzed at the station all the time and I'm afraid I may have participated in that a time or two."

"Well I'm sure he's forgiven all of you. I would love to ride up with you and surprisingly still remember how. Do you still have Cochise?"

"Yes I do. The other two horses are Tracker and Nevada. Both are mountain trained although I'm not sure where they came from exactly. I'm assuming the same school of hard knocks as Cochise."

"I think I remember Nevada. She's a mare, right, a Pinto?"

We discussed horses for a bit, she talked to her sons about the next day, and then I left directions to the trailhead where we would form up. On the way back to camp I stopped by a florist and picked up a wreath. At a nearby lumber yard there were things needed to make its placement permanent…at least for a little while.

The next day was perfect weather for horseback riding. Paula came and I introduced her to Tom who immediately hugged her and gave his condolences. What a sweet guy. Tom explained a little about his background and made her feel most welcome. The trail itself hadn't changed in all those years other than it was a little more worn and perhaps a little wider.

As I led the way up the mountain, I could visualize Mike riding ahead. The trees were bigger and the forest a little more overgrown but Cochise still hit the ground with his shoes making the same sounds that echoed the same way through the canyons. His ears were alert with head moving back and forth as if any minute now the logs would roll down the side and catch him. I had to admit it was a little nerve-wracking for me, but the sway of Cochise and knowing that Tom was behind me covering my back made it okay. At the bend before the place where the accident had happened, Cochise stopped. I just sat there and looked down the valley. The skies were clear, blue and sunny with little puffy clouds off in the distance. There were no threats, no logs, no bad guys, and no fear. All that was left was a peaceful view with a natural beauty, three older but wiser horses, and three people, two of which were left with a big hole in their hearts for a guy who had given them both a whole lot while he was alive.

"You can see him, can't you?" Paula had brought Nevada up on the inside and was just behind me.

"I was able to on the way up here, but now I can't. It's as if he's gone beyond the bend. Cochise is the one who stopped. Maybe we should walk the horses from here. It gets a little narrow in a few feet and we are only about 30 feet from the area."

The three of us dismounted and walked the rest of the way. I was surprised to find that someone had driven a metal pole into the rock and mounted a plaque with Mike's name and a few details of the ambush. You could see bullet dings on the pole where hunters and pranksters took pot shots to amuse themselves. Paula and I secured the wreath to the pole and I stepped back. Paula stayed and put something else on the wreath. When she stepped back I could see it was a laminated picture of her adult sons and their families, the families he had not lived to see. There was also a photo of Mike in dress uniform and their wedding picture.

Tom asked me to hold the horses for him and he walked over and placed something on the wreath also. When he came back to the mounts he helped Paula up and held Cochise. I walked over to the wreath and fished out of my jeans pocket two shiny objects dangling on a chain that I had been carrying around for a long time. They were symbolic, they had been updated a time or two, but their significance was beyond doubt. Carefully they were hung to withstand winds, rains, and snows for as long as possible. Returning to Cochise I mounted and Tom turned the horses to avoid having a horse getting skittish on that narrow section. When he wheeled Cochise around, I could see that he had left his department shoulder patches and insignia on the wreath as a sign of respect and brotherhood for a fallen officer.

Tom led out and Paula followed. She turned and blew a kiss good bye. Before I left I turned Cochise to face the marker, stood tall in the saddle and snapped a salute. "It's been an honor. I'll never forget you, Mike. Rest easy." The reflecting sunlight off the twin objects seemed to send a coded agreement.

Tonight the horses would eat hearty and hopefully we would all sleep well. Tom and I were finishing our bourbons before putting out the fire and calling it a day. Tom asked, "What did you hang on Mike's wreath? It looked like gold nuggets."

I laughed. "If we had gold nuggets that size, we wouldn't be worried about gas costs on the way home." I took a sip of my drink and savored the moment. "They were two symbols of a promise made 20 years ago and finally fulfilled."

Tom wasn't enjoying the suspense. "Well, you telling me or not?"

I smiled, "Just dragging it out for fun. Its two empty .40 caliber casings with the recent engravings...To-MJ on one and... From-JB on the other. I've carried two empty casings from every service weapon I've had since Mike was killed, knowing someday I'd kill the son of a bitch and hang them around his neck. This was the next best thing."

Happy Birthday, Mike.

A SPECIAL THANKS

Special thanks to Mark Perez, his staff, and JMC (editing) for all of their hard work on this reprint. I am not an easy person to convince or correct when it comes to my "precious and perfect" book. It took tender care and much patience that really amazes me these folks would bother to give for such a small unknown work. Don't know why they bothered but I'm glad they did … I think I'll be a better writer IF I ever write another book.

Thank you Mark and thank you to your team at Author Reputation.